PERFECT

What Reviewers Say About Kris Bryant's Work

EF5, *Novella in* Stranded Hearts

"In *EF5* there is destruction and chaos but I adored it because I can't resist anything with a tornado in it. They fascinate me, and the way Alyssa and Emerson work together, even though Alyssa has no obligation to do so, means they have a life changing experience that only strengthens the instant attraction they shared."—*LESBIreviewed*

Home

"*Home* is a very sweet second-chance romance that will make you smile. It is an angst-less joy, perfect for a bad day."—*Hsinju's Lit Log*

Scent

"Oh. Kris Bryant. Once again you've given us a beautiful comfort read to help us escape all that 2020 has thrown at us. This series featuring the senses has been a pleasure to read. …I think what makes Bryant's books so readable is the way she builds the reader's interest in her mains before allowing them to interact. This is a sweet and happy sigh kind of read. Perfect for these chilly winter nights when you want to escape the world and step into a caramel infused world where HEAs really do come true."—*Late Night Lesbian Reads*

Lucky

"The characters—both main and secondary, including the furry ones—are wonderful (I loved coming across Piper and Shaylie from Falling), there's just the right amount of angst and the sexy scenes are really hot. It's Kris Bryant, you guys, no surprise there."—*Jude in the Stars*

Tinsel

"This story was the perfect length for this cute romance. What made this especially endearing were the relationships Jess has with her best friend, Mo, and her mother. You cannot go wrong by purchasing this cute little nugget. A really sweet romance with a cat playing cupid."—*Bookvark*

Against All Odds—*(co-authored with Maggie Cummings and M. Ullrich)*

"*Against All Odds* by Kris Bryant, Maggie Cummings and M. Ullrich is an emotional and captivating story about being able to face a tragedy head on and move on with your life, learning to appreciate the simple things we take for granted and finding love where you least expect it."—*Lesbian Review*

"I started reading the book trying to dissect the writing and ended up forgetting all about the fact that three people were involved in writing it because the story just grabbed me by the ears and dragged me along for the ride. ...[A] really great romantic suspense that manages both parts of the equation perfectly. This is a book you won't be able to put down."—*C-Spot Reviews*

"This story tugged at my heartstrings and it hit all the right notes for me because these wonderful authors allowed me to peep into the hearts and minds of the characters. The vivid descriptions of Peyton, Tory and the perpetrator's personalities allowed me to have a deeper understanding of what makes them tick and I was able to form a clear picture of them in my mind."—*Lesbian Review*

Temptation

"This book has a great first line. I was hooked from the start. There was so much to like about this story, though. The interactions. The tension. The jealousy. I liked how Cassie falls for Brooke's son before she ever falls for Brooke. I love a good forbidden love story."—*Bookvark*

"This book is a bag of kettle corn—sweet, savory and you won't stop until you finish it in one binge-worthy sitting. *Temptation* is a fun, fluffy and ultimately satisfying lesbian romance that hits all the right notes."—*To Be Read Book Reviews*

Falling

"This is a story you don't want to pass on. A fabulous read that you will have a hard time putting down. Maybe don't read it as you board your plane though. This is an easy 5 stars!"—*Romantic Reader Blog*

"This was a nice, romantic read. There is enough romantic tension to keep the plot moving, and I enjoyed the supporting characters' and their romance as much as the main plot."—*Kissing Backwards*

Listen

"[A] sweet romance with a touch of angst and lots of music."
—*C-Spot Reviews*

"If you suffer from anxiety, know someone who suffers from anxiety, or want an insight to how it may impact on someone's daily life, I urge you to pick this book up. In fact, I urge all readers who enjoy a good lesbian romance to grab a copy."—*Love Bytes Reviews*

"If you're looking for a little bit of fluffy(ish), light romance in your life, give this one a listen. The characters' passion for music (and each other) is heartwarming, and I was rooting for them the entire book."—*Kissing Backwards*

"Ms. Bryant describes this soundscape with some exquisite metaphors, it's true what they say that music is everywhere. The whole book is beautifully written and makes the reader's heart to go out with people suffering from anxiety or any sort of mental health issue."—*Lez Review Books*

Forget Me Not

"Told in the first person, from Grace's point of view, we are privy to Grace's inner musings and her vulnerabilities. ...Bryant crafts clever wording to infuse Grace with a sharp-witted personality, which clearly covers her insecurities. ...This story is filled with loving familial interactions, caring friends, romantic interludes and tantalizing sex scenes. The dialogue, both among the characters and within Grace's head, is refreshing, original, and sometimes comical. *Forget Me Not* is a fresh perspective on a romantic theme, and an entertaining read."—*Lambda Literary Review*

"[I]t just hits the right note all the way. ...[A] very good read if you are looking for a sweet romance."—*Lez Review Books*

Shameless—*Writing as Brit Ryder*

"[Kris Bryant] has a way of giving insight into the other main protagonist by using a few clever techniques and involving the secondary characters to add back-stories and extra pieces of important information. The pace of the book was excellent, it was never rushed but I was never bored or waiting for a chapter to finish...this epilogue made my heart swell to the point I almost lunged off the sofa to do a happy dance."—*Les Rêveur*

Not Guilty—*Writing as Brit Ryder*

"Kris Bryant, aka Brit Ryder, promised this story would be hot and she didn't lie! ...I love that the author is Kris Bryant who, under that name, writes romance with a lot of emotions. As Brit Ryder, she lets chemistry take the lead and it's pretty amazing too."—*Jude in the Stars*

Whirlwind Romance

"Ms. Bryant's descriptions were written with such passion and colorful detail that you could feel the tension and the excitement along with the characters..."—*Inked Rainbow Reviews*

Taste

"*Taste* is a student/teacher romance set in a culinary school. If the premise makes you wonder whether this book will make you want to eat something tasty, the answer is: yes."—*Lesbian Review*

Jolt—*Lambda Literary Award Finalist*

"[*Jolt*] is a magnificent love story. Two women hurt by their previous lovers and each in their own way trying to make sense out of life and times. When they meet at a gay and lesbian friendly summer camp, they both feel as if lightening has struck. This is so beautifully involving, I have already reread it twice. Amazing!" —*Rainbow Book Reviews*

Touch

"The sexual chemistry in this book is off the hook. Kris Bryant writes my favorite sex scenes in lesbian romantic fiction." —*Les Rêveur*

Breakthrough

"Looking for a fun and funny light read with hella cute animal antics, and a smoking hot butch ranger? Look no further. …In this well written, first-person narrative, Kris Bryant's characters are well developed, and their push/pull romance hits all the right beats, making it a delightful read just in time for beach reading."—*Writing While Distracted*

"Kris Bryant has written several enjoyable contemporary romances, and *Breakthrough* is no exception. It's interesting and clearly well-researched, giving us information about Alaska and issues like poaching and conservation in a way that's engaging and never comes across as an info dump. She also delivers her best character work to date, going deeper with Kennedy and Brynn than we've seen in previous stories. If you're a fan of Kris Bryant, you won't want to miss this book, and if you're a fan of romance in general, you'll want to pick it up, too."—*Lambda Literary Review*

By the Author

Jolt

Whirlwind Romance

Just Say Yes

Taste

Forget-Me-Not

Shameless (writing as Brit Ryder)

Touch

Breakthrough

Against All Odds
(written with M. Ullrich and Maggie Cummings)

Listen

Falling

Tinsel

Temptation

Lucky

Home

Scent

Not Guilty (writing as Brit Ryder)

Always

Forever

EF5 (Stranded Hearts Novella Collection)

Serendipity

Catch

Cherish

Dreamer

Perfect

PERFECT

by

Kris Bryant

2024

PERFECT

ISBN 13: 978-1-63679-601-7

This Trade Paperback Original Is Published By
Bold Strokes Books, Inc.
P.O. Box 249
Valley Falls, NY 12185

First Edition: September 2024

CREDITS
EDITORS: ASHLEY TILLMAN AND CINDY CRESAP
PRODUCTION DESIGN: SUSAN RAMUNDO
COVER DESIGN BY DEB B

Acknowledgments

Inclusion is so important as we write our books. While it's fantastic to see so much sapphic literature available, it's equally important for all our alphabet family to see themselves in the pages of our books. I was blown away by how many people read *Forever* and wanted to see Alix get their own story. So, I did it. I opened up, and Alix came through loud and proud on the page.

I'd like to thank Bold Strokes Books for working with me. This is my ten-year anniversary with them (my debut, *Jolt*, was published in September 2014) and what a journey it's been! I've met my chosen family and best friends because I submitted the messiest manuscript in the history of books, but they accepted it and here I am today with over 20 published books under my belt.

I owe my success to my editor Ashley. We fight, we cry (okay, maybe that's just me), we laugh, we make it work. Stacia and Cindy polish my words, and will I ever learn grammar? The answer is no. I need them in my writing life.

I'd like to thank Tara Scott and Rey S. for their encouraging words while I wrote this love story. Love is different for everyone. Thank you to my sensitivity reader Ray R. for giving me valuable tips and suggestions. I thought I was killing it until I wasn't. I've learned a lot on this book journey.

Shout out to Deb for coming up with a companion cover that works with *Forever*. Covers can make or break a book before a word is even read. You do amazing work and I love you. Thank you for giving me the space to make my writing dreams come true.

This is the first book without my faithful sidekick, Molly. The house is quieter, my heart is heavier, and I miss her terribly. She will always be inside my heart and I will never pair with another animal like I did with her. I'll never get over losing her, but I have more love to give. I think I'm ready for the cat distribution system to find me.

Thank you to my friends, patrons, and readers who have lifted me up during two really bad years of my life. We all have to face hardships, and somehow we do it, but I'm pretty sure it's because we have this community and all the love and support we need. Blessed to be a part of it.

Dedication

To everyone who isn't afraid to be themselves

CHAPTER ONE

A lix Sommers stared up at the night hoping to see the flash of a shooting star streak across the Beverly Hills skyline so they could make the wish of being anywhere but here. Attending parties wasn't mandatory, but when the producer of *When Sparks Fly* threw a star-studded bash, it was highly recommended that the new host of the queer dating show attend.

Alix loosened the restrictive knot of their tie and undid the mother-of-pearl button that poked the middle of their throat. They took a deep breath and did a few shoulder rolls to release the tension that settled in between their shoulder blades as if the hanger was still inside their Brioni jacket. The heat, the party, the demands of Hollywood—everything was stifling, and Alix was becoming alarmingly grumpy.

When they stepped in as new host after the previous one ran off with the bachelorette, they didn't expect parties almost every night and weekly lunches with people who took pity on them for getting dumped on national television. Alix didn't have any hard feelings about Savannah. She had every right to find true love even if it wasn't with them. Their very public breakup stung, but it also opened the door to a new career, bigger dating pool, and attaining dreams they never thought possible. But right now, being home with a beer in one hand, the remote control in the other, and Woody, the twenty-pound recently rescued cat, snuggled up in by their side, beat any Hollywood party.

Where are you? I want you to meet someone.

Alix looked at their phone and sighed again. It was Sam, their agent, looking for them to meet another face to store in their overflowing memory bank. They couldn't remember the names of even ten percent of the people inside. Too many faces and not enough time to form even a slight connection. It was "hi" and "hello, nice to meet you" at least fifty times back-to-back and on to the next person who may or may not help them advance their career. Alix was perfectly fine being the first trans host of the show and nothing else, but Sam had other plans. He knew Alix was on the fast track to becoming the hottest nonbinary celebrity right now and was damn sure going to introduce them to everyone. Slipping outside for a moment alone was warranted, but Sam wouldn't see it that way.

Give me two minutes. I'll find you.

Mentally marking it as a quiet, private space to return to, Alix wound their way through the parked BMWs and fancy Italian cars and slipped inside the cool house that smelled of red wine, spices from hors d'oeuvres, and a lot of cologne.

"Alix, over here." Sam's voice rose above the chatter and softly playing music.

Alix gave a sharp head nod and weaved their way through the beautiful people they met earlier smiling and nodding and not remembering a single name. The woman Sam was with was a bombshell. All curves, legs, and Alix could already feel the spell when her light blue eyes bore into theirs. Whoever she was, Alix felt the welcoming tingles indicating an attractive woman was in proximity. "Hi, I'm Alix."

"This is Xander's wife, Kitty. She is a massive fan of the show and of you," Sam said.

The moment Sam said wife, Alix pumped the brakes. They managed to keep the polite smile on their face and keep their eyes focused on Kitty's stunning light blue ones instead of roaming her curvy body. "Hi, Kitty. Nice to meet you. Thank you for watching the show."

She purred her answer and placed her hand on Alix's lapel, dangerously close to their nipple. "You can thank me for making this all happen. *When Sparks Fly* was kind of my idea." She pulled her hand back and bit the tip of her finger and smiled. The flirting instantly made Alix uncomfortable. They looked around for Xander, the show's producer and birthday boy, afraid he would get the wrong idea.

"Kitty is a good person to have on your side. And if there's anyone you want to meet in Hollywood, Kitty will make it happen. She has the best connections," Sam said. He raised a brow at Alix and gave a small wink as though they knew exactly what he meant. They didn't. Alix was still wet behind the ears and Hollywood was overwhelming.

"Well, thank you for that," Alix told Kitty. They shot Sam a slightly confused look.

"What are your thoughts on the new bachelorette?" Kitty asked.

This was dangerous territory and Alix had been trained repeatedly by the show's public relations department on what was appropriate to say and what conversation to walk away from. "I think Heather is the perfect candidate. She's fun, the staff finds her engaging, and I wish her the best in finding love on the show. If there's a match to be made, I'm going to help find it and bring it to light." Alix did a silent cheer at nailing the question. Even Sam gave them a continuous nod throughout their whole speech.

"And who knows the show more than Alix? Am I right?" Sam asked.

Sam's interjection was annoying, but Alix knew he was just doing his job and expected them to do theirs.

"This isn't weird for you, right? I mean, you're not going to fall in love with the bachelorette and we'll have a repeat of last season, will we?" Kitty asked.

Alix held up their hands and waved them furiously back and forth. "Absolutely not. I'm taking a break from dating so that I can focus all my attention on my job. That's the most important thing right now." It wasn't, but Alix's heart was still a little sore from the show. Given how awkwardly things ended, no way were they going to jump into dating again anytime soon.

"But she's very similar to Savannah, right? I mean, except for the hair color. She's young, beautiful, ambitious, femme. All the same traits." Kitty was literally baiting Alix. Heather was also very demanding, attention-seeking, and way too flirty. She and Savannah were complete opposites, but Alix nodded and shot Kitty a small smile.

"Similar traits but a lot of different ones, too." Before Kitty could dig deeper, Alix quickly changed the subject. "I need a drink. Can I get something for either of you?" Alix took a few steps backward and waited for them to make a decision, hoping for a dismissal where they could make a quick getaway under the guise of needing alcohol. Alix knew women like Kitty who wanted to be helpful but had a high probability of causing more grief in the long run.

"I'll take another glass of champagne," Sam said. He turned to Kitty. "What do you say?" he asked. She nodded enthusiastically. Alix flashed a quick smile before heading toward the bar for some liquid courage and a few moments of peace. They needed to diffuse Kitty's intimate, flirty energy and shift it in a more professional direction.

"Alix. Are you enjoying yourself?" Xander asked from behind them.

Well, that lasted about seven seconds. Alix caught their eye roll before it reached a discoverable level. "It's a great party, Xander. Happy birthday." They pointed at the bar. "I just met your wife and am delivering champagne. Sam introduced us. Sounds like she's a fan of the show."

Xander grinned at them. His teeth were too white and his hair too perfect. And how could he look so cool and calm when Alix could feel the sweat gather around their waistband and in the small of their back? His level of perfection wasn't normal. "Oh, she's the one who put the bug in my ear. She has tons of gay friends who had been pushing for something queer on television. The first few seasons were rough, but after Lauren Lucas took over, it flew to the top ten in prime time. And you…" he paused and pointed at Alix slyly. "You are going to take it to the very top."

No pressure, Alix thought. "Thanks for that vote of confidence. I plan to do my very best." The show had shot several commercials but was focusing more on the bachelorette and taping interviews with this season's candidates. Alix wanted to be more involved, but Xander told them it was too soon. It would be another week before they needed to be on site daily. Alix was chomping at the bit to get started in their new role.

"Preliminary data says you're on fire. The world is excited to see you in action. Meanwhile, enjoy the party and get that drink to my wife. You're in good hands with her," Xander said. He dismissed Alix by tipping his snifter of a bourbon at them and winking.

What was up with everyone winking? Alix asked the bartender for an old-fashioned and two flutes of champagne. The drinks appeared in no time, and they begrudgingly rejoined Sam and Kitty. They were scrolling through pictures on Kitty's iPhone laughing at her dog who was adorably ugly.

"Alix. Let's take a selfie for the socials," Kitty said.

Part of the job, Alix thought. They sighed and shook off the negativity. Tonight was not the night to sulk. Kitty probably had hundreds of thousands of followers and could do a lot for them. And she seemed very nice and genuine which was perplexing since Xander was such a tool. They moved closer until Kitty's face was right next to theirs and smiled.

"Thank you, Alix. I'll be sure to tag you," Kitty said.

That felt like an appropriate time to slip away. "Thank you, Kitty. It was nice to meet you. Sam, I'll see you later." Alix turned before Kitty could make a fuss and beelined it for the side door. Not to leave, but to get away from the weight of Hollywood. These parties were grinding on their last nerve. And they never let up. It was either an A-list celebrity who wanted them there, or a producer's party, or even an impromptu concert where the network wanted all its big names to attend. Who said no to these invitations? Nobody.

Alix found a quiet place in front of parked cars away from the mansion and gave a quick sweep of their surroundings before speaking into their phone. "Call Buck." They held their phone up to their ear and waited. Whenever Alix felt the pressure of their newly found celebrity status, they reached out to the one person who grounded them. Buck Sommers was their rock. Not only was their brother the voice of reason, but he refused to give them any special treatment.

"What's up?"

At hearing the somewhat gruff voice on the other end, Alix felt their first genuine smile of the night.

"Bro, I'm hiding out. This has been a night."

"Too many sexy women around? Are you really hiding from them? That's sad," he said. They heard him pause and take a sip of something. He made a slight hissing sound after he swallowed. It had to be beer. They never understood why he tried so hard to like it.

"What's sad is you trying to pretend to like beer. Let me guess. The guys are around and you're watching the game."

Buck was a simple man. He ran their family tattoo shop, watched baseball with his friends, and spent every free minute outside in nature. Alix couldn't envision him settling down. Women tried to get close, but he always joked that he was allergic to relationships. Alix thought he was just scared. His high school sweetheart broke his heart and Alix believed he never recovered. Instead, he focused more on building the business.

"Extra innings. There's hope."

"Dreamer," Alix said.

"I think you have us confused. You're the one with stars in your eyes. And probably your bed."

Alix missed hearing his laugh even though it was at their expense. "Nah. No time for that. I'm too busy shooting promos, going to parties, and doing interviews every day." Their laugh was a bit too forced.

"It's getting to you, huh?" Buck said.

Alix exhaled a shaky breath. "I signed up for this."

"Whose party are you at tonight?" he asked.

"One of the bosses. I had to show up. It's not in my contract, but it was highly recommended." Alix did quote marks with one hand as though Buck could see them.

"It's probably too early to sneak away, huh?" he asked. Alix pulled the phone from their ear when shouts and slaps of high-fives drowned out whatever their brother was saying.

"Hey, listen. Go enjoy your game. I'll just catch up with you in a few days." They disconnected the call after little protest from him. They didn't get the exact support they needed but still felt lighter. One deep breath. Then another. On the third, they turned on the square heel of their harness boot ready to face the crowd again. What they didn't expect was for a woman who had quietly slipped between the valet cars right behind them to lose her footing on the cobblestone driveway and fall directly into their arms.

CHAPTER TWO

A re you okay?"
Gentle hands steadied her. Marianna struggled for composure and immediately pulled the hem of her dress down as it had risen to just below the junction of her thighs. Heat flooded her cheeks followed quickly by a wave of other emotions from this stranger's strong arms still encircling her.

"Stupid cobblestone." Marianna tried to joke, but her ankle throbbed with pain at the sudden twist and her voice came out shaky and at a higher pitch. She cleared her throat and managed to take a step back. Her ankle held her weight.

"Those stilettos mixed with these cobblestones are a bad combination. I did the exact same thing and I'm wearing boots. By the way, I'm Alix." They pointed to their boots. Marianna figured it was just a way to make her feel better. It worked.

Marianna knew she should've waited to change from her catering uniform into her hot girl outfit, but she was going to be the last one to Chloe's Vegas bachelorette party and needed to hit the ground running the minute the plane landed. Besides, her cousin Andrea was working the same catering shift and she was the best at doing Marianna's hair and makeup. Getting ready there seemed the most logical decision but one she was instantly regretting. These shoes were a bitch.

"Who knew it was so treacherous around here? I should've been paying attention, but I'm in a rush." Marianna bit her lip to stop talking. Hollywood people were the worst and even though Alix was extremely helpful, they were still wearing an expensive suit and attending an exclusive party. Clearly, they were part of a scene Marianna wanted nothing to do with.

Alix handed her the phone she'd dropped. The screen was cracked despite the hard case and protective glass and Marianna tried to stifle the groan. Stupid cobblestone, she thought again but kept it to herself.

"Would you like for me to call you a car? Or you can take mine. The driver will take you where you need to go." Alix pointed at a black Escalade lined up in a row of similar vehicles. "I won't need it for a while."

Marianna didn't think they were flaunting it, just trying to be helpful. Still. It confirmed her suspicions about Alix and she wasn't interested. "Thank you, but my ride should be here soon." Marianna picked up her overnight bag that looked more like an oversized purse and scanned the driveway for any sign of Brandon. She was extremely aware of Alix's lithe form and perfectly coiffed pompadour standing close. Too close. Not that uncomfortable level of nearness, but the welcoming kind that unnerved her.

"Who do you know at this party?" Alix asked.

Their voice was slightly raspy as though they had either been talking too much or not enough. It sounded sexy. No, wait. Not sexy. Marianna didn't have time for sexy now or later. It took a moment for the question to sink in. Shame and pride simultaneously fought inside her chest. She was proud of the success of her aunt's catering business, but she didn't want Alix to think she was the help. Tonight, she was Marianna Raines, hot twenty-six-year-old single woman who was on her way to Vegas to party with her friends. But Alix didn't know that. Marianna could've been anyone at that moment. She could've been a movie star or successful entertainment lawyer. What if she said astrophysicist or restaurateur? Not that Alix was asking, but it would be rude to ignore them. "My cousin." She kept her answer vague. Alix slowly nodded.

"I've been to a few of these parties, but I haven't seen you before." Alix took a step closer. "I would remember you." Alix was quietly confident and that unnerved Marianna. She brazenly matched Alix's intense gaze but was the first to look away.

"I'm more of a wallflower." That part was true. Plus, with her hair pulled back into a tight bun and very little makeup on, Marianna doubted Alix would see past the pressed white button-up shirt, black pants, and sensible shoes if they ran into each other inside.

"Well, it's nice to meet you, wallflower."

Marianna put her hands on her hips and debated if she should tell Alix her real name, but their moment was interrupted as a 1964 Rolls Royce Silver Cloud pulled up in front of them. It was her brother's favorite car in his small fleet, and she smiled. "Looks like my ride's here. Have a good evening. You should get back inside to all the fun." Marianna thumbed behind her at the ginormous mansion and all the beautiful people she weaved through to serve food they only nibbled at and champagne they gulped by the glass.

"Sorry I'm late." Brandon jumped out of the car and made a big production of gallantly opening the door for Marianna. He gave her a sly wink.

"No worries," she said. She shot Alix a quick, soft smile and slipped inside. The smoky windows were so dark that she didn't think Alix could see her so she took a moment to study them. Very attractive with a genuine smile. That probably got them a lot of dates. She leaned back in the seat when Brandon put the vintage car in drive and smoothly slid away.

"Who was that?" he asked.

His voice was playful and Marianna knew if she gave in, he would tease her all the way to the airport. She ignored his question. "What took you so long?"

He held up a hand. "Hey, I'm only five minutes late. Traffic sucks. Don't worry. I'll get you up there in time."

Marianna looked around at the crawling cars. "What time do you pick up your client?"

"A few hours. I gave myself enough of a cushion," he said.

Marianna's parents weren't happy when her brother decided to skip college and start a car service business. All his friends teased him for being so into cars and restoring them instead of gaming or going to bars, but he had a dream and Marianna was proud of him even if she didn't tell him as much as she should.

"Are you staying pretty busy?" She never wanted to burst his bubble, unlike their parents who thought accruing so much debt when he first started was a mistake. They thought Marianna was the responsible one because she had a steady career with benefits. She liked her job, but she would never see fast money unless she worked a second job. Her brother wasn't even thirty and he already had three beautifully restored vintage limos, two classic Rolls, five employees, and an impressive client list. His business seemed to be thriving.

"Busy enough. I only have a few clients who still request me personally. Even though I'd rather be at the shop tinkering around and let one of the other drivers take it, I'm not going to tell them no."

"Good for you for making it happen, bro," Marianna said. They weren't overly emotional or affectionate siblings, but she knew that if she ever needed him, he'd be there for her in a flash.

"Thanks. It's all coming together nicely. I'm looking at another old luxury car that will need a major overhaul, but it's very cool."

"I like your vintage rides. There's something so luxurious about being in a Rolls Royce or Bentley with soft leather seats and blackened windows."

Brandon's laugh boomed through the car. "That's what my whole business is built on."

"Thanks for picking me up. A ride to the airport would've killed my spending money for the party."

"Not a problem. I still can't believe Chloe is getting married."

Marianna watched as he shook his head slightly. She wondered if he ever regretted breaking up with Chloe. Their one-year relationship after high school was tumultuous, but they had several sweet moments, too. She treaded lightly in case hearing her name still stung. "I'm not surprised. But also, Connie seems to be a decent person. She treats Chloe like royalty," she said.

He waved her off. "I'm just glad she found somebody who can give her everything she wants. She's a good person. Tell her I said I'm happy for her."

"I will," Marianna said. She would wait until after the weekend to tell Chloe, not knowing if that would change her mood. Besides, this weekend was supposed to be about celebrating the last few weeks of being a single woman, not about old boyfriends. "When do you think you're going to settle down?" He laughed in response. She loved his laugh.

"When you do. Maybe we can have a sibling wedding," he said.

"I'm not even dating anyone. At least you've had a few dates recently."

"What about that sexy person you were just talking to?"

"Alix? That was nothing. We literally just met. I'll never see them again." Only she didn't really mean that. But if they met again, it would be at another Hollywood function and she would be serving overpriced hors d'oeuvres instead of wearing a cocktail dress, heels, and makeup that emphasized all her good traits. She shuddered when she pictured her bumping into them and the mortified look on their face when they realized she was a server and not somebody who once kind of flirted with them at a mansion one night.

Chloe and Jess met Marianna's cab at the casino's entrance. "You're here!" Chloe shouted. She was pulled into a big hug by both of them after sliding out of the back seat of a cab that smelled like stale cigar smoke and sickeningly sweet citrus air freshener.

"I'm so excited. Is everyone here?"

Jess shook her head. "The twins will be here in about half an hour. We have time to drop off your bag at the suite and grab another drink at the bar. We have a VIP table at the nightclub when everyone's here."

Upon closer inspection, Marianna noticed how Chloe's cheeks were pink and how Jess was slightly wobbly as she leaned against her. "Looks like I need to play catch up. Let's go." It was hard not to get caught up in their excitement. Plus, Vegas buzzed with an undefined energy. The weariness of working all day and all evening faded away when they walked into the casino. Even though it was almost one in the morning, the casino floor was full of people. Slot machines flashed with brightly colored lights and people were yelling and high-fiving one another.

"We're this way. I'm sending you the digital key." Chloe fumbled with her phone and smiled after successfully forwarding the email with the hotel information. It felt like a mile before they finally got to their suite.

"This place is amazing." Marianna gasped when Chloe opened the door and immediately made her way over to the floor-to-ceiling windows. The view of the strip was impressive. Millions of lights lit up the night as though day never left. "I can't believe you got this for such a good price." There were two queen-sized beds, a foldout couch, a bathroom that was almost the size of Marianna's one-bedroom apartment, and a powder room to the right of the entry door. She almost missed the awkward elbow nudge between Chloe and Jess in the reflection of the window. She sighed and bit her tongue. They were being sweet by helping her out financially, and as much as she wanted to be mad at them, she also didn't want to ruin the weekend.

"Good news. You get the couch all to yourself," Chloe said.

Marianna raised her arms in a cheer pose. "Woo-hoo! Let's get it ready because I'm sure the last thing we want to do when we stagger in here at daybreak is make a bed."

Chloe stacked the cushions in a pile out of the way so Marianna could unfold the bed. The process took thirty seconds. She dropped her bag on the firm, flat mattress.

"Let's go celebrate being single," Marianna said. She was curious as to why a vision of Alix popped in her head at that moment and a hint of sadness grazed her heart. She chalked it up to being slightly jealous of Chloe finding her person while she had no real prospects in sight.

CHAPTER THREE

Just give me your key and I'll take care of Romeo." Alix took their assistant, Tobey, by the shoulders. "Xander said they're done with me for the day. It'll be fine. Go take care of your daughter."

A stray sob slipped out from between Tobey's lips. Alix wanted to pull Tobey into a hug, but they were afraid that would prompt a complete breakdown and she needed to stay strong. Tobey had gotten a call five minutes before from her kid's day camp to report that her daughter had hit her head while playing.

"Are you sure? I don't know what time we'll be home." Tobey sniffled and quickly rummaged through her purse to find her keys.

"I promise I'm fine. Plus, Romeo loves me. We've got this." Alix gently pried the keys from Tobey's hands and worked the house key off the ring. She pulled up Tobey's contact information from her phone and recited her address. "Now go. Keep me posted," they said after Tobey confirmed.

Alix had never been to Tobey's place, but it didn't seem to be too far from the studio. Hopefully, there was a park nearby where they could walk Romeo and maybe find a pup cup at a coffee shop. It was a beautiful Saturday afternoon and Alix was excited to be out in the fresh air and sunshine.

They shot off a message to Denise, the show's director, just to be sure nothing was on the schedule the rest of the day and, after confirmation, slipped out the side door and crawled into their convertible. The sleek, silver two-seater was ridiculously expensive and pretentious, but after heartbreak and a decent Hollywood contract, Alix decided to splurge. It helped and today was the perfect day to put the ragtop down and get some much-needed vitamin D.

Alix found Tobey's apartment building and snagged a parking spot up the block. The landscaping was slightly shabby and the building could've used a fresh coat of paint, but overall held an element of seventies charm. Alix rode the small elevator to the fourth floor and unlocked Tobey's apartment.

"Romeo, Romeo! Wherefore art thou, Romeo?" Alix couldn't resist quoting Shakespeare because the situation was perfect. They elevated their voice to announce their arrival as to not startle the sweet pooch. Romeo trotted into the living room surprised to see them, but happy. Alix rubbed his fur. "Hi, boy. How are you? Do you want to go for a walk?"

They looked around for his leash and found it on the small table by the front door next to a Barbie missing one arm, a small gaming system, more keys, and a coffee of the month gift card. Romeo danced when Alix held up the leash. In seconds, they were out the door and Alix let Romeo lead the way. While he was busy tagging every tree and hedge, Alix found the nearest park on their phone.

The half-mile walk was refreshing, and Romeo was such a well-behaved dog. He knew how to heel, wait, sit, stay, and shake. They got a lot of attention walking him and even though they loved their cat, having a dog by their side was, indeed, a chick magnet. Several women stopped them to say hello to Romeo and give Alix flirtatious smiles. Sadly, now was not the time to start dating. *When Sparks Fly* was starting to film and Alix would be busy hosting the show. It wasn't fair to ask anyone to be at their beck and call because filming sometimes lasted until after midnight. Ironically, Alix was too tired to date.

Alix eyed a fruit cart parked near the playground. Realizing they skipped lunch, an uncomfortable emptiness rumbled in their stomach at the thought of devouring slices of fresh fruit with tajin. "What are the rules about dogs and fruit?" Romeo indicated by repeatedly licking his chops that everything was fine and he was allowed to have it, too. Alix eyed him warily and googled fruits safe for dogs. "I'll have a cup with everything on it and a cup of just mango and pineapple for him."

The twenty-something kid running the cart turned on the charm and tried drawing Alix into conversation. He had thick, black slicked-back hair and a spotless white T-shirt. He tossed a chunk of pineapple to Romeo. "How you been, Romeo? I haven't seen you in a while." He turned his attention back to Alix. "Where's Tobey?"

"She's tied up at work. I volunteered to take this big guy for a walk." Alix leaned down and stroked Romeo's back for emphasis.

"She has a great job. Working for a studio. I'm jealous."

"You're trying to get into Hollywood?"

He shrugged and handed them the cups. "Aren't we all?"

Alix smirked and shrugged back. "Thanks for the fruit."

They looked for a place to sit and share the spoils. It was a perfect afternoon. It wasn't too hot, the fruit tasted delicious, and people-watching was on the agenda. Romeo plopped down on the bench beside them and they sat in companionable silence with full bellies until a squirrel ran into their line of vision. Alix thought it was cute the way it sniffed the air and how its ears twitched at other squirrels chattering in the trees above. It was peaceful and adorable until Romeo sprang from the bench and chased it. Alix didn't have a tight enough hold on the leash and swore as it ripped from their fingers and bounced on the ground in Romeo's wake.

"Romeo! Get back here. Romeo! Come here, boy." Alix took off running after him. The new leather of their clunk Doc Martens oxfords dug painfully into their ankles, making them instantly regret wearing them. They shouted several more times, but Romeo wouldn't listen. A few people tried to intervene, but he slipped through their grasps and continued running. Alix couldn't imagine he was chasing the squirrel anymore but was galloping off into freedom. "Romeo, please stop!" Alix twisted their ankle on a broken curb, cursed, and slowed down. A woman off in the distance grabbed Romeo's leash and braced herself as he jerked to a stop. "Oh, my God, thank you so much!" Alix jogged up to her, completely winded, and bent over to catch their breath. When they reached out for the leash and finally looked at Romeo's captor, shock and excitement rippled through them. "Wallflower. Hello again." Recognition and a flicker of fear registered on the woman's face. Alix took a step back to give her space. "Thank you for stopping him. I would hate to fail on my first day of dog sitting."

"Alix, right?"

Alix nodded, desperate to know her name, but not wanting to overwhelm her. Something about her made Alix pause. "We never did get around to proper introductions, but you remembered. I'm Alix, they/them, and this is Romeo, he/him." Alix gave a small encouraging smile in between large gulps of breath hoping it would come across as a safe and non-threatening gesture. Romeo's tongue lolled out of his mouth as he, too, was trying to cool down. Alix would give him a stern lecture about running off later.

The woman looked at the panting dog. "It's nice to meet you, Romeo."

"Do you mind if we sit? My legs are kind of rubbery after sprinting and I did something weird to my ankle," Alix said.

"My yoga mat is over there. I have an extra water bottle that you two can share," the woman said.

"Thank you. We appreciate it." Alix wrapped Romeo's leash around their fist, ensuring any attempts at running off again would be thwarted after five feet. They poured water into their cupped hand while Romeo sloppily lapped it up. The woman handed Alix a fast-food napkin she found in the bottom of her yoga bag.

"So, dog walker by day, Hollywood hipster by night?" she asked.

Alix laughed and fell back on the grass. Romeo curled up beside them. "Not a hipster. More of a helper."

"I can definitely see that. You helped me the other night. Thank you again," she said.

She slipped on a thin T-shirt over her skimpy athleisure top. Not that Alix was staring, but it was hard not to notice.

"I would've hated to see you fall. That driveway was a deathtrap. I'm glad we both survived," Alix said.

"I shouldn't have worn those new shoes. Those were the real deathtrap," she said.

Alix rubbed their ankle gingerly. They understood how footwear needed to be broken in. Even though they added padding to the back of their shoes, the skin at their ankles was raw. Now wasn't the time to inspect. "Here's the funny part. I wore these today to break them in. I didn't realize I was going to be running a marathon chasing after a doggo."

"Glad I could help," she said.

Alix liked the way her smile lit up the space between them. "So, I guess that makes you a helper, too. Since we're being extremely vague which is totally fine, I'm going to guess you're a yoga instructor."

The woman shook her head. "Let's play a game. Tell me what you do in the simplest way possible." She tied her hair back in a ponytail. Alix noticed she was more relaxed now that her body was covered. "I'll go first. I'm not a yoga instructor, but I tell people what to do."

Alix slowly nodded as though contemplating the woman's words. "Strong. Bossy. A lot to think about there. Let me see. Simplest way possible?" At her nod, Alix blew out a breath. "I make people fall in love."

That got a head tilt and puzzled look. "Huh. That's a surprise. Now I'm very curious," she said.

"Hold up." Alix reached out and playfully tapped the woman's hand. "I've held you in my arms and now I know you're a boss of some sort, but I still don't know your name." The blush that feathered her cheeks was delightful. They wanted to tease her but held off because they had just met and their relationship was vulnerable—if it was even a relationship. Alix pushed just a bit. "You even know Romeo's name."

"Why Romeo?"

"I don't know. I'm assuming because Tobey, his person, loves love. And he looks like a heartbreaker. Look at those big, brown eyes." It just occurred to Alix that Tobey worked on *When Sparks Fly* so if anyone believed in love, it was her. That was actually really sweet. "And you're stalling again." Alix pushed a little harder. "I have an idea. Hear me out. What are you doing today?"

"What do you mean?" she asked.

Alix's heart started beating faster as an idea quickly formed. Tobey had sent a message that they would be home in an hour and that everything was fine with her daughter. "Well, I have the rest of the afternoon off. Maybe we can just make a fun day of it. Let's have this spontaneous afternoon where we do whatever we want. I know you don't know me, but we can take this time and just hang out. If that sounds like fun, just tell me your name. It can be your first name only. And if you want me and Romeo to slink off with broken hearts, don't tell me your name." Alix hoped their charm was enough to intrigue the stranger. The seconds felt like hours, and for a moment, Alix thought whatever this could have been between them was over before it begun.

"Marianna." She hesitated. "I use she pronouns."

A tickle worked itself up from the pit of Alix's stomach to press against their chest. They tried to keep their voice even and steady. "Marianna. I like that a lot. It suits you." Marianna smiled and blushed again. Alix liked the way she nervously wrapped a blade of grass around her finger and how the sunlight that filtered through the green leaves landed softly on her face. She didn't seem like the woman from the other night, and even though she was beautiful then, the woman in front of her stripped of makeup and wearing her curly hair in a ponytail was breathtaking.

"I'm not looking for anything right now." Her voice was almost a whisper and she looked everywhere but in Alix's eyes. That meant Marianna felt whatever was happening between them, too.

Even though Alix was in the same boat, they liked the lightheaded feeling they got sitting close to their mysterious woman who now had a name. "Oh, I'm not either. It's such a beautiful day and I know I'm about to lose my free time. And I could use a new friend in LA. How about I take Romeo home and meet you by the park entrance over there in an hour? We can grab a bite to eat and maybe take a walk on the beach?"

"Hmm. That sounds suspiciously like a date," Marianna said.

Alix shook their head. "Nope. Just a fun evening for two people who don't have time to date and just want to forget about life's problems for a short time. What do you say?" Alix was trying to remember what clothes they had in their emergency bag in the car because showing up wearing the same clothes wasn't an option and there wasn't enough time to go home. This was a moment they had to grasp with both hands. Marianna looked at her phone.

"Okay. I should be able to make it back here by then."

Alix patted their leg to get Romeo's attention. He heeled immediately. Great time to obey, they thought. "I'll see you in an hour." Alix stopped and turned. "Hey, Marianna." There it was. That tiny tug on the ribbon of their attraction when Marianna's eyes met theirs. "Thanks for saving me today."

CHAPTER FOUR

Out of millions of people in LA, you ran into the same person twice within two weeks? How is that even possible?" Andrea's voice screeched through Marianna's car speakers two octaves higher than normal. She quickly turned down the volume.

"It's weird, right? But good." A momentary panic fluttered in her stomach. Was this a good idea? She didn't know a thing about Alix, which was the point, but also slightly unnerving.

"Tell me everything. Leave nothing out," Andrea said.

"I don't have a lot of time. I'm supposed to meet them in ten minutes, and I just parked. I wanted somebody to know what I'm doing or at least where I am. Check my location and make sure it's not in the middle of the ocean later tonight." Marianna's blood pressure spiked at the thought of doing something so exciting and so reckless.

"Will do. Good luck, have fun, and don't get murdered."

"Thanks, cousin." Marianna disconnected the call and took a deep breath before leaving her car. It was ridiculous that she drove the short distance to the park, but she wasn't going to sweat again around Alix. Plus, she didn't know how long they would be out, and she didn't want to walk home in the dark. She didn't know what to expect so she'd dressed for anything. Her summer dress was classy but comfortable and she knew she could walk for miles in her fashionable sandals. She smiled fondly when she remembered how effortlessly Alix caught her and how their eyes sparkled playfully even though it was a mortifying moment for her.

Marianna slowed when she approached the entrance to the park. She didn't want to seem too excited, but it was hard once she saw Alix. For someone who wasn't ready for a relationship, they looked fantastic.

"Are you ready to be spontaneous?" Alix asked.

It was hard not to stare at them because even though they weren't dressed as formally as they were the night of the party, they still looked great and smelled amazing. How did they get ready so quickly? "Yes, I am."

"I'm at your mercy since I'm not familiar with this neighborhood. What's a good place around here to hang out?"

"Are you new to this area or LA?" Marianna asked.

"I just moved here a little over a year ago from Portland. For my job."

"As a person who makes people fall in love." Marianna couldn't help but tease. She was enjoying the magical sweet spot when a person only saw the good in somebody they were just getting to know.

Alix laughed. "Yes, and it's very time-consuming, but I should take more time out to sightsee and learn Santa Monica and Hollywood and all the amazing touristy spots, but I'm also lazy and somewhat of a homebody. What about you? Born and raised in LA?"

Marianna nodded. "Something like that. My mom met my dad while he was stationed in Long Beach. I've always lived here."

"I'm jealous of people who have roots."

"You don't have roots in Portland?" Marianna asked. She couldn't fathom being away from her family.

"My brother and I own a tattoo parlor there, but my parents live on the East Coast. We bounced around a lot when I was a kid. I followed my brother to Portland knowing we'd always do something with our art."

"I think that's cool. You both followed your dreams." She pointed to the ink on Alix's arms. "Do you design your own tattoos?" She was fascinated as Alix explained the larger tattoos and the difference between theirs and the ones their brother, Buck, designed.

"Do you have any tattoos?" Alix took a step to the side and gave Marianna a quick look over. "I don't see any."

"No. Not because I don't like them, I just haven't found anything I like," she said. Most of her friends had boring tattoos like flowers or hearts. Chloe even had Connie tattooed on her heart. Marianna didn't have anything she loved or believed in that much to make it a permanent part of her body.

"Well, if you ever come up with anything, you now know a tattoo artist."

Marianna was trying to figure out how a tattoo artist could make somebody fall in love but drew a blank. She changed the subject. "What do you think of California so far?" Everything Alix said told her that they weren't a part of the Hollywood scene, yet they first met at a party for a big producer. Why was Alix there?

"That's a tough question. I love the beach and the warm weather, but I'm still getting used to the people."

"I get it. Me, too," Marianna said.

"But you're from here. What do you mean?"

Marianna didn't want the conversation to go down this path. She had her reasons, and talking about ex-girlfriends this soon in their budding friendship felt like a downer. "Let's just say I'm not a fan of the people in the Hollywood scene."

"Ouch. Sounds like a bad experience," Alix said.

Marianna's shoulders involuntarily tensed. Was she in the mood to talk about Vee? Their breakup wasn't that long ago. Or even Brandi who refused to go public with their relationship because she was afraid of alienating potential agents? "Not worth talking about." She shrugged off the tension. The last thing she wanted to talk about was a relationship that ended badly and without warning. She was thankful Alix didn't push. "I have an idea. How about we grab a coffee or a cup of tea? There's a cute little coffee shop about two blocks away."

"That sounds great. Are you more of a coffee drinker or tea drinker?" they asked.

"Both really. I only drink coffee in the morning, but I like tea, hot or cold, in the afternoon."

"Isn't it funny that people can drink super hot coffee all day long and nobody questions it, but when you say you drink hot tea in the afternoon, they have this weird reaction like it's too hot outside, why would you do that to yourself?" Alix walked two steps ahead so they could turn around and face Marianna. They continued walking only backward completely unaware of what was in their path and it made Marianna nervous. She was ready to grab Alix if they stumbled. The longer Alix stared at her, the more nervous she became. Blue eyes always fascinated her, and Alix's were the color of sapphires. Everyone in Marianna's family had brown eyes except her father who had light blue. Ever since she could remember, she wished for blue eyes like his. Instead, she got his long eyelashes and his height, but inherited her mother's wavy brown hair and chestnut-colored eyes.

"It doesn't make sense, right?" Marianna liked how playful Alix seemed. Who thought about things like tea versus coffee and the arguments for and against? "Now, you're from Portland so you must be a coffee snob."

Alix held their hand over their heart and turned back around so they were right beside Marianna again. "I mean, you're not wrong. I know a good cup of coffee, but when I'm desperate, I'll drink sludge."

Marianna wrinkled her nose. She tolerated coffee because elementary school hours were hard and the caffeine gave her the energy needed to keep up with eight-and nine-year-olds, but nothing hit the spot like a good cup of ginseng green tea. "Truthfully, I only like coffee if it's doctored up. Cream, sugar, a shot of vanilla." Alix looked horrified.

"Why would you do that? I mean, coffee is meant to be enjoyed untainted," they said.

Marianna put her hand on her hip. "Didn't you just talk about judgy people?"

"You're right. I'll have a cup of tea with you and I will undoubtedly enjoy it."

She liked how easy Alix was to talk to. She was horrible at small talk. It was refreshing to be around somebody who naturally kept the conversation going. "Good news. It's right around the corner."

"Is this your neighborhood or just a place you like to go?" Alix asked.

"I don't live far away. My entire family lives within a twenty-mile radius of here."

"You're so lucky. At least Portland is a direct flight, but I'm about to be slammed at work. I won't see my brother for a few months."

That stung Marianna's heart. She saw her family frequently and couldn't imagine waiting months between visits. "Can he come down here?" She smiled when Alix opened the door to Wooden Box Coffee for her.

"He does want to come down here for a baseball game. There are one hundred and sixty-two games a season, not including any playoff games. I'm sure I can get away for one of them," Alix said. They turned to Marianna. "What do you recommend? Earl Grey? Or sencha?" Marianna noticed how Alix barely held back the grimace when they said sencha.

"It's a horrible tea. It's not even good iced. How do you feel about bubble tea?"

"Something cool sounds great. What's your favorite?" Alix asked.

"I love the brown sugar milk tea," Marianna said. Before she could get her wallet, Alix had ordered two teas and tapped their phone on the payment terminal. "Thank you, but you didn't have to do that."

"Today was my idea so my treat. Let's grab a seat over there to get out of the sun for a bit," Alix said. Several people smiled at them as they weaved between the bistro tables to one nestled in a corner. It was the perfect spot for a private conversation and made for a nice, light date. Even though this wasn't a date, Marianna reminded herself.

"Excuse me for just a minute," Alix said.

She watched as they walked to the back of the café and disappeared under a sign marked restrooms. She took the time alone to check her makeup, which was perfect, and check her phone for any messages. Andrea had snapped a photo of Marianna's location. *Good, you're still alive. Keep me posted.*

She dropped a thumbs up on the message and put her phone back in her purse. Alix was on their way back when they were stopped by two very attractive women who Alix obviously knew. They both hugged them and got a selfie. "And you said you didn't have a lot of friends."

"Oh, I don't. And I wouldn't really call them friends. They aren't sitting with me drinking bubble tea and talking about baseball and dogs and all the fun things in life."

The words fell so effortlessly from Alix's lips. Marianna should've been put off by their smoothness, but Alix was too engaging. And they were focused solely on her. "We've only talked about Romeo. Do you have any dogs yourself or are you the kind of person who dog sits or babysits to have the experience but then can give them back when you're done?"

"I have a fat cat."

Marianna cocked her head and pursed her lips. "Is that really a nice thing to say?"

"Woody doesn't seem to mind. As a matter of fact, he's pretty confident and comfortable in his skin. I mean fur," Alix said. They pulled out their phone and showed Marianna a photo of a robust black-and-white cat with gold eyes.

"He's beautiful."

"He knows it, too. The few friends I do have come over to hang out with him. And drink my beer. What about you. Do you have any pets?"

Marianna didn't have the time for pets. "I don't, but my parents have a pug named Cookie."

"Aw. That's an adorable name. I feel like all pugs are sweet. Is Cookie?"

Marianna nodded. "She's as sweet as her name and very well-behaved."

"Is that a dig at Romeo?" Alix asked.

Marianna raised her eyebrow and shrugged. "I'm sure he's a good boy, but he's too big for my comfort level. I'm more of a lap dog kind of girl."

Their conversation flowed so easily that when Alix suggested dinner somewhere, Marianna was surprised that three hours had passed. "Wow. Definitely. What are you hungry for?" she asked.

"I have no dietary restrictions. I love everything. Whatever you're in the mood for." Alix pulled out their phone and rattled off restaurants nearby. "We can Lyft."

Marianna shrugged. "It's prime time for dinner. We might have to wait."

Alix rested their forearms on the table, an action that brought them into Marianna's space. Neither one moved. "You tell me what restaurant is good and I'll get us in."

CHAPTER FIVE

Y ou didn't tell me you were a foodie." Alix sat back in the chair stuffed and surprised they were contemplating dessert but pushed that temptation down. Camera weight was a real thing and Alix was very critical of themselves. Televisions were high-definition and very large. "I will come back to this restaurant again." They wanted to impress Marianna by getting them into an upscale restaurant where people were on a waiting list for months, but instead, Marianna waltzed them into the most charming restaurant, Clovr, with brightly colored dishes and thick, oak tables with padded benches. Marianna's friend got them a table near the bar although the outside dining space was adorable.

"I learned everything from my aunt. She's a wonderful cook and has a very successful catering business." Marianna pushed the empty old-fashioned glass to the side and reached for her glass of water. Alix eyed the abandoned Luxardo cherry in her glass and refrained from asking for it. She would ask Marianna's bartending friend, Jess, for an extra in the next drink.

"Speaking of following dreams, it seems like several people in your family followed their dreams. Your brother, your aunt. Even your uncle with his motorized surfboard business. I think that's great," they said.

"Can I get you another drink?" Jess swooped into the conversation as if reading Alix's mind.

Alix pointed at Marianna's glass. "I'll have one of those with an extra cherry."

"Same," Marianna said.

Alix caught the wink Marianna's friend shot her and looked away as though pretending they didn't see it. They waited until Jess was out of earshot. "So, how do you know her?"

"I've known her since we were in grade school. She's trying to get her big break into Hollywood but bartends here most nights. She always said if I needed a table, to give her a call," Marianna said.

"Are you close?"

"She's part of my inner circle. She's a good egg."

"What does she want to do in Hollywood?" Alix asked.

Marianna gaped at them. "Have you seen her? She's made for the camera. She's beautiful. Right now, she models for some LA-based designers. I know she loves it, but she really wants to be in the movies."

Alix caught Marianna's eye roll. She really didn't like the industry. "Is she good? Do you know? Does she have an agency?" Not that Alix could help, but maybe they could squirrel Jess's information away and pull it out if they ever crossed paths with somebody who was looking for someone like her.

"She was great in high school and she did some plays at the community college," Marianna said.

"I have no idea how hard it is to get an audition," Alix said. Their only experience with it was sending in a video of them explaining why they should be a contestant on *When Sparks Fly*. Everything else just fell into place whether they wanted it or not.

"Apparently, it's not easy." This time a frown slid into place as an apparent unpleasant memory clouded Marianna's features.

"If you want to talk about it, I'm a great listener," they said.

Marianna sighed. "I've been out my whole life and my first real girlfriend after college decided she wanted to stay in the closet. At first, I thought she was embarrassed of me, but it turns out, she was afraid of getting typecast because of her sexuality. And then my last girlfriend dumped me the second she got on a show. I was her free ride."

Her words were heated so Alix treaded lightly. "No wonder you're so wary of Hollywood types. That's got to be hard in a place like LA. Tobey, Romeo's mom, told me dating around here is difficult." Alix was about to change the topic, but Jess's delivery of fresh drinks made the segue easier.

"What do you have planned after this?" Jess asked. She placed both drinks on the table and gracefully picked up the empty glasses.

"We're winging it tonight," Alix said. They weren't sure what Marianna told Jess before arriving so wanted to keep it as vague as possible.

"That's great. Most people aren't spontaneous enough. If you need any suggestions, I'll be at the bar." She winked again at Marianna who blushed and quickly tried to cover it up by taking a sip of the fresh drink.

"I like your friend. She's nice," Alix said, hoping it didn't sound like they were interested in her. "I hope she gets what she wants. I mean, she got us a table at this swanky little restaurant. And judging by the fact that every table has been full since we got here, it was a nice favor. You'll have to tell her thank you if we don't see her again tonight." The stools were full of happy people drinking alcohol and Jess was moving like a pinball behind the bar bouncing from one end to the other, filling drink orders and smiling at the customers. Alix took the opportunity to slide into a different conversation. They told Marianna about the time they decided to spend a summer in Provincetown bartending but it only lasted three weeks. They were terrible at it because they spent more time talking to the patrons instead of getting drink orders out correctly or in a timely manner. They spent the rest of the summer selling saltwater taffy and working part-time at a housekeeping business. It wasn't the summer they planned, but it was one of the best summers of their life.

"I've never been there," Marianna said.

"My parents live in western Massachusetts. It was a four-hour drive and when you're eighteen, it's a lot, but it's an amazing place and every queer should go there. How did you spend your summers as a teen?"

"I spent them here. I worked for my aunt's catering business starting when I was fifteen. It was always going to be that. I knew that when I was old enough, I would work for her. I did babysit a lot though, too. I feel like my summers growing up were boring and typical." There was a comfortable lull in the conversation and Alix took the opportunity to look at Marianna. She was so refreshing and something unfamiliar tugged at Alix's heart. Hope, which disappeared from Alix's life when Savannah turned them down, was finding its way back to them.

Marianna pointed to Alix's almost empty drink. "Do you want to order anything else?"

"No, thank you. Any more alcohol and I'll fall asleep. I'm not ready to do that." Alix wanted the night to keep on moving in the magical direction it was headed. It was exhilarating to be with somebody who wanted to get to know them. It was obvious that Marianna didn't know who they were and Alix was impressed that she didn't probe. She was taking this situationship to heart and keeping it light enough to honor the suggestion Alix made at the start of the afternoon. Sometimes the conversation took a darker turn, but Marianna didn't shy away from tough subjects like addiction or politics. But Alix noticed when the topic got close to love lives, Marianna changed the subject. She wasn't going to give Alix anything but the bare minimum, and even though it wasn't Alix's business, they wanted to know everything about Marianna.

"Are you up for a walk? Or have you had enough of me yet?" The small quiver in their stomach told them they were nervous about Marianna's answer.

"It's such a nice night. Let's walk off the meal," Marianna said.

"Let me just grab the check and we can go." Alix wasn't sure if they should pay Jess or flag their waitress.

"It's already taken care of. You got the bubble teas and I got dinner," she said.

"Well, that's not fair at all. Let's go find one of those swanky bars so I can drop fifty dollars on fru-fru drinks for us. I'll feel better about it," Alix said. They could tell Marianna was about to protest, but their playful banter was interrupted.

"Are you leaving so soon?"

Jess rolled up as though on cue. Marianna stood and enveloped her friend in a hug. "Yes, we have plans. Thank you for dinner. I owe you," Marianna said.

Alix reached out their hand to shake Jess's and was immediately pulled into a hug. It was a surprise, but they didn't mind. It felt nice and friendly. Jess gave them warm vibes. "Yes, thank you. The food was great. Thanks for recommending the eggplant. It was delicious."

"She doesn't bring anyone here so you must be special," Jess whispered before she released them.

Pride bubbled up in Alix's chest even though there wasn't any reason. They didn't know Marianna that well and even though they both said they were too busy to date, they were going to take advantage of tonight until one of them dropped from exhaustion. It wasn't going to be Alix. This was too much fun. They gave Jess a friendly good-bye wave and followed Marianna through the restaurant until they reached the front door.

"Show me your world," Alix said. Marianna's smile was already affecting Alix. Maintaining a friendship without catching feelings was going to be hard with her. She was smart, quiet, and beautiful. It was obvious she loved her family and friends. Her foundation was strong.

"Okay, there's a bar about three blocks away. It's not as swanky as you want, but I can tell them to double the price of the drinks," she said.

And funny. She had a quiet sense of humor that Alix appreciated more than people with large ones. Wallflower was still the perfect description. "Well, let's not go that far. What's your favorite drink?"

"I like a nice glass of wine. Or a spicy bourbon," she said.

"Very sophisticated. I'm trying out new bourbons bound and determined to find one I like. Usually, my go-to is a mojito."

"Tell me your worst alcohol experience. The time you swore off alcohol for good," Marianna said.

Alix took a deep breath. It was during their stint on *When Sparks Fly* during a horribly hot day while playing water polo in the pool. There was so much free time waiting around for dates and cocktail parties. That day was a disaster for several contestants. One of the things Alix suggested to Xander was less alcohol and more workout equipment or board games at the mansion. He didn't take their advice. It made their stomach turn just thinking about it. Given Marianna's aversion to Hollywood and celebrities, Alix kept it vague.

"It was last year when I first moved here. A bunch of people got together at a pool party. Too much sun and liquor and not enough water. I felt like crap for the entire next day. It took a while to be able to have more than just a sip of alcohol here and there," they said.

"Sounds awful. Mine was the night I left the party when we first met. I went to Vegas for a bachelorette party and I made the mistake of trying to play catch-up." Marianna put her hand on her head and Alix smiled. "I didn't drink the rest of the weekend."

"That's kind of what Vegas is about, right?" They lightly touched Marianna's arm. "Listen, let's skip the alcohol and find ice cream or dessert instead. Crepes sound yummy. Something around here is open late." Alix pulled out their phone and quickly typed in all night diner and found a cute place. "We can jump in a Lyft and be there in eleven minutes. How does that sound?"

"That sounds perfect."

Spending time with Marianna was so enjoyable that Alix forgot about the heaviness of the show recording in less than two days and how their life was going to be long days, hard nights, and smiling for the camera take after take. It was going to be grueling. Was it fair to even start a relationship? Marianna deserved a friend who could be there for her when she called. Alix's schedule was too unpredictable. They were going to have to keep it more casual than they wanted.

❖

They both reached for the bottle of wine at the same time. Alix wiped the sand from the neck and handed it to Marianna. She smiled and brought the almost-empty bottle up to her lips making Alix inwardly sigh at how perfect her mouth was. They looked off into the distance. The moon was bright and the ocean dark. There was something slightly romantic about sharing a bottle of pinot grigio at a beach at three in the morning. This was how Alix wanted to spend their nights off.

"When did you come out as trans? If you don't want to talk about it, I understand." Marianna pushed the bottle back into the sand, crossed her arms over her knees, and looked at Alix.

"To the world? About four years ago. To myself? Way before that. I never felt comfortable with either side of the binary. Growing up was hard because I was labeled a tomboy, but that still meant everyone saw me as a girl wanting to be a boy and that's not it. I feel most comfortable being on the line between the two." Alix waved a hand at their clothes and short hair. "Obviously my gender expression is more masc, but I like being nonbinary. It fits me."

Marianna nodded. "It fits you perfectly. And I love this." She touched the tips of one of Alix's perfectly manicured short fingernails. The translucent purple nearly glowed in the moonlight.

"Thank you. When did you know you were queer?" Alix asked.

"I knew in grade school. I had a crush on my best friend who was straight. She broke my heart when she dated the captain of the boys' soccer team," Marianna said.

"That's the worst. Falling for a straight girl." Alix said. They paused. "Did you ever date anyone from your inner circle like Jess?"

Marianna burst out laughing. Alix liked the way her fingers wrapped around their forearm as she balanced herself and gave Alix a little reassuring squeeze whether she realized it or not. "Oh, God, no. I've seen too many friends date and then when they break up, hanging out together is awkward for everyone. Also, as beautiful as she is, I just see her as a friend." Her voice lowered as though somebody could overhear them. "She's slightly high maintenance. I've had my fair share of that and I'm not interested."

Alix slowly nodded. "Okay, so you like low maintenance. Maybe even people who take charge of situations. Got it." Even in the moonlight, they could tell Marianna was blushing. "Did you date a lot in high school? What was it like for you?"

Marianna shrugged. "High school was hard. I mean, you're not wrong about labeling me a wallflower. I've always been the quiet one."

Alix playfully wagged a finger at her. "The quiet ones are the ones you have to watch out for. In a good way, of course." They softly bumped their shoulder against hers and watched as she aimlessly drew figure eights in the sand.

"I was voted most likely to be found in the library. They weren't wrong. My superpower is knowledge. Socially awkward but the person you want on your trivia team," Marianna said.

"Ooh. Sexy and smart. I'll take it."

She shook her head. "I had popular friends, but I wasn't really in the popular crowd. They were the fun ones. I was somebody who tutored them sometimes. Except for Chloe and Jess. Well, that's not true. I helped them pass Algebra."

Alix wanted to rub away the worry line on Marianna's forehead with their thumb. Instead, they held their hands up. "See? Sexy and smart. You're an amazing person, Marianna Raines, and I'm glad we're friends." Alix reeled in the compliments, not wanting to scare her off. They reached for the bottle, feeling sophomoric knowing that her lips were just on the rim, and drank the rest of the wine.

"I'm glad, too."

"Sadly, we should probably get out of here. I didn't mean to keep you out this late." Alix stood and reached for Marianna's hand. Her fingers were soft and her nails slightly dug in their palms as Alix gently pulled her up. "The ocean is lovely even at night."

"I can't remember the last time I was at the beach this late. I was always told not to because it's not safe, but we really haven't been bothered," Marianna said.

Alix pointed to a few bars off in the distance. "Even though they're already closed, there are people there in case there's a problem." They pulled up Lyft and pointed at the closest bar. "Our Lyft driver will be there in fifteen minutes."

The Acura was waiting for them in the parking lot when they arrived. Alix held the car door open and slipped inside after

Marianna. Their thigh was pressed against hers and neither one moved to create space. It thrilled Alix but also made them realize that this night was coming to an end and a soft wave of sadness rolled over them. When the Lyft driver dropped them off, Alix noticed Marianna wasn't in a big hurry to get away either.

"I can't believe we stayed up half the night," Marianna said. She rubbed her face and stifled a yawn behind her palm.

"I had a great time. Thank you for showing me a little piece of your world." Alix leaned their hip against Marianna's car. "I know we said we were just keeping it casual because we both are busy right now, but could I have your number? Maybe we can text from time to time. You know, as friends." The look on Marianna's face gave Alix their answer and it wasn't what they wanted.

She put her hand on Alix's forearm. "We should probably just leave it up to fate. I know that sounds ridiculous, but I'm about to be slammed at work and you said you're going to be busy, too," she said.

"How about this. If you're available next Sunday, let's meet at Wooden Box Coffee at nine. If you can't make it, I'll understand." Sunday mornings were always open. The contestants slept in and the staff wasn't expected until noon. Alix slid their hands in their pockets to keep from fidgeting. They didn't want Marianna to know that they were anxious for her response and tried to appear as casual as possible.

"That sounds like *An Affair to Remember*," Marianna said.

Alix could tell she was wavering. "I thought you didn't watch television."

"That movie is from the fifties. And it's cinema. Also, it's like *Sleepless in Seattle* but not as creepy. Take your pick," she said.

"Movies are okay, but television shows are bad. Okay, got it." A tiny nagging feeling crept into the forefront of Alix's mind. Now was the time to come clean, especially if there was a friendship in the making. Or more. They tamped down their last thought. Too soon. It was too soon to think about that.

"I'd rather read. Or work out. Or sleep," Marianna said.

"Don't even tell me you don't have a television." Alix gasped in mock disbelief. "Or do you stream from your phone or a tablet?"

"All of it. Honestly, I'm tired when I get home. I turn on music or watch a cooking show while I veg. I need mindless shows that don't have any drama. I can't watch television or movies that make me uncomfortable. I want to power down at the end of the day or on the weekends," she said.

"There's where we differ. I watch a lot of television. And a lot of sports. I love baseball, football, hockey, and golf," Alix said.

"And all of those are stressful. Will the home team win the game or not? Competition makes me nervous. Same with reality shows. I don't like watching people be mean to others just to win some prize. It's like drama sells."

Alix felt their heart sink at Marianna's words. "Maybe you can look at it like it's more like a degree of uncertainty. Will they or won't they? It's still fun to cheer people on. And let's be honest, most decent people win on reality shows. They keep the troublemakers for drama."

Marianna shook her head. "Why have drama? It's unnecessary. And, again, stressful."

Alix shrugged knowing full well why. "Ratings. Plus, people like watching other people say and do things they never would. It's a whole thing. Apparently, there's a science to it."

They were both stalling. Alix toed a loose pebble and rubbed their neck. They hoped Marianna would take them up on their offer. Honestly, they weren't even sure if they could get away, but as the host, they had more freedom than being a contestant. They would make it work. "Okay, I'm going to go. Go home. Get some sleep. Thank you for a nice, spontaneous thirteen hours of carefree, no-strings-attached fun. Is a hug out of the question?" Alix asked.

"Another chance to hold me." Marianna's eyes widened in surprise. "I'm so sorry. I didn't mean it that way."

Alix laughed. "You're not wrong. Come here." They held open their arms and smiled when the warmth of Marianna's body pressed against theirs. The contact was brief, but it energized Alix.

"Thank you again. Hopefully, we'll see each other a week from today," Alix said.

Marianna slipped into her car and slowly pulled away. Alix gave a quick wave and walked across the street to their convertible. Last night, this morning, however they wanted to put it, was the most fun Alix had in months.

CHAPTER SIX

W hy on earth did Marianna agree to teach summer school? She looked at the packed classroom. They combined the second and third graders into one room and every one of them looked bored and tired. She didn't blame them. She was only there for the extra paycheck, and the kids were there because they needed daycare. "Since this is the first day, why don't we do something fun."

A few kids perked up. After reviewing the curriculum, Marianna had decided she was going to rely on educational games to keep the kids sharp. Most of summer school was just extended daycare. This was her second year so she knew the tricks but wanted the kids to be excited to be in school. She turned on the Smartboard to show ten lines of ten single numbers and divided the class into two groups.

"Who loves math?" she asked. She expected the boos and groans. Nobody liked math at eight thirty in the morning. "Let me phrase it a different way. Who loves math enough that winning this game will give them extra playground time?" That woke them up. The room filled with excitement as the kids sat up straighter. She split the classroom in half. "Everybody on this side is Team Fire and everyone on this side is Team Ice." She waited for them to finish mimicking whooshing sounds of fire and hissing sounds of ice. "Okay, okay. Let me explain how the game is played."

At least the game kept the kids entertained and Marianna's mind mostly off Alix. Did she make the right decision not to give

Alix her number? Was that dumb? She couldn't remember the last time she stayed out that late. Maybe that was the problem. She made a bad decision because she was overtired. Was that even a thing? She sighed. Alix was great, but maybe too great and she learned the hard way that the big personalities weren't for her. Vee was always the life of the party and the person who was always in front of the camera. It was going to take a lot for her to trust bold people again.

"Ms. Raines?"

The tiny voice snapped her back to reality. "Yes?"

"Is my answer correct?"

She mentally scolded herself and focused on the numbers the student was pointing to. "Yes, you got it." Team Fire erupted into victorious shouts of joy. "Looks like Team Fire gets fifteen extra minutes at recess." Marianna had checked with her teacher's assistant who was more than happy to hang outside in the fresh air with the winners. It was a successful learning game and fun for the students. She decided she would start every week with the math game.

By the time summer school let out for the day, Marianna was exhausted. She set her bag on the coffee table and dropped on the couch. Chloe had texted her several times, apparently forgetting that Marianna was teaching this summer.

Where are you?

Hello? We're doing final fittings this weekend. What day is good for you?

Marianna groaned. Chloe was getting married in a few weeks. As happy as she was for her friend, she was dreading it. She'd invited her cousin even though she knew several people who were going solo.

Sorry. First day of summer school. I'm free either day.

Oh, shit! I forgot. How was it?

Marianna laughed. *Exactly how you would think. It's going to be a long month.*

You're the bravest person I know. Everyone is down for Sunday. Meet at eleven?

Marianna was trying not to think about Alix's invitation, but it buzzed around her brain like a bee to a flower. She had gone back and forth a thousand times. Should she go and see Alix again or just leave it as a perfect night? Even though she and Alix talked about how they needed only friendship now and nothing more, Marianna felt it could quickly turn and she wasn't emotionally prepared to screw up another relationship. She typed out, then quickly erased the message where she said she was having coffee with a friend.

See you then. She tossed the phone at the end of the couch and scowled. Why couldn't she stop thinking about Alix? It was because for the first time in a long time, somebody took the time to really get to know her. It felt respectful and Marianna hadn't felt that in a long time. If she met with Alix Sunday morning, she would have to leave after an hour and a half. That was harmless, right? She nodded and convinced herself it was safe and Alix needed friends. Who better to show them around than somebody who had lived in the area her whole life?

❖

Marianna didn't want to be early. She tossed and turned most of the night worried she'd oversleep and ended up getting to Wooden Box fifteen minutes early. She smiled when she saw Alix already at a table. "Hi." She hoped the rush she felt was just the heat of the early summer morning and not the nearness of Alix.

"Hi. I'm glad you made it. What can I order for you?" Alix did that thing where their dark blue eyes were focused solely on her and in the beginning, it was unnerving, but today it felt different.

"Oh, you don't have to order for me. I'll just run up to the counter. Can I get you anything to eat? Have you had breakfast?" Marianna grasped the back of the chair and rocked it gently as she waited. It felt like time stopped as they stared at one another. Alix didn't look as fresh and pressed like before, but still sexy as hell.

"My team and I just had breakfast an hour ago. We just got done working," they said.

"Wait. You haven't been to bed yet?" Marianna gaped at Alix. "What time did your day start?"

"Grab your coffee and we'll talk about it."

Marianna quickly ordered a latte and even though her stomach rumbled, she passed on the coffee cake. Eating alone in front of people was unnerving, especially those who made her blush. She grabbed her latte and made her way back to the same table they sat at before. "Tell me about your day or night or whatever?"

Alix waved Marianna off. "It's not a big deal. We're just working on a project that took longer than we thought."

"You must be so tired. When do you have to go back to work? Or is today your day off?" Marianna asked. And she thought her days were long and hard. Alix checked their watch.

"I have a little bit of time. Tell me about your week."

The leaf design on Marianna's latte gently separated as she blew on the top of it to cool it. She regretted not getting tea but was so nervous ordering knowing Alix was watching her that she panicked and ordered the first thing she saw. "It was as exhausting as I thought it would be." Which was weird because she taught every day during the regular school year, but trying to keep education interesting when the kids wanted to be anywhere but school was harder in summer when the weather was great.

"I bet bossing people around is hard work." Alix winked.

Marianna was surprised at the jolt that shot through her veins at Alix's wink. What was happening to her? "You make my job sound more badass than it really is. This wallflower isn't that bossy." She took a small sip and swallowed the strong brew without grimacing. "Why did making people fall in love take all night?" She laughed at how sexual that sounded.

"You can lead a horse to water…" Alix's voice trailed off.

"What does that even mean?"

"But you can't make it drink?" Alix looked at her expectantly. "Seriously? You've never heard that?" They sounded incredulous.

Marianna shook her head.

"I mean, I can set the scene and create the perfect atmosphere, but I can't make people fall in love." Alix shrugged.

"Okay, I get it now. Somehow, I find it hard to believe, though. You're very persuasive," Marianna said. Was that a blush that colored Alix's cheeks?

"I don't know about that. I didn't get your phone number. Talk about a blow to the ego," they said.

Without even thinking, Marianna slid her phone across the table, bumping Alix's coffee cup hard enough to slosh some over the lip. "Oops. I'm so sorry."

Alix picked up the phone and typed their name and number. They handed Marianna back her phone. "Any time you need somebody to talk to or text, just hit me up."

This was a big trust move for Marianna and a part of her felt like Alix knew that. She nodded and put her phone back in her purse pretending the weight of it didn't feel like a ton. "I'll do that."

"Big plans for the day?" Alix asked. Marianna wondered if they were going to offer up another spontaneous afternoon. Sadly, she wouldn't be able to accept because Chloe would drag out the fitting and it would turn into a late lunch.

"I have a fitting at eleven. Remember that bachelorette party?"

"For Chloe, right?" It was nice that Alix remembered.

"Yes. She's getting married in two weeks. Today is the final fitting."

"Are you the maid of honor?"

"A bridesmaid. Jess is the maid of honor. There are five of us in the party."

"I love weddings," Alix said with a smile.

"Because you make people fall in love. Have you been to many weddings for people you've made fall in love?" Marianna asked.

"All together?" Alix looked up as they counted on their fingers. After two rounds of counting, they looked at Marianna. "Zero."

"What? What do you mean? You don't strike me as somebody who fails."

Alix's eyebrow raised slightly. "Well, I'm just getting started. Ask me in a few months."

"Well, now I'm officially intrigued." Marianna sat back in her chair and crossed her arms. This back and forth had been cute, but now she was very curious about what Alix did for a living. She never got the chance. Alix's phone chimed and they stood after reading the message.

"I'm so sorry, Marianna. I have to go." The sweet, playful smile on Alix's face was replaced with a straight line as they read the message again.

"Oh, no. It's okay. Go do what you have to do," she said. She liked how Alix's voice softened when they said her name.

"Text or call me sometime? I'd like to try this again when work isn't blowing up my phone," Alix said.

Marianna nodded. "Sure." She stood when Alix moved closer.

"I'm sorry again," they said. There was a pause as they looked at one another. Marianna noticed the slight blue tint under Alix's eyes and how their body language screamed exhaustion. She hugged Alix and watched as they hustled to the door and disappeared. It wasn't even nine thirty. She pulled up her contact list and smiled when they found Alix's name. Alix Sommers. She wanted to text them right away, but swiped out of contacts and pulled up a game she played to kill time. It was too early to go to the bridal shop and too late to go home. She pushed her coffee away and ordered a tea. When she became aware that she either needed to order another tea or give up the table, she headed to the final fitting. She could hang out in her car until everyone showed up.

"You're never this chipper on a Sunday morning. Especially after hell week." Chloe met Marianna as she parked. "We're the first ones here. Can you tell I'm excited?"

"You're practically glowing," Marianna said.

"I'm just happy I found my forever person, you know? It's been a rough road." She looked horrified and corrected herself. "Except for your brother. I mean, Brandon was always great. We just didn't fit together."

Marianna gave her a hug and smiled. "He told me to tell you he's really happy for you."

Chloe's dimples popped up on her cheeks. "Did he really?"

Marianna nodded. "Connie is a great person and everyone knows it. I'm really happy for you, too."

"I'm guessing Brandon's not going to be your date at the wedding. We still have you down as a plus-one. I'm not giving up hope. Any prospects besides Andrea? Don't get me wrong. Your cousin's great."

Marianna hesitated. How fun would it be to invite Alix to Chloe's wedding, as a friend, given that their job was this very thing? "I might. I have a new friend that I might ask. They're really busy so I don't know if they can get away." That was the perfect reason to shoot Alix a text.

"Oh, do tell." Chloe slinked closer as though Marianna was going to tell her the biggest secret. Marianna playfully pushed her away.

"Nothing to tell. Yet. But if things turn, I'll let you know."

Chloe threw up her arms. "Well, tell me something. We've waited a long time for you to think about another person since Vee."

"Right now we are just new friends. They are new to the area and I've been showing them around," Marianna said.

"Well, regardless, you look happy. Sometimes a new friend is the perfect remedy for a quick bounce back," Chloe said. She pointed as Jess and the twins pulled up. "We'll talk more later. Let's go get beautiful."

The sales associate unlocked the door at eleven and ushered them inside. "Your dresses are hanging up for you. There are mimosas, muffins, and fruit if you're hungry." She pointed to the long table far away from the dressing rooms. The message was clear. Don't eat or drink while trying on dresses.

"My mom will be here in about ten minutes. She's excited to see how they look," Chloe said.

It wasn't that Chloe's mother was intolerable—she just wanted things a certain way. The dresses changed from a pale green to lilac because of her. Marianna thought the change was better, but it was Chloe's wedding and she deserved to have it her way. After the fiasco on her way to Vegas, Marianna begged for shorter heels for fear of tripping and because she was so much taller than the rest of the party, Chloe agreed to one-and-a-half inch heels instead of three-and-a-half. The bridal shop had dyed the shoes to match the dress and today was the moment of truth. Was everything going to match?

"You even put on makeup for the final fitting. That's smart," Jess said.

Even though that wasn't the reason she had makeup and styled her hair, she just nodded. "I want to see what's going to work with my skin tone and the dress."

"But Chloe hired stylists for hair and makeup. They'll be able to do magic. They won't have to do much with us." Jess gave an exaggerated wink.

Marianna thought Jess was the prettiest in the wedding party. Her blond hair was straight and lovely and her large boobs perky and all hers. Not that Marianna lacked, but she wasn't confident like Jess was. Jess got all the attention whenever they went out. Alix was right. Marianna was a wallflower but that was okay. She grabbed her dress off the rack and slipped into one of the rooms. The dress wasn't too tight and the slight flare allowed her room to move, dance, sit, and sprawl out if she wanted.

"You all look so wonderful!"

Chloe's mom already had a plate of food and was sitting on the chaise nibbling on a strawberry. The associate was hovering in case she got too close to the dresses. Marianna smiled knowing full well Chloe's mom knew exactly what she was doing based on her tiny smirk as she put the leafy crown on her plate and licked her fingers.

"My waist is loose. I might need a little taken in."

Jess pulled the fabric away from her waist showing the give of her dress. Marianna frowned. This would be Jess's third alteration. She shot Chloe a look. There was concern on Chloe's face, too. Whenever Jess didn't get a part she auditioned for, she always thought it was because she wasn't pretty enough or thin enough. It was a cycle and Chloe and Marianna would have to have another conversation with Jess about their concerns.

"My dress is fine," Marianna said. She sat down across from Chloe's mom, careful to stay out of reach.

"You look lovely, Marianna. How is your family doing?"

"Everyone's busy and healthy. We're all doing well. Thank you for asking."

Chloe's mom leaned closer. "I heard you might have a date for the wedding. I'm so glad you're getting over Vee. She was never good enough for you."

Marianna gritted her teeth. She literally told Chloe fifteen minutes ago. When did Chloe have time to tell anyone?

"It's a long shot and I might not even extend the invitation. It might be nice just to have fun with my friends and not have to worry about somebody new in the group," she said. Did she believe it? Absolutely not. Did she say it with conviction? Also, no, but everyone was respectful enough to not question her. She'd been through too much.

CHAPTER SEVEN

I'm sorry I'm late."

Alix lobbed their apology to everyone within hearing distance and slid into the chair for hair and makeup. They had decided to ask for forgiveness rather than permission. They really wanted to see Marianna again even if it was just for twenty minutes. At least now Marianna could reach out if she wanted. They looked at their phone again.

"Expecting an important call?" Mandee, the show's makeup artist, asked. She tsked and slightly shook her head after scrutinizing Alix's face. Their paths rarely crossed during the last season since the contestants had their own hair and makeup team, but Mandee stepped in to do all the makeup during the week in Mexico. It was the one perk Alix missed most when they left the mansion—having somebody do all the hard work. Hair was relatively easy, but Alix never got the hang of makeup. Mandee was a genius and made them look refreshed and glowing in front of the camera.

"Maybe," Alix said. It wasn't anyone's business. Alix liked Mandee but she wasn't overly friendly. She was proficient at her job but hadn't warmed up to them. But then, Alix wasn't making the effort either. They tried harder. "Just a new friend."

"Like a friend-friend or just a friend?" She emphasized the last friend by dragging out the word.

"Right now, just a friend. But there's hope for something more."

"Good for you. Was it an organic meeting or did you use an app?" she asked.

Alix shuddered at the thought of using a dating app in Hollywood. Especially since most of the people on the queer sites were aware of the show. "Organic. We met at Xander's birthday party. She literally fell into my arms."

Mandee stopped moisturizing Alix's face. "Well, if that isn't the most romantic thing I've ever heard, I don't know what is."

Alix wanted to smile, but Mandee's face massage was making it difficult. "She was wearing these ridiculously high heels and tripped on a cobblestone and then plunk! Crashed into me and I caught her before she fell."

"Aren't you the knight in shining armor. Did you get her number then?"

Alix laughed. "This is going to sound ridiculous, but no. I saw her a few weeks later in the park. I was walking Tobey's dog Romeo and he got away from me. Marianna, that's her name, was in the park doing yoga and grabbed his leash."

"So, she returned the favor. That's cool."

"We went out that night, as friends, and just agreed to hang out, have fun, not talk about our jobs or our pasts and ended up staying out all night. It was the most fun I've had since moving to LA," Alix said.

"So, does she know what you do for a living?" Mandee asked.

"She doesn't know about me being the host of *When Sparks Fly*. At all. It's nice," Alix said.

"Don't most queer people know about our show? I mean it made primetime last season and was plastered all over social media."

"It's kind of strange, isn't it? She said she doesn't watch much TV." Alix frowned and shook their head. "Maybe she doesn't have a lot of queer friends. You know how the straight world is self-absorbed."

"Ouch. Not everyone."

Mandee gave Alix a stern look. Alix sighed. Forward progress with Mandee just took a step back. "I'm sorry. I just meant from ratings and information gathering, most straight people aren't meeting in groups to watch our show, but a lot of queer people had watch parties for shows like *The Bachelor* and *The Bachelorette*."

"We all want love."

"Just not equal television time." Alix couldn't figure out why she was fighting this fight with Mandee. It wasn't her fault. "I'm sorry. I'm just tired and I'm not making any sense. You've always been so supportive of us and the show. Forgive me." Regret uncoiled in their stomach and Alix grasped for anything neutral to talk about. Before they could blurt something boring about the weather, their phone dinged.

"Is it her?" Mandee stopped spreading the second moisturizer to give Alix time to check.

The number wasn't saved in their phone, but the words were definitely from Marianna.

Did you make it back on time? Or are you in trouble?

"It's her." Alix quickly added Marianna to their contact list and starred her in their favorites.

"You can text her back. I can wait." Mandee stood with her weight on one hip and both hands away from Alix's face.

Alix took Mandee up on her offer, whether she was being sarcastic or not. *I was only a few minutes late and nobody yelled at me so all is good.*

Great. Try to find time to rest today. Talk to you later.

Alix sent a thumbs-up emoji and tucked their phone in their pocket. "Thanks for that."

Mandee gave a small nod and started contour lines. Alix tried hard not to smile and focused on being in the moment. They were professional. It was just a text. They received hundreds of texts daily. Maybe not from tall, beautiful women with long wavy hair who may or may not be interested in them, but still. The count was high.

Denise Lawry, the director of *When Sparks Fly*, slid into Alix's peripheral. "Are you good to go? I know it was a long night and everyone's tired, but emotions are high and we want to capitalize on that."

Alix cracked an eye open to look at Denise. Was she this cold when Alix was a contestant? What things did she say about them?

"I get it. As soon as Mandee is done, I'll head over to wardrobe. Shouldn't take too long. Are the contestants up and moving around?" Noon was the average time the women started stirring. Right now, their private conversations with one another were being recorded and reviewed with a fine-tooth comb.

"I'll have Alix out of the chair in fifteen minutes. They should be on set in twenty," Mandee said. She shooed Denise back and quickened the pace. "Last night was hard for everyone. Don't let Denise get to you. She has a good heart. She's just overwhelmed. Last season was pretty bonkers with everything that happened with Savannah and Lauren. She's hoping for normal problems this time around like tears and arguments. Last night didn't disappoint."

Alix blew out a deep breath. "We just got started. I feel like our season was really tame compared to this one. How can so many women say they're already in love with Heather Winemore? They've only known her for two weeks."

Mandee playfully tapped the end of her brush on Alix's nose. "Don't knock love at first sight. Maybe their feelings are legitimate." They both laughed.

"You're right. I know I didn't do this to further my career on television yet here I am, ready to stand in front of cameras."

"And you're finding people outside of the show to connect with. You must get a ton of fan mail. Any prospects besides her?" Mandee pointed to Alix's phone.

Alix was hesitant to discuss their personal life on the set. It wasn't professional and they weren't sure who was close enough to overhear. Opening up to Mandee was one thing, but more people were in earshot now. Discretion was a must, especially now that they were in the limelight more. "I've been busy getting situated in my new place. And learning things around here."

"What about all those parties?" Mandee asked.

Alix refrained from rolling their eyes. "They are more for meeting people in the industry than for meeting potential partners."

"Must be tough. I'm glad I have a boyfriend. The dating scene is hideous, especially here," Mandee said.

"So, I've heard." Both Tobey and Marianna said the same thing.

"Let me spray your face and get you to wardrobe. We don't want to keep Denise waiting."

Alix was on the set within the twenty minutes Mandee promised. Today was a group date. Alix would be heavily involved which meant a lot of camera time. They left their phone with Tobey while one of the set's sound mixers discreetly hid their microphone in their clothing. Even though it was getting easier to be in front of the camera, Alix still felt beads of sweat along their waistband. It was embarrassing because the sound mixer had to double tape the microphone cord so it would stay in place.

They picked up the schedule for today and practiced sounding casual and encouraging. Thankfully, Alix only had to introduce the date card to the women and then slip away until everybody got ready. After filming the quick scene, Alix tried to relax and unplug, but the pull to scroll on their phone and check text messages was too strong. Tobey handed them their phone on her way to wardrobe to pick up their next outfit. It seemed like such a waste. Were they doing enough? Should they be more involved? Nobody really gave them direction unless there was a camera nearby. Maybe Alix should reach out to Lauren for pointers but they were worried Savannah might not like that.

Have you made anybody fall in love yet?

Alix smirked at Marianna's text and quickly looked around to see if anyone was watching. *Not yet, but I'm working on it. How's your day bossing people?*

Shrug. Somebody has to do it. But so far it's been mostly good.

Mostly good? Anybody getting fired? Alix tried hard to chill and not let the pull of their conversation take over, but it was hard not to be fully invested. Marianna was on their mind entirely too much. Especially since both agreed that friendship was the only thing on the table at the moment. Maybe it was the thrill of the chase. But what were they chasing?

No. I'm really at their mercy. One day they'll figure out their power over me, but for right now, I have the upper hand.

Alix laughed out loud. Their phone vibrated with emails for work and messages from other people popped up on their screen.

Alix ignored everything. They wanted to keep the banter with Marianna alive. *I pity them.*

You think that. Wait until you meet them.

Alix froze and immediately wondered why or when they would meet Marianna's co-workers. Bubbles popped up before they could respond.

At least I have the weekends off.

Lucky you. Love stops for no one. Alix dropped a sad face followed with a wink emoji.

When's your next day off?

Why? Do you want to do something? Tomorrow was a blackout day. No filming, no wardrobe, no makeup. It was a day to relax. After last night and this morning, everyone needed time off. Alix vowed to lie on the couch with Woody and stream the latest episodes of *The Great British Baking Show* in between naps. It was the perfect day. One their body and brain desperately needed. But here they were, ready to throw it all away if the cute girl said yes. *My next day off is tomorrow. Then I don't know.*

That has to be hard. Not knowing. How do you know what to look forward to?

"Alix. Denise wants to go over a few things before the group date gets underway," Tobey said. She put her hands on her hips. "How are you already wrinkled?"

Alix stood and looked at their clothes. "I literally just sat down."

"You've been here half an hour and probably missed out on lunch." Tobey dug out an apple from her backpack. "I don't know when we'll get a dinner break." She looked down at Alix's phone. "Finish your message first. Looks important. All those happy faces and words."

Alix smiled softly as they caught the apple in midair from Tobey. "Thanks for thinking of me."

"I'd get in so much trouble if you passed out. Also, make sure you stay hydrated. It's hot and most of the group date will be outside."

Alix loved pickleball and was excited to help announce the match. They were getting help from one of the quarterbacks from the

Los Angeles Rams and Alix promised themself not to act starstruck. Sports was life. They played disc golf, pickleball, and softball back home in Portland. Watching baseball with Buck was one of their favorite pastimes. Alix sent Marianna a quick text. *Gotta go. Boss wants me but I'll chat with you later. Thanks for making my day.* They hit send before changing their mind. It was okay to be excited about a new friend.

CHAPTER EIGHT

"Why don't you just invite Alix?" Andrea asked.

Marianna chewed on her bottom lip as she thought about her cousin's idea. "Would it be weird to invite an almost stranger to a wedding? They probably wouldn't be able to go because they work every day." Andrea was fixing a charcuterie board while Marianna was cutting up fruit for the family meal. Once a month, the extended family got together for Sunday dinner. She chewed on a juicy strawberry while fielding questions her mind and her cousin threw at her.

"Are they a server?" Andrea asked.

"What?" Marianna looked at her cousin.

"I'm trying to figure out what job they have. Usually food or retail don't have set schedules. Those schedules are announced weekly or biweekly." Andrea continued dicing cheese and throwing out job possibilities. "Neither of those jobs have anything to do with falling in love. Maybe they were stretching the truth. People love food, right?"

Guilt weighed her down because she wasn't entirely truthful to Alix about what she did for a living. Being a boss sounded a lot better than a third-grade teacher. She was proud of her students and what she was doing, but it wasn't a sexy job. "We know about the power of food. And even though this back and forth is cute and fun, maybe it's time to come clean."

"Invite them to the wedding. You'll have more fun with them," Andrea said.

"Isn't that kind of weird? We've only hung out a handful of times." What if Alix said no?

"What do you think, Pops? Should Marianna invite a new person in her life to Chloe's wedding? Or do you think it's too soon?"

Marianna's uncle entered the kitchen and hugged them both. "Why wouldn't you? Are you dating?"

Marianna felt the heat rise up from deep inside and color her cheeks. Her uncle Bill was notorious for teasing all the kids. "No, we're just friends."

"Friends for now, but I have hope," Andrea said. She nodded as if she knew Alix even though she'd never met them. "I can just tell by the way you talk about Alix. You haven't been this happy or all about your phone since that skank Vee dumped you. She better hope she never runs into me again." She muttered something low that only Marianna could hear. She acted shocked and nudged Andrea with her elbow.

"She wasn't completely bad," Marianna said. The words tasted bitter leaving her mouth. "I mean, everyone here loved her for at least part of the time, right? You even got her a Christmas present."

"Only because we drew names and sadly, I got hers. I hope the necklace I bought at the thrift store rots off her neck," she said.

Marianna knew Andrea was hurt by Vee, too. They used to talk all the time about fashion and what celebrities were wearing. Marianna had tuned them out. She hated how obsessed Vee was about famous people and what they wore to events. When Vee signed with an agent, Marianna knew she was serious about acting. Getting in front of the camera was more important than their relationship. Vee stopped contributing rent money so she could buy expensive clothes to look the part. She would hold Marianna and apologize until she felt Marianna soften and give in. To compensate, Marianna worked as many catering jobs as she could. When Vee got her first acting gig, she packed up and moved out leaving Marianna all the bills and a rude note.

"I believe in karma. She'll get what's coming to her." Marianna couldn't afford to break the lease, but once it was up, she moved to a tiny apartment on the other side of the building that was big enough for only her.

"I hope whatever she does in this life, she fails," Andrea said. She never hid her feelings. Marianna respected her for that even if her words often stung.

"I just hope I never see her again," Marianna said.

"Well, she's no longer a part of our lives so we can put her behind us," Bill said. He snatched another piece of cheese from Andrea's board. "You should invite Alix. If you present it like a group of people going as friends, it won't seem so much like a date."

Andrea smacked his hand when he reached for more. "Even though he's spoiling his appetite by filling up on cheese, he's right. Just tell them a group of people are going and it'll be a good time. Wait. Even better. Tell them it's a great place to meet new friends."

Marianna slowly nodded as she thought about every scenario that could come from her asking Alix to be her plus-one. Alix reading too much into it, Alix saying no and never talking to her again, or worse, Alix saying yes and hoping for more than friendship. Chloe's wedding wasn't casual. It was a traditional black-tie wedding with expensive champagne and over a hundred guests. She turned to Andrea and frowned. "But I already asked you. That's not fair to you. You were looking forward to it."

"I'm looking forward to you going out and having fun. And that dress? With professional hair and makeup done? Chloe is going to ask you to sit far away from her because you'll be the one everyone will be looking at," Andrea said.

Marianna blushed. She liked getting dolled up because it made her feel beautiful and she hadn't felt that way in a long time. "Chloe is stunning. She and Connie are gorgeous together. And Jess is perfect. I just hope I survive the photo shoot." As good as she felt looking her best, she wasn't photogenic at all. It was a good thing she wasn't on the socials because her selfies were hideous. Her teaching mentor had recommended that she not have active social media accounts and since she was avoiding Vee, deleting them a few years ago was an easy decision.

"Quit worrying. You'll be fine. Send Alix a text right now before you talk yourself out of it. Hopefully they can make it. If they can't then I'll go and we'll still have fun," Andrea said.

Marianna took a deep breath and picked up her phone. "What do I say?"

Andrea leaned over her shoulder. "Say hey, next Saturday I'm going to my friend's wedding and I wanted to know if you wanted to be my plus-one. Don't say date or go with me because that implies too much. And add it'll be a great place to meet new people because she has a hundred guests."

"I think it's more like one sixty."

"Just say a lot. A lot of people." Andrea pointed at Marianna's phone ready to grab it if she didn't type fast.

"Okay, okay. Give me a minute to type something noncommittal," she said. She typed, erased, typed more words, erased some and scowled at Andrea who was huffing and pacing beside her.

"Read it to me before you send," she demanded.

So, listen. My friend is getting married next Saturday and I'm going with a group of friends and wanted to know if you wanted to go. Lots of fun people and great food. If you're not working, do you want to go?

Marianna read the text to Andrea who rolled her eyes and reached for the phone. "Too late," Marianna said and hit send. She set the phone on the kitchen counter and shrugged like her heart wasn't fluttering in her chest and panic wasn't squeezing her throat. She swallowed hard and tried to get her anxiety under control. It was a simple invitation. Relax, she told herself. Andrea high-fived her.

"Now we wait," she said.

"Now we wait," Marianna echoed. She flipped the sound on so she wouldn't miss a message and turned her attention back to chopping fruit and made small talk with family members who floated in and out of the kitchen. When dinner was ready, Marianna glanced at her phone one last time before leaving it on the counter and taking her place at the table. Maybe she scared Alix away.

"Quit worrying about it. They're probably busy with work stuff. You said they have long days so maybe they haven't seen your message." Andrea put her hand on Marianna's knee and gave an encouraging squeeze. "They'll say yes."

Marianna had just taken a bite of pasta when she heard the ding. Andrea's eyes met hers in silent excitement. Both jumped up from the table and raced into the kitchen.

"Is it Alix?" Andrea asked. She rested her chin on Marianna's shoulder to try to see the screen.

Let me see if I'm on the schedule that day and I'll get back to you. Sounds like fun.

"Oh, they said it sounded like fun. Perfect!" Andrea said.

Marianna clutched her phone close. It felt like a date. Deep down in the corners of her heart, regardless of what her brain repeated, it felt like a date. She casually put her phone on the counter as if the weight of it and Alix's words didn't burn into her skin.

"You need to answer them," Andrea said.

"I know," Marianna snapped and immediately reached out for Andrea's hand. The stress of this moment wasn't Andrea's fault. "I'm sorry. It's all a little overwhelming."

"Girls. Are you going to join us?" Carrie, Marianna's aunt, yelled from the dining room.

Marianna sent a short and sweet message to Alix before rejoining the family. "I'm sorry for jumping up like that. I was waiting on an important message." Marianna waved her phone before sliding it into her pocket. She adjusted her napkin in her lap for five seconds. She waited for the quiet space to be filled by several conversations happening at once and was disappointed when that obviously wasn't going to happen.

"And? What did they say?" Bill asked.

"What are we talking about?" Carrie asked.

"Marianna just asked someone to go to Chloe's wedding," he said.

"I thought Andrea was going with you?" Carrie sounded confused and looked pointedly at her and Andrea expecting one of them to start talking.

"Mom, it's okay. Alix is a new friend and I thought Mar should invite them to the wedding. I said I'd be backup in case they couldn't make it."

Marianna dug her nails into her palm, hating the attention. It was the only bad thing about family dinners. She was perfectly fine listening to everyone else's conversation. She hadn't even told her mother about Alix. There really wasn't anything to tell her, was there?

"How come I don't know about this person?" Marianna's mother, Anna, asked.

She felt heat on her cheeks and couldn't remember a time when she was this embarrassed. "Mom, Alix is just a person I literally ran into one night and our paths keep crossing."

"Hey, wait. Is that who I saw you with the night I picked you up to go to the airport?" Brandon asked.

It was getting worse. Her family was relentless. She shot Brandon a look that made him press his lips together and shrug.

"What does Alix do? How did you meet? What's the story there? Is this more than friendship?" Too many questions were fired at her at once. Slipping away from the table wasn't an option, but just when she had enough and was ready to excuse herself to hide in the bathroom until the meal was done, Andrea stepped in.

"Alix is just a friend. New to the area and Marianna has been introducing them around. It's all just very casual. Alix said they wanted to meet more people. I thought the wedding would be great since there are a lot of people going and Chloe and Jess are so nice and outgoing. Let's leave Marianna alone. Besides, I have news I've been waiting to share. Can we focus on me again?" Andrea asked.

"What's going on? What else don't I know?" Carrie threw her arms up dramatically as though nobody told her anything ever.

"I just signed with an agent. It's that woman who is connected to all the cooking shows."

The entire table roared with enthusiasm and Marianna was so thankful her cousin pulled the attention away from her. "That's amazing, cousin. Congratulations." That Andrea didn't tell her sooner stung a bit, but Marianna had been so self-involved that maybe Andrea hadn't been able to.

"We'll talk about Alix later," her mother whispered to Marianna. One-on-one with her mother was easy. All eyes on her were hard. Since she flipped her phone to vibrate instead of ring, she couldn't help but smile when she felt another text come through. It was hard to be discreet with her family, but she very slowly pulled her phone from her pocket and looked down.

I can get away for about three hours in the evening. Hopefully it's a short wedding.

Marianna was glad gravity kept her from floating away. *You can always skip the wedding and just meet me at the reception.* Alix was more than accommodating and Marianna felt a tinge of guilt that Alix was doing everything possible to fit into her schedule. But to be fair, Alix had only invited her to coffee.

That's sounds like a plan. Okay, gotta run. Thank you for thinking of me.

You bet. I'll talk to you later.

Marianna discreetly handed her phone to Andrea who read the messages and gave her a hearty thumbs-up.

CHAPTER NINE

The reception was held at a hotel that was relatively close to the studio. Alix asked Tobey to find them a nice suit and begged Mandee to fix their hair in a fun style. Tobey found the light gray suit they wore to the first candle ceremony, a blue shirt that matched the color of their eyes, and a thin tie with tiny silver hearts. Alix looked at themself in the mirror and couldn't help but smirk because damn, they looked hot. If Marianna couldn't see that, well then, she really only wanted to be friends.

"You look phenomenal, boss," Mandee said.

"I don't know what you did with my hair, but I fucking love it." Alix looked closer in the mirror. Too bad the show wanted them to look a certain way every time because this was funky and fun.

"They don't want you to run away with a contestant so we have to do boring, but still sexy. Hold still and let me spray it before it falls," she said. Alix covered their eyes as Mandee sprayed far more hairspray than normal. She tugged off the paper smock that was protecting their clothes and pointed to the door. "Okay, be back here by nine."

"Or I'll turn into a pumpkin?"

"More like the contestants will be too drunk to have coherent conversations. It'll make for bad television," she said.

Alix cringed remembering trying to film good television with people who were falling over drunk. They were just as guilty. "Good point, and thanks for the tip." Alix looked at their watch.

That gave them four hours. The timing was perfect. Chloe and Connie's reception was starting soon so they wouldn't be too early or fashionably late. Alix slid into the waiting SUV and gave the driver the address. In an attempt to not sweat, they opened all vents and took several deep breaths to relax. By the time the car pulled into the hotel parking lot, outward Alix was chill, but inward Alix was starting to feel the excitement of seeing Marianna again.

I'm here. What ballroom?

Alix waited in the car until Marianna responded. They didn't have to wait long.

Ballroom A. Apparently there are three weddings here this weekend. I'll be there soon. Out back taking photos.

Great! I'll see you inside. Now that Alix had confirmation, they put their phone in their suit pocket and stepped out of the car. They usually felt uncomfortable when people whispered around them, but nothing could put them in a foul mood. Fame still felt weird, but it was something Alix was starting to embrace more. They followed the signs up to the second floor where Ballroom A was at the end of the hall.

"Hey, aren't you on that bachelorette show?"

A very drunk couple making out against a column stopped slobbering on each other to stare at Alix. Clumsy and giggling, they invaded Alix's personal space without regard.

Alix calmly took a step back. "Hi. Yes, I'm Alix Sommers."

The taller of the two women was pinching a beer bottle between her forefinger and thumb while her date was spilling the contents of her glass on the red and orange carpet. At least it was white wine, Alix thought.

"Wait. Are you here to marry someone? Like the people on the show? Are they getting married here?" She moved closer pulling her girlfriend behind her, waiting for their answer with a very wide smile on her face as though she just figured out a big secret and couldn't wait to tease or share.

"I'm just here with a friend," Alix said. They looked at their watch indicating they needed to be moving along, but the couple was too drunk to notice or care.

"Cool. Cool. Hey, can we get a selfie with you?"

Lines and boundaries. On one hand, exposure was good, but on the other hand, Alix deserved privacy, too. Plus, this couple was wasted, and their loudness was starting to draw attention. "Sure, but I have to be somewhere in about a minute." Alix took one of the women's phones and snapped three photos not caring how they turned out. "Thanks. Have a great time." Alix quickly put space between them. Ballroom A was straight ahead. They slipped into the double doors and headed straight to one of the bars outlining the room. Liquid courage in the form of a mojito felt like an old friend. They cupped the glass firmly and looked around. There must've been two hundred people milling about waiting for the wedding party.

"You look familiar. Which bride's side are you on?"

An older woman wearing a simple but classy gown slid up next to Alix and gave them a full up and down as though trying to place them and check them out at the same time.

"I'm here as a plus-one. On Chloe's side," Alix said. At least that's what they thought. Marianna talked about Chloe and being in the wedding party so they just assumed.

"I know everyone. Who are you here with?" she asked.

Alix wouldn't call her aggressive, but she was determined to find out more about them. They took their drink and moved to the side so the next person in their bar line could order. The woman glided with them.

"I'm sorry. Hello, I'm Jennifer. Well, one of a handful of Jennifers. I'm friends with Chloe. Her mom is my best friend. I'm killing time until they return from taking wedding photos somewhere."

"I'm Alix. I'm friends with Marianna."

"Hi, Alix. Wait. I know I've seen you before. Have you been seeing Marianna for long?" She paused and stared even harder. She gasped. "Are you on television?" she asked.

Alix nodded. "I'm the new host of *When Sparks Fly*. We're filming now."

Jennifer's demeanor changed. Her body language shifted from interrogator to flirt. "I'm surprised Marianna didn't say anything. It must be so much fun to work in Hollywood. All the perks and rubbing elbows with movie stars. It must be so rewarding."

Alix slowly sipped their drink and tried to scan the room again without it being so obvious that they didn't want to get cornered by Jennifer. She was nice, but Alix's energy was ramping up and they wanted to see Marianna again, not make small talk. Even though they texted daily, it wasn't the same as seeing her in person. They focused on Jennifer's words and tried to answer question after question. "It's very rewarding. I'm very fortunate." Those were brainless, canned answers. "Who's my favorite movie star? Oh, I can't answer that. There are too many great ones." And a slew of not-so-great ones, Alix silently added. "I'm pretty new to the scene."

"Now how did you and Marianna meet? I'm so curious," Jennifer said.

It was the question they didn't want to answer without Marianna present. Marianna still didn't know about Alix's professional life. They needed to have a private conversation about it. It was fun at the beginning, but now shit was getting real and people were finding out before Marianna. That wasn't cool. Alix pretended they were getting a call and pulled out their phone. "I'm so sorry, Jennifer, but I have to take this." Alix held the phone up to their ear and walked away. A few people who were sitting at tables recognized them, but they kept on walking until they found a quiet corner away from everyone with a clear view of the door. Hopefully, Marianna would show up before they needed another drink or somebody else approached them. When their phone rang for real, Alix smiled at the name. "I'm here."

"I'm on my way. We got held up taking photos."

"I met a Jennifer. Apparently, there are five at the wedding. This one ran me through the ringer."

"That was probably Chloe's mom's friend. She's always curious about people. I'm sorry about that. She can be a lot. Don't worry. I'll save you in two minutes."

Alix liked how breathless Marianna sounded. She didn't have to call them because she was going to be at the event very soon, but she did and that meant everything to Alix. "Can I get you anything from the bar?"

"Rum and Coke?"

"I'll greet you with it," Alix said.

"See you soon."

Alix disconnected the call and made their way back to the bar, careful to avoid Jennifer and any probing questions she might have about their relationship. With a new mojito and a rum and Coke in hand, Alix turned to face the front door right when Marianna and the rest of the wedding party walked in. The applause and the disc jockey were deafening, but Alix only heard a pleasant hum as their eyes bored into Marianna. It was as if Marianna knew exactly where to look for a moment and shot Alix a smile before turning her attention to the crowd who had gathered to greet them. Every couple of seconds, Marianna would look at Alix. After patiently counting to ten, Alix made their way straight to her like a bee to a flower.

"You look amazing." Alix put the drinks on a high table, reached for Marianna's hands, and pulled her into a gentle hug. They smiled when Marianna leaned into their body. She smelled like orange blossom and felt warm in Alix's arms. The hug lasted a second longer than most hugs and that made Alix smile harder. They reached back and handed Marianna her drink.

"I'm so glad you're here. I'm sorry photos took longer than expected," she said.

"I haven't been here long." Alix tried to soak in Marianna's beauty with her peripheral vision but gave up and blatantly stared. "You really look nice. I mean, you always do, but there's just something about weddings." Alix shrugged and reeled back the intensity. They took a sip of the mojito and quickly looked away for a moment to gather themselves. Anything to snap out of this trance that Marianna put them in.

"You look very nice as well," Marianna said.

Before Alix had a chance to respond, they were interrupted by a woman who literally squeezed her tiny body between theirs.

Alix knew they were a part of the wedding party because they were dressed exactly like Marianna. "Hi, I'm Olympia, Marianna's friend. You must be Alix."

Alix had to take a step back to shake her hand. "I am. Nice to meet you, Olympia."

"Olympia's one of the twins. Her sister, Ophelia, is at the bar," Marianna said.

Olympia turned to Marianna. "Why didn't you tell me you were dating the Alix?" She quickly lowered her voice. "Do I need to be quiet?" She looked around. "Is the paparazzi here?"

Marianna furrowed her brow and glanced between the two of them. "What are you talking about? Do you know each other?" she asked.

It was now or never with Marianna. "Olympia, will you please excuse us for a minute?" Alix knew they would tell her tonight, but they wanted it to be on their terms, not some overzealous friend dying to be the one to deliver a news bomb. "We'll be right back."

Alix held Marianna's hand and led her to a quieter corner. Now that the wedding party had arrived, dinner would be served soon and this conversation had to happen before they sat down. Too many people had already recognized them.

They sat at a high top and Alix took a deep breath. "Remember when I told you I make people fall in love?" Marianna nodded. Alix reached out again and linked their fingers. Marianna didn't pull away. That was a good sign. "I really enjoyed the way we got to know each other. Chance meeting, then another. It's been so refreshing meeting somebody organically."

Marianna smiled shyly and nodded. "It's been fun. But why is all of this coming out now? How do you know Olympia? Have you met her before?" she asked.

Alix was quick to deny. "No, but she's probably seen me before. As has one of the Jennifers." Marianna's smile was starting to falter. "I wanted to tell you before, but we were having such a great time getting to know one another and I know how you feel about Hollywood so I was nervous." Alix clamped their mouth shut when Marianna pulled their hand away. "I'm not an actor, but

I host the queer dating show *When Sparks Fly*. I was a contestant last season, didn't win, and they asked me to be the new host when the last one ran away with the bachelorette." Alix's eyes bored Marianna's as they anxiously waited for the news to sink in. Her shoulders dropped a fraction while Alix's heart sank.

"I remember people talking about the show."

"And you never saw it? I mean, not that I care, I'm just surprised." Alix wanted to run their fingers through their hair but remembered Mandee styled it to perfection and dropped their hands onto their hips instead. Marianna hadn't had a reaction and Alix wasn't sure if that was a good thing or not. "You're not talking and that scares me." Alix saw a flurry of different emotions play across Marianna's face. Just when they thought it was over before it began, Marianna held out her hand.

"Hi, I'm Marianna, and I'm a third-grade teacher at Franklin Elementary School. It's nice to meet you, Alix."

CHAPTER TEN

Marianna had a choice. She could walk away from this budding relationship with Alix and stay true to her stance on not dating people in Hollywood, or she could lean into it and continue this fun and flirtatious rapport. After months of feeling down and not attractive, she crashed into Alix and her life changed for the better. Her heart was light when she woke up every morning and she checked her phone a lot. Even the other teachers at work noticed she seemed friendlier. The choice was simple.

"It's so nice to meet you, third grade teacher, boss of children," Alix said.

"Are you disappointed?" Marianna asked. Here was a Hollywood celebrity as her guest at a friend's wedding and she worked at an elementary school.

"What do you mean disappointed? I think teachers are completely underrated. It's an amazing job," they said.

"The kids are fun at this age. They're starting to find their humor and understand the world a little bit better. It's exciting to see them grow right in front of my eyes." Marianna couldn't help but smile thinking of the kids. Summer school was a whole different beast, but no less rewarding than the regular school year.

"I think it's great you're a teacher. Are you disappointed in who I am?"

Marianna almost snorted. "You're famous."

Alix shrugged. "I'm not. A little over a year ago I was tattooing strangers. Now I'm making them fall in love."

• 97 •

Marianna had so many questions now that she knew what Alix did for a living. "What happened on your show?"

"When I was a contestant?" Alix's voice got a little higher. "Well, I crashed and burned, but they liked how I was in front of the camera, and they offered me the job. I'm not a natural and I need a lot of tutelage. I had a teacher who helped me for months." Alix emphasized the word teacher and gave her hand a quick squeeze.

"What did you need to learn?" Marianna was surprised. Alix was so smooth and easy to talk to. She wondered what could they possibly need help with?

"Small talk and how to fill in the gap when people aren't talking. Or worse, when too much has been said. Damage control is a real thing," Alix said.

"Why didn't you win, or do you not want to talk about it? I guess I can just binge the season," Marianna said. Alix stiffened immediately and their sweet smile became more of a pinch. She wished she would've kept her mouth shut. She touched their hand. "I'm sorry. I'm sure it wasn't an easy time in your life. I have no desire to watch somebody hurt you. Never mind. I won't watch it."

"I had a connection with the bachelorette, Savannah, but that was over a year ago. I'm happy she found love. She and Lauren are perfect for one another. It was just hard for all of it to be out there for the world to see."

Marianna believed them. She hated her most recent breakup and only a handful of people knew Vee. She couldn't fathom the whole world witnessing her emotional breakdown. "I'm sorry that happened to you. Sometimes things don't work out, but I feel like it's for the best."

"Definitely for the best," Alix said.

Marianna smiled and felt a rush of flutters when Alix's eyes met hers. She didn't want to flirt but it felt freeing and exciting. What was happening? Why the sudden change? Oh, right. They were at a wedding and emotions were soft and tender on this special day.

"Marianna!"

Marianna looked up to see Chloe's mom wave her over.

"Oh, it's dinner time. We should probably go to our table before they give the welcome speech." She stopped in front of Alix when they stood to follow her. "Thank you for telling me the truth. Not that you weren't being truthful before, but at least now I won't be surprised if somebody comes up and wants to take a selfie. It won't feel so weird."

"Honestly, it still feels weird to me. It's hard to find the balance with fans of the show, especially when I'm at a private affair. If I don't act or do something a certain way, it'll be all over social media. And then I'll be canceled and will have to give up my life here and go back to drawing for a living," Alix said.

"Well, we don't want that, do we?" There she was, flirting again.

"No. Not at all. Come on. Let's go meet your friends."

Alix's hand on the small of her back gave her unexpected chills. It was the wedding. It had to be. How many times had she dabbed her eyes dry from all the feels?

"Marianna, who's your lovely date?" Chloe's mom asked.

"Everyone, this is Alix. They were sweet enough to agree to be my date tonight," she said. She hoped everyone picked up on Alix's pronouns and would use them accordingly.

"It's nice to meet you all," Alix said.

Alix pulled out the chair for Marianna and unbuttoned their suit jacket button as they sat. It was such a smooth and confident move and truthfully, hot. They fielded questions from the group as servers placed plates in front of all of them.

"I picked the vegetarian dish for both of us. Just in case," Marianna said.

Alix touched her hand. "Thank you. It looks and smells delicious."

Marianna didn't miss the knowing looks from her friends. She didn't even mind them. Even though Alix was everything she wasn't looking for, it felt good to be by their side. She looked around to see if anyone recognized Alix. Several people were recording the front of the room, but Marianna wasn't sure if it was because they were at the wedding party table or because of Alix. She smiled brightly either way and sat up straighter. Alix checked their watch several times throughout the dinner and the toasts. She leaned over and whispered to Alix between the best man and the maid of honor's extremely long toasts. "If you have to go, I understand." She felt Alix's fingers on hers.

"I'm good until about eight. I was kind of hoping to get you out on the dance floor before I have to leave," they said. It was seven thirty and her friends were wordy, plus Chloe and Connie had come up with a couples' dance to start them off.

"I don't think we're going to be that lucky."

Alix frowned. "That's too bad. You'll just have to make it up to me."

Marianna nodded. "Hmm. Sounds like fun." She softly pushed Alix's shoulder, wanting to drape her arm around it instead. The wedding was making her sappy. She only had a few sips of her rum and Coke so her touchy-feely behavior wasn't fueled by alcohol.

"Ladies and gentlemen. Now that dinner is over, how about we welcome the happily married couple Chloe and Connie Davenport to the dance floor for the first dance." It was because of Alix that Marianna noticed the use of "ladies and gentlemen" to address the crowd. She thought people had moved away from the traditional salutation—especially at a queer wedding. On top of that, the disc jockey was obnoxious with his sound effects and loud voice, but he did manage to get the crowd's attention. He played a soft, slow instrumental song and as soon as the crowd softened as they watched Chloe and Connie, the music changed and Chloe kicked off her shoes and Connie tossed her tuxedo jacket. Marianna laughed and clapped along with the other guests to their highly practiced and incredibly awkward dance.

"I'm so sorry, Marianna, but I have to go. My driver's almost here. I have to get back to the show." Alix pointed at the newlyweds. "And this is a riot. I hope you'll send me video of this later."

Marianna nodded her head in the direction of the door. "I'll walk you out." They slipped out of the ballroom easily enough since everyone's attention was elsewhere. She wasn't sure if she grabbed Alix's hand or they grabbed hers. Either way she felt warm and safe as a thrill rippled through her. On a whim, she pulled Alix into a side door of Ballroom B where another wedding was in full swing.

"What are you doing? Are we crashing this wedding?" Alix's laughter told Marianna they weren't too worried about it.

"You said you wanted to dance with me so let's dance for about fifteen seconds," she said.

For fourteen seconds, Marianna was pressed up against Alix. They swayed together effortlessly as though they'd been dancing as a couple for years. Marianna tried hard to not to read anything into it because it was just a dance. When Alix's phone buzzed, Marianna felt their shoulders slump a little. They pulled away from her.

"Thank you for the dance," Alix said.

"Thank you for being my date to this wedding." It wasn't technically a date and Alix didn't get to hang out a long time and they barely got to meet all her friends as planned, but Marianna couldn't remember when she felt such a high with another person. She almost regretted saying the word date, but when Alix leaned in and placed the softest, lightest kiss on the sweet spot at the corner of her mouth, she knew that this had become so much more.

❖

Chloe playfully grabbed Marianna from behind and twirled her. "Where's Alix?"

"They had to get back to work," she said. As much as she wanted to have quality time with one of her best friends and unpack this treasure of new feelings, today was Chloe's day. She hugged her. "You can meet them some other time."

"They're definitely hot and had the attention of most the room. I was almost a little jealous," she said with a smile.

Marianna held Chloe's hand. "So, about that. Turns out Alix is the host of some queer dating show."

Chloe gasped. "Wait. *When Sparks Fly?* That queer dating show?"

Marianna shrugged. "You know I don't watch television."

"And you just found out tonight?" Chloe made a sweeping motion with her arm from one end of the room to the other. "Apparently, a lot of these people knew. It makes sense now. Everyone recording on their phones. And I thought they were recording us."

Marianna groaned. "I'm sorry. I didn't mean to take away from your special day. Go enjoy your wedding. We can talk about this when you get back from your honeymoon. I'll arrange a coffee date. You come back with amazing stories of Jamaica."

"I'm going to google them the minute things wind down here." Chloe pointed at her before Connie dragged her away for another dance.

"This is so exciting. You should've told us you were dating a celebrity." Olympia sat in the chair Chloe vacated.

"We're not dating. We're just hanging out and having fun."

"Hm. I don't know if I believe that. You were pretty close with your heads together and their hand on you almost the whole time."

Marianna pulled out her phone and did exactly what Chloe wanted to do. Olympia peered over her shoulder. Obviously, this wasn't something she was going to get to do on her own unless she slipped away again and found a private corner in the hotel. Olympia pointed to Marianna's phone.

"That's a great picture of them."

Marianna blew out a slow breath. She wasn't wrong at all. "There are so many. I mean, as the contestant, as the new host. Look, there are even photos of Alix with Jodie Foster and Elliot Page."

"Oh, look at the money they raised for GLAAD." Olympia squeezed Marianna with excitement. "I know you don't like Hollywood types, but maybe Alix is different."

Deep in her heart, Marianna knew this was true. Alix was nothing like Vee. They were extremely attentive and seemed to be so genuine, whereas Vee, although beautiful, was cold and selfish.

Olympia put her hand on Marianna's arm. "Let's obsess later. You can internet-stalk Alix after the party. Come on. Let's dance."

Marianna placed the phone face down on the table and finished her watered-down rum and Coke. "You're right. Let's dance."

CHAPTER ELEVEN

Not having a social media presence was a blessing for Marianna, Alix thought as they scrolled. A photo of them dancing with her for that brief, yet wonderful moment in time had been captured by an unknown person and surfaced with the caption *who's the woman with our favorite Hollywood queer?* If Marianna hadn't discovered it by now, her friends surely showed her. Alix decided to test the waters.

Good morning. How was the rest of your night? Alix was on a quick break and knew there wasn't a lot of time. When the bubbles appeared, they sat up straight in their chair and clutched their phone. A knock at the door startled them. "Yes?" Tobey poked her head in.

"You're being requested. Denise wants to have a word with you before we start recording. Do you have a minute for her?"

"Sure," Alix said. They glanced at the time. "How long until we need to record?" They looked in the mirror to see if they were camera-ready.

"You've got about thirty minutes. Mandee will have plenty of time to check you."

"Got it. Any idea what she wants to discuss?" Did Alix do something wrong? They shook off the feeling. If it was bad, Denise would have found them herself. "I can be there in five minutes."

"Okay, I'll let her know."

Alix waited until Tobey closed the door to look at their phone. The bubbles were still there. Was Marianna writing a book? They tossed their phone on the vanity and marched down the hall to find out what was so important that Denise needed to talk to them right now. The mansion was always crowded right before filming started. Denise was nowhere to be found. Alix wove through the crew standing around, looking for her. Somebody grabbed their arm and pulled them to a stop. It took several moments for Alix to process that one of the contestants, Violet, stood in front of them. She slinked closer to Alix causing them to take a step back and bump against a tall metal floor vase causing it to wobble precariously. They were instantly on alert.

"What can I help you with, Violet?"

"We never get a chance to talk. There's some time before we have to leave for the group date." She put her hand on Alix's forearm.

"Is there something specific you wanted to talk about?" Alix frantically looked around for Tobey. Everything about this screamed inappropriate, but they had to tread lightly.

"I feel bad for what happened to you on the show and I wanted to let you know that I was always rooting for you. But also I'm glad that she turned you down or else you wouldn't be here." Violet stepped closer so she was in Alix's personal space. "You're doing a great job, in case you needed to hear it." The effort she put forth to make her voice raspy was equal parts hilarious and creepy.

Alix stepped away. They put their hands in their pockets to force Violet to let go of their arm. "Thank you for sharing. I appreciate you saying that. I'm sorry, but I need to go. Denise is looking for me. I'll see you on the set."

"Wait. I also wanted to explore this little spark you and I have," she said.

They froze. "No, Violet. There's no spark here." Alix started praying to Buddha or Dolly Parton that no one was close enough to hear this conversation.

Violet giggled, undeterred. "You're always so friendly and flirty with me. Don't think I haven't noticed you paying attention to me."

Was she delusional? Alix barely gave her the time of day. "You know, I'm friendly to everyone. I'm sorry if you misread me, but there's nothing here."

Violet's bottom lip pouted out. "Are you sure? We could just skip all of this and pull a Lauren and Savannah. I would never leave you like that. You're too special. Savannah got it wrong."

Alix was officially panicked. "Let's keep this professional. I'll see you on set, okay?"

"Hey, Alix? Do you have a minute?" Xander popped up out of nowhere and Alix almost hugged him out of relief.

"Sure, what's up?" Alix motioned for him to follow them down the hall away from Violet. The last thing Alix needed was for this to blow up in their face for all the wrong reasons.

Xander opened the door to one of the small offices the crew used as a conference room. "Have a seat."

Alix knew it was bad to be seen with a contestant flirting with them but wasn't going to say anything unless he did. They hoped he had heard them giving Violet the brush-off. Xander motioned for them to sit and pulled up a chair directly in front of them. In such close quarters, Alix had to applaud him for always looking his best. His pink shirt still looked fresh and pressed and the charcoal gray suit snugged his broad shoulders and emphasized his muscular physique. The only thing Alix didn't like was that he wore his cordovan oxfords without socks.

He scooted the chair closer so that their knees were almost touching. It was unnerving. "What was just happening with Violet?"

Telling the truth would be a blow to the show. They'd already cut two contestants and brought in replacements because of hook-ups after only a few recordings. They were too far in the process to start from scratch so the new contestants brought out raging jealousy that made for great television but terrible for the emotional side of the process. Replacing another for flirting with the host would be impossible at this point. Alix couldn't afford to lose their job before it even got off the ground and Xander couldn't afford to start over. Alix was going to have to walk a fine line.

"Oh, that was nothing. Violet wanted to tell me she watched last season and she was sad at how it turned out."

"Alix, I need to be very clear. There is to be no contact with the contestants outside of filming."

Alix held their hands up. "I completely agree and it won't happen again."

"I'll be honest, between flirting with a contestant on set and last night, you're making me nervous." He squared his shoulders and leaned into their personal space. Alix didn't flinch.

"I can assure you I wasn't flirting with Violet. Apparently, personal space isn't big here on the set, but what you saw was an innocent conversation." Alix changed the topic as smoothly as they could. "Now, what about last night? What happened?" Sweat popped up on their temples. Alix grabbed a tissue from a box on the table and dabbed it dry. Ruining Mandee's makeup was more of a crime than visibly sweating in front of the boss.

"I'm sure you saw the photo that's circulating online of you with a woman. I know you don't really have rules and your time is definitely your time, but I really want this season of *When Sparks Fly* to be about Heather and the contestants."

"I understand completely. I was at a friend's wedding. I kept a low profile," Alix said. His words bothered them. What they did on their time was personal. "Honestly, isn't any press good press when it comes to the show? Even if I'm out on my own time?"

"Oh, we're not telling you that you can't go out and have fun, we're just asking that it not blow up so the world becomes more interested in your dating life than what's happening on the show. We have to nail this show given what happened last season."

"I thought *Sparks* had the highest rating ever last season? And wasn't the entire season in the top ten most streamed shows last year?" Alix asked.

"It was a success by those standards. But the studio doesn't want a repeat of that. We have a formula that works," he said.

"I can't imagine a photo at a wedding causing such a stir. If nothing else, it might draw more queers to watch it." Alix shrugged. Why was Xander making this into such a big deal? He was always sending them to this or that party. They cracked their neck to relieve the pressure that had been building since he sat down. "Look, Xander. Sometimes I hang out with my friends. Nowhere in my contract does it say I can't have a life."

"No, no. That's not what I'm saying." He held his hands up defensively as though Alix's words were threatening. "It's just easier to be able to control the narrative if we know about it ahead of time. Maybe you can tone it down until the show is done filming and the season is underway? We just want the focus to be moving forward instead of hanging onto the past. You understand that, right?"

Alix leaned back in their chair. They didn't like it when people were in their personal space bubble, especially their boss. He wasn't a threatening man, but clearly he liked to get his point across. "I get it. I'll keep my get-togethers more private until the show is underway. Everyone's going to fall in love with Heather. She's perfect as the bachelorette."

They bit the insides of their cheeks to keep from busting out laughing. This season was going to be a hot mess. The bachelorette was a difficult and high-maintenance woman. Alix hoped she would find a connection by the end of the show, but the odds weren't in her favor. She said a lot of rude things during the one-on-one camera time that would have to be heavily edited. There was still time though, and it was Alix's job to fan the spark.

Xander tapped their knee. "Thanks, sport."

"Sure thing. Good talk." Alix forced a smile and nodded at Xander.

He fired his finger guns at them and winked. They let out a sigh of relief when he walked off. Alix hustled back to their room and locked the door. The last ten minutes were awful. Their phone buzzed, reminding Alix they were in the middle of another important conversation that had to happen.

Once again, I drank too much, but it was a lot of fun. Did you make it back on time?

Marianna didn't know about the photo. Nobody knew or her friends didn't tell her yet. *Can I call you?*

Sure.

Alix counted to five and hit the call button. "Good afternoon." They heard Marianna stifle a yawn.

"I can't believe it's almost one." Her gravelly voice was making Alix's stomach flutter.

"What time did you get home?" they asked.

"The sun was almost up."

"Did I wake you?" Alix knew all about all-nighters and early mornings.

"No, I stirred about twenty minutes ago. I need caffeine," she said.

"So, I wanted to tell you that somebody posted a pic of you and me online. When we were dancing at that other wedding. You can't really see your face and no one has identified you, but I wanted you to be aware." The seconds were painfully slow as Alix cringed and waited for Marianna to blow up.

"Okay. What do we do?" She didn't sound upset.

Alix smiled. Her reaction was a good surprise. "Are you okay with this? I know that you struggle with the Hollywood lifestyle and this invades your privacy."

Marianna sighed. "I'm fine. I guess I should've said that I don't like self-centered people trying to get famous. Half of my friends are trying to make it without a lot of success. I feel like the wrong people are getting their big breaks. You're not like that. I can tell you are very different from Vee and Brandi." She paused and Alix held their breath. "What do we do about the photo?"

Alix almost crumbled to the floor in relief. "Nothing. I just wanted you to know. I don't think anything's going to come of it."

"Thanks. I'll have to look it up once I wake up."

Alix heard rustling and assumed she was getting out of bed. "Is it time for coffee?"

A small laugh. "Definitely. I can't sleep the day away. I have to work tomorrow and I don't have a plan. Summer school is almost over though and I'm pretty sure if it's not fun, the kids are going to revolt."

"We'll have to get together and talk about our jobs. I'd like to know more about what you do."

"After this week, I'll have more time to work with your schedule," Marianna said.

Alix couldn't believe Marianna was being cool about everything. They thought for sure she would have shut down at the photo online, but she blew right past it. Maybe she didn't realize what that meant. Or how tenacious the media could be if they wanted to know something. Alix was new to it all, too, but it was part of their job to be prepared for it. Out of the corner of their eye, Alix saw Denise waving them over.

"Blackout day is Wednesday so if you want to do dinner, that would be great. Or we could hang out at my place." Low key, Alix kept silently repeating. "The director is waving me over so I need to go but I'll call you soon." They disconnected the call and trotted over to Denise. Shooting wasn't supposed to start for another fifteen minutes. "What's going on?"

She pointed to the women sitting on the bench ready to head out for their group date. "It's showtime."

❖

"Woody, I wish you could be on set with me. You'd be the real star."

Alix plopped down on the sofa and thumbed through the mail which was nothing but a stack of grocery store flyers and letters addressed to current resident, trying to sell all kinds of insurance from home to car to affordable internet. Tobey took care of the fan mail at the studio. Woody looked up when they sat down, rolled over, and offered up his belly for rubs which Alix happily obliged. It felt good to be home. Maybe laying low was the best advice. They could get out of all the parties and shake off the stress. Looking out the window at the evening sky was going to help, too. Alix's rental house wasn't big, but the view was everything and totally worth it. They picked up their phone and hit their first contact.

"Bro, when are you coming down for a visit? I need to know when I should ask for the suite." Alix loved hearing their brother's deep rumbling laughter.

"I can take a Sunday off. Or are there any Monday games? That way I won't miss work," he said.

It stung a bit that he didn't make visiting them a priority, but business was booming. Alix helped Buck buy the space next door since they'd moved to California. "Hang on. Let me check." Alix slipped their AirPods in and scrolled on their phone. "They play at home on the twenty-fourth. Let me find out the schedule and let you know. We're halfway through filming so I'm not sure when I need to be at the mansion."

"How's that going?" he asked.

Alix signed a nondisclosure agreement with the studio and no matter how many times they told Buck, he still asked. "It's fine. Normal drama, you know."

"Can I go on set with you?" he asked.

Alix wasn't sure. It was a closed set, but Mandee's boyfriend and Kitty were always lingering. Why couldn't Buck? "I'll check, but I don't think it's a problem."

"It would just be cool to see the mansion. It looks massive on television."

Even though Buck knew what happened on the show last season, Alix didn't think he actually watched the show. The only time he could be found in front of the television set was when there was a ballgame on. He never watched movies or game shows. "Even as handsome as you claim to be, none of the women will be interested in you. You know that, right?"

"Easy, tiger. I just like to brag about you and I'm proud of your growth over the last year. Plus, you helped boost our business. We now have health insurance. What tattoo studio has health insurance? So many people want to rent space all because you showed off your tats on national television."

Alix laughed. "It's not like I did it on purpose." For some reason, everyone on the show was fascinated with their tattoos. Most of them were their own design, but some were Buck's. Having Savannah trace them with her fingertip on the show last season didn't hurt. Alix was surprised they didn't bleep the name of their business. "I'll shoot my boss a message and text you the best day.

Everything else good?" Alix learned not to ask if things were okay with Buck. He got defensive immediately.

"Yes. Status quo."

Alix hated awkward silences. "Good. Okay, I'll talk to you soon."

Alix ended the call and went back to stroking Woody's soft fur. As exciting as Hollywood, the glitz, and attention were, sometimes Alix missed the simplicity of their former life. Hanging out with Buck and the other artists was everyday life. They fought sometimes. Being in a small space sometimes seemed like a lot, but they worked through their differences. It seemed like a lifetime ago and was making Alix nostalgic. It was time for a quick trip to Portland. They wanted to see the new shop anyway.

CHAPTER TWELVE

Y ou have got to be kidding me!" Marianna stopped short when she entered Clovr. She and Alix agreed to meet there to save time. Besides, Alix really enjoyed the food and the press wouldn't think twice about covering a small out-of-the-way restaurant. She marched straight up to a couple sitting at a table that faced the front door. "Mom! Dad! What are you doing here?"

"Oh, hi, sweetie. You mentioned the restaurant and we haven't been here in a few months so we decided to have a quick dinner. Oh, wait. Is tonight your date with Alix? We won't interrupt. You don't mind, do you?" her mother asked. Marianna stared at her father who looked away guiltily.

"Do not make a big deal about this. Alix has enough problems with people taking photos and posting them online. I want this to be a safe space for them," she said.

"We're not taking pictures. We're going to eat a nice dinner and then go home," her mother said.

Marianna wanted to stomp her foot like a child. She wasn't ready to introduce Alix to her parents. She didn't know what path their relationship was headed down. Were they friends? Was it going to be more? Alix didn't have a lot of spare time since they were in the thick of the show. The first episode was dropping soon and then Alix would be recognized more than they were now. That would probably dictate the direction of their relationship more than anything.

Marianna looked around the restaurant in case any other family members had decided to have dinner here, too. Thankfully, it seemed to be a normal Wednesday night. She hoped her parents' food would arrive before Alix and they would scamper off and allow Marianna to introduce them to Alix on her terms, not theirs. No such luck. Alix breezed through the front door confidently and their eyes met Marianna's immediately. She had no choice but to smile and wave them over. She greeted Alix with a quick hug. "Alix, I'd like for you to meet my parents, Anna and Jack Raines."

Alix held out their hand. "It's so nice to meet you. What a great surprise." They looked at Marianna with the biggest smile and a perfectly arched eyebrow.

"My parents decided to have dinner here because when I mentioned it two nights ago, it sounded like a good idea even though it has nothing to do with meeting you." Her heavily veiled sarcasm was noted with a curt nod from Alix.

"I love this place. Good choice," Alix said.

"Would you like to join us?" her mother asked.

Marianna couldn't help but glare at her mother's audacity. She quickly answered. "Thank you, but no. We have the booth in the back. It's a little more private."

"Your parents can join us if that's okay with you," Alix said.

Marianna bit back her groan. Alix was just being kind. They had no idea how tenacious her mother could be. She placed her hand on her mother's shoulder and gave it a gentle squeeze. "I think that's fine."

"I'll tell our waiter we're switching tables," her father said. He excused himself and bolted from the table.

"So, Alix, Marianna tells us you work in television." Her mother led the way to the booth that Marianna pointed to earlier but looked over her shoulder when she addressed Alix.

"That's right. I mean, when in Hollywood, right?" Alix waited until Marianna and her mother slid into the booth before sitting. "I host a dating show." They waved it off like it was no big deal, but Marianna knew it was huge. After reading about the show online and how the last season really boosted viewership, she knew it was a stressful job. A lot was riding on Alix to keep the success level up. The fact that they were here at all amazed Marianna. Time was precious and they were making her family feel welcome. Massive bonus points in Marianna's book.

"A dating show? That sounds like a lot of fun. What's it called?" her mother asked.

Marianna rolled her eyes hard. Her mom knew more about the show than she did at this point. Alix probably knew, too, but respectfully played along. "It's called *When Sparks Fly*. It's like *The Bachelorette* but all the contestants are lesbians or queer."

"The waiter will bring our entrees out with theirs when they order." Her father sat across from Alix. They shared a sweet smile that made Marianna grin. "What are we talking about?"

"*When Sparks Fly*. The dating show Alix hosts," her mother said.

Marianna caught the look her mother shot her father. He played along smoothly. "Well, that sounds fun, but I bet it's a lot of hard work."

"It's a lot of late nights, but so far, it's been a dream come true. I'm not a natural in front of the camera, so I'm working hard to come across a little more relaxed than I feel."

"Oh, come on. You can't be serious. You are nothing but charming. They can't teach that. That's all you," her mother said.

"Well, thank you. They have to edit me a lot. I say 'um' quite a bit. Directors don't like that."

"What's been the most rewarding part of the job? Meeting other celebrities?" her father asked. Apparently, now he was invested. Marianna stepped in.

"You know, this is my date, not an inquisition. Let's not talk about Hollywood because Alix has interviews almost daily."

Her mother held up her hands. "You're right. I'm sorry," she said.

Alix smiled. "It's fine. Your parents have every right to ask me all the questions."

Marianna put her hand on Alix's forearm. "That doesn't mean you have to answer."

"Okay. Let's talk about something else. Alix, what are your hobbies?" her father asked.

They were interrupted by the waiter who placed four glasses of water on the table. Marianna drank half her glass while he rattled off the specials. Marianna noticed Alix was giving him their full attention. Maybe that was the real Alix and Hollywood hadn't changed them. Maybe Vee and Brandi were just really bad decisions. She was hoping for a lull in the conversation after they placed their orders, but no such luck. Her mother pounced.

"We were talking about your hobbies," her mother said as she brought the conversation back to Alix.

"I like to draw." Alix stretched their arms out to show their forearm tattoos. They were lovely and Marianna liked looking at them when Alix wasn't paying attention. Which was almost never because they were very attentive.

"I can see that," her mother said.

Marianna's mom wasn't a fan of tattoos and was angry with Brandon when he got his, but here she was, fawning over Alix's arm. The two were deep into conversation about Alix's job in Portland and how many repeat customers they had. Her mother even asked what body part was the weirdest place somebody wanted a tattoo. To be fair, it was an interesting question. Marianna was curious, too.

"Dad, why don't you show Alix your tattoos?" Marianna asked with a straight face. When her father joined the Air Force, he and his buddies went out one night and all got the same tattoo. It was an American flag with dog tags draped over it. Marianna was sure he loved it up until he retired from the military.

"The one with your names?" He rolled up his sleeve and showed Alix a heart with Anna, Marianna, and Brandon tattooed inside. It was a sweet gesture, and he was very young when he did it, but it didn't age well. "It's a bit rough but it's near and dear to me."

"I was talking about the other one," Marianna said.

"You want me to take my shirt off in a restaurant?" he asked. He pretended to stand, but Marianna grabbed his arm.

"No, Dad. Please." This kind of teasing was supposed to happen long after they got to know Alix, not on the day they met them.

Marianna was mortified. She felt a slight bump from Alix's knee against hers and she sighed with relief. Alix was trying to comfort her.

"It's okay. This is what parents do," they whispered.

The rest of the night went smoothly. Marianna was able to relax and have fun with her family and decided maybe having them meet Alix was for the best.

"Have a great evening, you two." Her mother practically sang it as she and her father left the restaurant.

"I know it's getting late and you need to work in the morning. How about a quick walk around the block to have a few minutes to ourselves?" Alix said. They dropped cash on the table as a tip because her father paid for dinner before they left.

Marianna couldn't help but smile at the way Alix gently held her hand. Their grasp felt so natural and their skin so warm. Marianna didn't question it. "I'm sorry about our date getting hijacked by my family. I know your time is precious," she said.

"At least we got that part out of the way. And your parents are really cool," they said.

"What time do you have to be on set? At the set? What's the right wording?"

"On set," they said. They looked at their watch. "I owe them a good night's sleep so that my makeup artist, Mandee, doesn't have to pile on the coverup. I probably have an hour. What did you have in mind?"

Marianna thought of the little bar at the corner. Then she thought about the bench at the end of the block where they could people watch and get to know one another better. "How about we go to my place for a nightcap?" She froze. Why did she say that? And did people even say that? Did she even have any alcohol? She wracked her brain trying to remember if the place was clean when she left. "I only said that because I don't live far." She pointed at her car. "It's about a five-minute drive."

"I could follow you," Alix said. "Do you have parking?"

"Oh, sure. There's always a spot in visitor parking." What was she thinking? Inviting a celebrity over to her apartment? Gah. Too late to back out now. Marianna crawled into her practical four-door sedan and waited until Alix's convertible pulled up next to her.

"Follow me," Marianna said. She tried to discreetly look at herself in the rearview mirror to ensure her makeup was fresh and she didn't have food stuck in her teeth. She motioned for Alix to park in visitors' parking while she pulled into her reserved spot. Immediately, she started apologizing. "Look. I don't know how I left my place. It might be a little messy and I don't know what I was thinking."

Alix grabbed her hand and pulled her close. "We can just take a walk around your neighborhood instead. I don't want you to feel uncomfortable. Looks like you have plenty of cute sidewalks and streetlights," they said.

It couldn't be that bad. "No, it's okay. Let's go." She unlocked her door with confidence and turned on the light to a very tidy apartment. She discreetly blew out a sigh of relief. "Welcome. Make yourself at home."

"I like your place. It's so warm and friendly," Alix said. They grabbed a throw pillow on the couch and sat.

Marianna checked the refrigerator and the bar. "Well, I have cold beer or I can make you a rum and Coke. Slim pickings, I'm afraid." She grabbed a beer for herself that she didn't open. She was too nervous.

"I'll take a rum and Coke. Thank you. I love the big windows. You can't beat natural light." Alix looked around the room. "How long have you lived here?"

"About three months. I lived in a spacious two-bedroom with a balcony on the other side of the building but downsized when Vee and I broke up." She didn't want to go into detail, so she kept it light. "It's better for me. Less to keep clean."

Alix laughed. "I get it. My rental is small. Woody sheds so I'm forever wiping the floors down. Maybe you need a cat. How do you feel about pets?"

"Never had one. I'm not against them or anything. We just never had the time growing up and I never thought about it when I moved out."

"We always had dogs growing up. I never had a cat before, but when I got here, I was lonely and I found Woody at the local shelter. He's totally chill and the best cat. Loves everyone but also doesn't care about anything other than sleeping and eating. Which I totally support."

Marianna handed Alix their drink and sat on the sofa with enough space between them but close enough for personal contact, if that was on the table. "Maybe when I get a bigger place. Five hundred square feet doesn't seem like a big enough space for me and a furball. Knowing my luck, I'll get a cat with a big personality."

"They really work with you. And eventually they'll grow up and slow down. You could always get an older rescue cat like I did. Woody's about ten. I mean, no pressure. I just like to see animals find good homes and I know this would be a good home," they said.

It was the way Alix looked at her over the rim of the glass. None of her other friends looked at her like that. A slight shiver tickled up her spine. There was something happening between them. Ignoring their obvious attraction, Marianna kept the conversation moving forward. She was afraid that if she stopped, the spark would ignite and their relationship would cross a line that they both agreed in the very beginning that they wouldn't cross. Never mind the small kiss that happened at the wedding they crashed. Alix's lips landed mostly on Marianna's cheek. But the part that landed on her mouth felt like sweet fire that quickly spread and flamed the soft space between her thighs. "What do you normally do on your day off?" Marianna asked.

"I'm in bed all day." They weren't being flirtatious, but Marianna couldn't help but feel like it was a double entendre. Her brow shot up and she cocked her head. "Really?"

"Even though I have my own private space at the mansion and on set, it's hard to rest or even relax. I'm so nervous every time we film. I thought it would be easier than being a contestant, but it's very stressful."

Marianna softened at Alix's vulnerability and tucked thoughts of kissing them away. "I'm positive you are very good at your new job. You're obviously very popular with the queer community and there is so much chatter online about you." She watched as Alix moved closer.

"How do you really feel about that?" they asked. They were in her personal space and Marianna didn't balk.

"What do you mean?" She didn't want to assume. She didn't want to put any words out there in the universe that she couldn't take back.

"With me being in Hollywood?" They motioned their finger back-and-forth between them. "And whatever is going on with us. I'd like to continue it."

Marianna was going to play innocent but gave up. The attraction was too hard to ignore and denying it would be ridiculous.

"Now that you know me better and we've known each other for over a month, I'd like to pursue something more than friendship," Alix said. "Like go out on an actual date. I mean, this feels like a date, but I mean when we have time and with both of us knowing it's a date." Alix paused and reached for Marianna's hand. "I promise I'm not like them. I'm not like your ex-girlfriends. I'm new to the scene and it doesn't appeal to me. I told you the night we met I was outside to get away from everybody for a minute. It's a lot, even for me. I like chilling and spending time with you and your family."

"They are a lot and are very nosy and will want to know everything about you. Wait until you meet my cousin Andrea. She is very persistent," Marianna said.

"I'm looking forward to it," Alix said. They leaned forward and tucked Marianna's hair behind her ear. She almost leaned into Alix's palm but caught herself. "What do you say? Will you go out to dinner with me? And I pick the place and pick you up and we cross the line together?" They ran their thumb slowly along Marianna's bottom lip. "It's a stupid line anyway. How am I supposed to sit by you and not want to kiss you every time we're together?"

Marianna watched as Alix slowly leaned forward until their lips were a breath away from hers.

"May I kiss you?" they asked.

Marianna barely nodded before feeling Alix's soft, plump lips against hers. They were warm and after about five seconds, became more demanding, matching Marianna's energy. Alix slipped their hand in Marianna's hair and wrapped it around their fingers before holding her close. They gently sucked her bottom lip inside their mouth and ran their tongue softly across it. Marianna moaned and ran her hands up Alix's arms to rest on their shoulders. She loved how soft and hard Alix felt under her fingertips.

"I probably should go," Alix said. They placed another swift kiss on her lips.

She moaned again. Stop doing that, she told herself. "You need some rest. Go home. Get some sleep. Send me a message when you can," Marianna said. She stood and pulled Alix up who was playfully pouting for having to leave.

Alix pulled her into a nice hug. "Thank you for the perfect night and for giving us a chance."

Marianna leaned against her doorframe. "Send me a message when you get home safely." She closed the door and fell on her couch. Her feelings for Alix were bouncing all over the place. She was excited yet guarded. Her lips still tingled and tasted like Alix's rum. She hoped she was making the right decision. As much as she believed Alix, why was she always drawn to people in the industry?

CHAPTER THIRTEEN

Tobey handed Alix the schedule for today. "Are you bringing anyone to the viewing party?"

Alix struggled internally about inviting Marianna. They wanted to, but also wanted to introduce Marianna slowly into their world. The viewing party was going to be massive. The entire crew, studio staff, and their plus-ones would all show up at the network studio. It was the first event they were legit excited to attend but they knew their nerves would be raw as the world would be watching. Giving Marianna the attention she deserved was going to be hard at a party that size. Maybe they would just invite her to the set one day.

"I haven't decided," Alix said.

"Wait. Is there somebody?" Tobey asked. She moved closer for intel so that their conversation wasn't overheard by the wrong people. Gossip paid and Alix was a sought-after single in Hollywood even if they ignored all advances.

Alix nodded and smiled. "There is. But she's shy and I think this would be a bit too much. I need to have a conversation with her first. When do you need to know by?"

"Um, you're pretty much the star of the show so really you can invite whomever you want, whenever you want. I'm sure nobody's going to say anything." Tobey gave Alix an encouraging smile. "I say invite her and if you or she get overwhelmed, then I will step in and make sure she gets home safely, or I'll give her a tour."

"That's not fair to you. You're just as invested in the show as everyone else," Alix said.

"Then have her invite a friend. I can't imagine somebody in her life not wanting to be at a Hollywood party." Tobey put her hands on her hips and tapped her foot waiting for Alix to commit.

"You know, that's kind of a great idea." Alix figured Marianna could invite her cousin or Jess. "Let me text her real quick."

"Why don't you just call her?" Tobey held up the schedule. "Again, you're the star and they'll wait."

Alix whipped out their phone. "Call Marianna," they said into the speaker.

Tobey wagged her eyebrows. "Oh, fancy name for a fancy girl." She stepped back so Alix could have some privacy.

"Marianna, hi, it's Alix. Do you have a minute?" Were they sweating? They stepped closer to an air conditioning vent and welcomed the cool air. "So, I know this is kind of last minute, but we're having a viewing party of the first episode of *Sparks* when it airs on Thursday and I wanted to know if you and your cousin or one of your other friends like Jess would like to be my guests? I'm not going to lie. It's a big party, but they have the first episode up on all the TVs and in the theater and it's supposed to be a lot of fun." Alix stopped talking because if they felt overwhelmed, then Marianna was probably drowning.

"Wow. That's a lot to process," she said.

"You don't have to go. I'm just trying to figure out when I'm going to be able to see you during the next few weeks because the show's going on location for private getaways for the bachelorette and the remaining contestants and then we're doing hometown dates. That will take over two weeks." Alix took a deep breath. "Hopefully, all of this makes sense."

"It does. Even though I never watched *When Sparks Fly*, I watched *The Bachelorette* in middle school with Aunt Carrie. I remember the hometown dates back then."

"So, even though we won't really have alone time before I leave, at least I'll get to see you if you come to the party." Alix felt their blood race at an alarming speed, wondering if she was going to say yes. Her pause made Alix close their eyes and silently pray for Aphrodite or Venus to step in and help Marianna say yes.

"How big is big?" she asked.

Alix leaned their head against the wall and blew out a breath. "It's a lot of people, but more like people from the show—the producers, the director, stage managers. There might be a famous person or two, but nothing like Xander's party."

"Can I think about it?"

Alix's heart thudded in their stomach. It wasn't a no, but it wasn't a resounding yes either. "Oh, definitely. I want to ensure you are comfortable and you are okay being around…" Alix paused. They were Hollywood, too. "Being around people you might not like to be around. That's why I suggested your cousin and Jess. Really, anyone who you think might have fun."

"Thank you for thinking of me. You really don't mind if I think about it? Like instead of answering right now?"

Alix wanted to spend as much time as possible on the phone with her, but now wasn't the time. "Of course. I need to get back to the set, but please let me know either way tomorrow so I can give the boss a head count." Alix was gently pushing knowing Tobey was right about them having freedom to invite people. They disconnected the call feeling disappointed but trying to hold onto hope. Now it was time to focus on work. "What's the plan for today?" they asked Tobey.

There were only six bachelorettes left. Tonight was a candle ceremony, and in four days, the show was relocating to Vancouver Island where Heather had one-on-one dates with the remaining five. After that, it was hometown dates. Alix expected to be on the road for three solid weeks. They picked a crappy time to start up a relationship, but Marianna was somebody Alix didn't want to let slip through their fingers.

❖

"Really? That's great. This will be a great opportunity for Andrea and Jess to rub elbows with people in the industry. I'll send a car for you all around five. It starts at seven. Is that going to work?" Alix tried to contain their excitement, but it was hard. It was a massive step for Marianna.

"Since school is out, I'm available whenever. And the girls can get the night off no problem," Marianna said.

"Just so you know, it's not as fancy as a red carpet, but there will be journalists taking photos and asking a lot of questions. What are you comfortable telling people?" Alix cringed as they waited for Marianna's answer.

"Since I'm with two other people, we can say we're your guests. I'd like to keep us private for as long as we can. If that's okay with you," she said.

"Definitely. Besides, we still have to have a proper first date." Alix's mind was already spinning trying to work out the details for that special day. They even asked for suggestions from Tobey. She would have the best ideas since this was her town and she had a lot of pull with a lot of people. If anyone could get them into a cool first date kind of place, Tobey could.

"But not until you get back in about two to three weeks, right?"

Alix rubbed their hand over their face. Was it two or three? Everything was running together. "Unfortunately, that's right. But when I get back, we'll almost be done shooting and then the season is over. I'm not sure what my role is then, but I'm sure it won't be at the stress level it's at right now."

"Do you like it so far?" Marianna asked.

Not a single person asked them that question. Out of all the interviews with prominent television shows, newspapers, online magazines, nobody asked if they were enjoying themselves. "Yes and no. It's still stressful, but I like watching the contestants fall in love." They barked a short laugh. "Sounds weird coming from me. Most people think people on reality shows are there to get famous and mostly that's true, but there's always a small chance love will blossom. That there are people there for the right reasons. I saw it firsthand. I didn't know what was happening at the time, but I still believe in it."

"I think that's sweet. They picked the right person for the job," Marianna said.

"Thank you. I hope it comes across on television." Alix wasn't sure if they could talk about the show to Marianna since everything was so hush-hush. They wanted to tell her how the director wanted to keep a contestant who was downright mean to everyone except for Heather because it made for "good television." They would check their contract again before having in-depth conversations about the show. Not that Marianna watched, but just in case she decided to in support.

"You are one of the most genuine people I know. You'll come across as a star." Marianna's voice lowered when she said star. Marianna had bad luck twice. Alix refused to be the third.

"You're very sweet to say that. I guess we'll find out tomorrow." Alix's energy was explosive and it was hard to rein it in. "I have to get back to it." They paused to ensure Marianna knew she was still very much on their mind. "I'm excited to see you again. I miss you." It was weird saying that they missed her this soon into the relationship, but it was true. "Okay, let me know when you get to the studio." Alix disconnected before they said something else embarrassing. "Good news. Marianna and her friends are coming tomorrow night. Do I give her flowers? What do I do?" Tobey put her hand on Alix's shoulder.

"I need you to relax. That's why you have me. I take care of things like this," she said.

"I want to be a part of it, too, though."

Tobey nodded. "I know. And that's what makes you sweet. I can't wait to meet this special girl."

Alix ran their fingers through their hair. "Do I need to get her friends something, too?"

"Here's the good news. Everyone in attendance will get a party favor. It's not as elaborate as an awards show, but they have some nice trinkets and small bottles of champagne," Tobey said.

Alix watched as she jotted down notes on her iPad. "That's great, but I want it to include something special from me."

Tobey looked up. "I can order flower bouquets. Small and easy enough to carry. I'll make them cute. Trust me."

"I do. Thank you." Alix already decided to swing by Wooden Box Coffee and pick up some loose-leaf tea and coffee beans. "How's everybody feeling? I can tell there's a buzz, but I don't know if it's because of the viewing party or because we're packing up and heading north."

"Probably both. This place is bonkers whenever there's a relocation."

This was Tobey's fourth year as the assistant to the host of *When Sparks Fly*. At first it was hard for Alix to relinquish control, but it became evident that Tobey knew the best way to do everything and Alix had to let go. "Okay, put me to work."

Unlike most long nights, the wrap ended with excitement. The bachelorette lit the candles of the contestants she wanted, including one everyone disliked. It pained Alix to see some of the women go home because they seemed to have feelings for Heather, but she'd only cared for three women since the beginning. Denise begged her to have an open heart because picking this soon would kill the show. When Heather stomped and pouted, the lawyers reminded her she had signed a contract. A closed-door meeting left her in tears and made her a little sweeter in front of the cameras. She informed Alix that she didn't care who they kept as long as the three she was warming up to the most stayed. That meant the show kept the troublemakers including Maven the whiny nasally trust fund baby and Violet the mean girl. Alix remembered all the contestants from their show who were high-maintenance and vied for camera time. To some, it was to get famous. For them, it was to find love. That's what made this show worth it. That's why Alix took the job.

"Try to get here by three in the afternoon so we can get you in the chair," Mandee said. Alix looked at the clock. It was two in the morning. It almost didn't make sense going home, but it would be nice to sleep in their own bed next to a warm body, even if it was an oversized cat.

"I will. And I'll drink lots of water." Alix never liked hearing Mandee cluck her tongue like an old lady scolding her for not taking care of themself.

"Do that and get some sleep. Unplug. Let's be proactive on getting rid of those dark circles under your eyes," Mandee said.

She wasn't wrong. Alix saluted her, said good-bye to Tobey, and bounced down the stairs of the mansion to their convertible. Tomorrow was everything. There was so much advertising this week about the show and Alix always cringed when they saw their own commercials and billboards. Everything was ramping up to this moment and Alix wondered how they were going to keep their promise of getting any sleep with the professional and personal promises of tomorrow.

CHAPTER FOURTEEN

O h, my God, I'm so excited!" Andrea squeezed Marianna's hand to the point it hurt. They, along with Jess, were sandwiched in the back seat of an SUV that Alix sent to collect them.

"Ow. Careful. I just had my nails done," Marianna said.

"And they look amazing. You look beautiful tonight. I did a great job," Andrea said.

As much as Marianna wanted to give her shit, she was one hundred percent correct. Her cousin was great at so many different things. "Maybe instead of joining a cooking show, you can do makeup and hair for weddings. You do an excellent job." Andrea smiled at her compliment and shrugged.

"And give up my dream? No way. But also, I know your complexion and hair so I will always do a great job. But you did a great job with me, too," Andrea said.

"Now you're just bullshitting me. You did your own makeup and I held your hair up while you pinned it. That's all I did." Marianna always knew Andrea was great at dishing out her own compliments but was terrible at receiving them. Andrea blatantly ignored her.

"Thanks for helping me get ready, too," Jess said.

Andrea rolled her eyes. "You wake up perfect every day. I brushed your hair. That was it." She moved closer to Jess. "I wish my skin was as smooth as yours."

Jess playfully pushed her away. "I wonder who's going to be there? I know you said it's mostly people from the show, but don't celebrities watch these shows?"

"Probably more of the queer celebs," Marianna said.

"That's cool, too. Just seeing famous people is always a kick," Andrea said.

"You see them all the time." Marianna refused to gawk at the celebrities she helped serve over the years. Only a handful were ever nice or muttered a polite thank you.

Andrea put her head on Marianna's shoulder. "Except this time I get to pretend I'm one of them. Should we have cover stories? Like let's be whomever we want. I can pretend I'm Cate Blanchett's personal chef. Jess, you can pretend you're a movie star because someday you will be."

Marianna moved, forcing Andrea to lift her head. "Nobody's faking anything. Just tell people the truth." She pointed at Andrea. "You're a chef." She pointed at Jess. "And you're a model. The truth works for you both in this environment. It doesn't for me."

"Everyone respects educators," Andrea said.

Marianna rolled her eyes. "Nobody respects third grade teachers. Not even the kids. Maybe I'll say I'm in the catering business. That's true."

"You should talk that over with Alix. Maybe they already told people about you. I can't imagine their assistant doesn't know," Andrea said.

Marianna sighed. "Hopefully, they'll greet us and we can have a moment to figure that out. I can't believe my parents have met Alix but you still haven't."

"Your parents rave about them. More than anyone else you've ever dated. Hell, more than anyone I've ever dated. I can't wait. Tonight is going to be so exciting."

It was hard not to feed off their energy. This was a dream come true for them. They'd never been to anything like this as attendees. Neither had Marianna, but it wasn't on her top five list of things to do in Hollywood. "I'm excited, too." She was looking forward to seeing Alix in their element. Hell, she was happy to see Alix for any reason.

"We're almost there. Are we in line?" Andrea pressed her forehead against the window to try to see the line in front of her. "I wonder who's in the Lexus SUV in front of us?"

"If the paparazzi catch you with your face against the glass, you'll be the laughing stock of Hollywood," Marianna said. Andrea sat back at once and rubbed the makeup off the window.

"I was just trying to see if I recognize anyone," she said.

Marianna pulled out her phone. *We're in line. I'm not sure how long it will take. We're like five or six cars back.*

This is Tobey, Alix's assistant. I'll be out in a few minutes to greet you. Alix is at a photo shoot right now but should be done soon.

The fact that Alix's phone wasn't with them threw Marianna for a loop. It was a reminder to never send Alix any private messages or photos, not that she was thinking that, but just in case. *Okay. Thank you.*

"So, Alix's assistant, Tobey, is taking us in. Alix is tied up," Marianna said. She tucked her phone back into her clutch. It stung a bit knowing she wouldn't see Alix right away. Andrea squeezed her hand.

"It's okay. They'll be out soon enough," she said. She leaned forward and pointed. "Wait a minute. Isn't that Keely O'Neal? Her girlfriend is so cute."

"Who's Keely O'Neal?" Marianna asked.

Andrea shook her head. "You really are the worst gay in the history of gays. She's the forward for Angel City." She blew out an exasperated breath. "Women's soccer? Hello? Well, I'm going to have to find her and say hello. She's great, trust me."

"Sit back. We're next. We don't want to seem too eager," Marianna said. She noticed an attractive woman standing off to the side. She bet that was Tobey and a pang of jealousy swept through her. She was beautiful in her black knee-length cocktail dress and her auburn hair styled in a classic bun with small tendrils that framed her oval face. She was probably in her early thirties with flawless skin and a toned body. This was who was taking care of Alix daily? The jealousy grew more insistent. "Here we go. Let's have fun tonight."

"Hello, you must be Marianna." She shook her hand. "And you must be Jess and Andrea. I'm Tobey. Welcome to the viewing party." She stood back as they slipped out of the car.

"We're excited to be here." Andrea grabbed Jess's hand and pulled her along.

Tobey turned her attention to Marianna. "Alix is only a few minutes out. They asked that I bring you inside not in front of the press. Follow me." They followed her through a side door that required not only a key card, but a code she had to punch in.

"It's cool that she knew you were Marianna." Andrea's voice was a low whisper that she thought only Marianna could hear.

"It's my job to know who's who," Tobey said. She stopped and turned. "I understand you helped Alix with Romeo. Thank you. Alix was a hot mess that day, but it was sweet that they volunteered to help me."

Marianna's laugh sounded foreign as it bubbled out of her mouth. "That was quite a day. And you have the sweetest dog."

"You mean Romeo the escape artist? He's a handful, but a real lover." Tobey gave Marianna a soft, reassuring smile.

Marianna understood. Tobey wasn't interested in Alix. She was there to help them and the show and make it the best it could be. "Does he ever get to be on set?"

"Only if we're in the studio. He's too much of a distraction at the mansion," Tobey said.

The hum of chatter was getting louder and Marianna's pulse was spiking. Andrea linked arms with her and when Tobey opened the door to the studio, she couldn't help but be impressed.

"Here are your party favors. Alix made sure to add something personal for all of you." Tobey handed them each a golden bag with thick braided handles.

Andrea didn't hesitate and opened her bag. "Wow. Is that Cameron Dalton's skin care package? That's amazing. Oh, is that a forever bracelet from Catbird? I love all of this."

"Thank you," Marianna said. She looked around for a place to set them, afraid of accidentally forgetting them given the excitement of the evening.

"Why don't I lock them up while you all have a great time? I'll check on Alix and let you know how much longer it'll be," Tobey said.

"Great. Thank you." Marianna handed the three bags to Tobey and watched her disappear. At least she had friends by her side to help her talk to people. As if reading her mind, Andrea grabbed her hand.

"Come on. Let's meet some of these people. The idea is to mingle, right? Plus, I know Keely is here somewhere."

Marianna grabbed a glass of champagne from a passing waiter. Liquid courage, she thought. Jess quietly squealed when she recognized an agent and made a beeline for him. Andrea immediately found a couple who were just as excited to experience this as much as she was and drew them into conversation. Marianna didn't want to interrupt either of her friends so she slowly made her way along the back wall of the studio looking at the lights and trying not to stare at the people in the room.

"Hello, wallflower."

Marianna's heart felt like it jumped into her throat not from fear, but from the nearness of Alix. She turned and without thinking, cupped Alix's face. "Hello." She placed a small kiss on Alix's lips, surprising both of them.

"I'm so glad you made it," they said.

Alix was breathless and excited to see her. Not once did they look around the room. They only had eyes for her, and that attention made her feel like she was floating. "Thank you for inviting us." Marianna looked behind her. "They're both out there making friends. Definitely not wallflowers." She grabbed Alix's hand. "How are you feeling? Are you nervous? Excited? Happy? You look amazing, by the way. Amazing." She gave Alix a thumbs up.

Alix linked their fingers together with hers and pulled her closer for another small kiss. "I'm pumped but also nervous. Thank you again for coming out. Did you get your bag?"

"I saw that you put some Wooden Box's tea in there, but I didn't see everything. Tobey said she was putting the bags in your office."

Alix thumbed behind them. "She sent me to find you. We can take a tour before the show starts." Alix looked at their watch. "We have time."

"Do you want me to grab the girls? Well, at least Andrea since you haven't officially met. She's now over there with somebody who plays soccer." Marianna pointed her cousin out. Alix pulled her close.

"Or we can just sneak off together," Alix said.

"Andrea looks like she's fine." Marianna couldn't stop staring at Alix. Their eyes were such a beautiful blue color. She didn't know eyes could twinkle until she met them.

"You didn't even look," Alix teased her.

"I have eyes in the back of my head. I'm a teacher, remember? Besides, she's always fine. Come on. Show me your workplace if you're sure we have time. I don't want to get you into trouble," Marianna said.

"As long as we're back here by a few minutes before seven, we should be good."

They slipped behind a black curtain and walked down a long hallway. "It sounds all posh but really it's a lot of metal, lights, and makeshift offices."

"It changes with every show?" Marianna asked.

"Some shows get cancelled, and the studio just takes the bones and gives it to the next up-and-coming show. Plus, sets are used when we're not filming so everything has to be pretty generic," Alix said. They leaned against a door and pointed to their name. "This is my office." Alix pushed open the door to allow Marianna to enter.

"Oh, I love it. It's exactly what I thought it would be like," Marianna said. She walked around the room and sat on the plush couch.

"It folds out into a bed," Alix said but quickly backpedaled. "I mean, you know that sometimes I only have a few hours before shoots and it doesn't make sense for me to go all the way home.

Most of the time, I'm at the mansion and I have a small room there. Oh, hell. I'll shut up. Now I'm just embarrassing myself."

Marianna laughed. "It's okay. I completely understand what you meant. It makes sense. All the long days and even longer nights. So, is this where they do your hair and makeup?"

"No. That's usually done on the set. This is just a safe space to decompress and go through emails and itineraries for the day when I'm not at the mansion. I should use this space more, but I feel like I should hang around at the mansion. I remember Lauren, the previous host, was always around to answer questions or be available for anything."

"Or she could have been hanging around to spend more time with Savannah. Remember self-care," Marianna said. She felt like an ass for bringing up Savannah, but she didn't want Alix to run out of steam trying to be available every minute for every single person.

"I didn't think about that. Maybe I should slow down a bit."

When Alix sat next to her on the couch, their knees touched. "I'm glad you're here. Thank you. I really appreciate it."

"Thank you for inviting me," Marianna said. This polite back and forth game was starting to irritate her. She just wanted Alix to kiss her. Something that would equally settle her nerves and kickstart her heart. She spent hours on her look tonight hoping Alix would be bold now that they had established a brief outline of their relationship. And Marianna had already made the first move by kissing them on the mouth. Sure, it was more of a friendly peck, but the electricity from that flash of a kiss raised Marianna's libido from the dead. She wanted more. She wanted to know if Alix felt it, too. "Now that you have me in a private space, what are we going to do about it?" Was her idea of flirting okay, or did it come across as desperate? She slid closer to Alix. Her intent was clear. Thankfully, Alix didn't disappoint.

They stood and pulled Marianna into their arms. "I'm going to kiss you is what I'm going to do about it," Alix said right before their lips claimed Marianna's in a full-blown kiss. The kind that made her clutch Alix's jacket for fear she would float away into oblivion.

Alix's mouth was warm and their probing tongue soft but demanding. Their hands burned against her skin and Marianna felt herself melt against their body. She lost track of everything and allowed the precious moment to envelop her. The way Alix always smelled clean like soap and spicy like sandalwood. And their lips were so soft and yet so demanding. How their tongue felt smooth against hers and how they tasted minty and warm. Marianna moaned and wrapped her arms around Alix's shoulders and deepened the kiss. She couldn't get close enough to Alix. She knew now wasn't the time or place, but just those few moments of passion made her head and heart spin.

The knock on the door separated them fast as though they had been doing something wrong. Alix groaned and turned on their heel. "Who is it?"

"Alix? It's Tobey. We're getting close to time. I wanted to give you a ten-minute heads up," she said.

Marianna looked at the clock above the door. Had they really been in Alix's office for twenty minutes? Time flew. She wrapped her arms around Alix's waist and rested her cheek on their shoulder.

"Okay, we'll be out there soon. Thank you for letting us know," they said. Alix turned back to face Marianna. "Where did the time go?" They kissed her again and again while gently pulling her toward the door.

Marianna finally broke their embrace. "Let's go. I don't want you to be late on one of the biggest nights of your life."

Alix kissed the back of her hand before clasping it in theirs and guiding them back through the maze of gray hallways with names of people she didn't recognize. They didn't let go of her hand when they got to the studio. "Let's go meet your cousin. That should give me a few moments to make my rounds before the show starts," Alix said.

They walked over to where Andrea was drinking champagne with two people Marianna recognized but couldn't recall their names. "Excuse me." Marianna tapped Andrea on her arm. "I don't mean to interrupt, but I want to introduce you to Alix."

Andrea's face lit up. She excused herself and gave Alix a hug. "It's so nice to meet you. Finally."

"I've heard so much about you," Alix said.

"Thank you for inviting us to this event. I've already met some pretty great people and I've only been here for about thirty minutes."

"And it's just getting started. Now, if you'll excuse me, I have to say a few words to the crowd before the show starts." Alix kissed Marianna and smiled at Andrea before slipping away to the front where couches and armchairs were scattered in front of a giant screen.

Andrea nudged Marianna and gave her a look. "Oh, my. Alix isn't just hot but smoking hot. And adorable. How is that possible? Hot and adorable?"

Marianna couldn't have stopped smiling any more than she could've stopped time or the sun from rising. "Sexy when they want to be and adorable all the time. That's the best way I can describe them."

Andrea slapped the table. "That's exactly it. I'm happy for you, cousin. It's good to see a smile on your face again. And for all the right reasons. I approve. I definitely approve."

"Everyone. Can I have your attention. It's almost showtime and I wanted to thank you all for coming and supporting this show. It's important to have diversity on television, and even though I didn't have any luck on *When Sparks Fly*, it's my honor to help the next batch of people looking for love," Alix said. The applause and whistles made them blush. Marianna was bursting with pride. Alix looked at her and winked. Andrea squeezed her hand.

"I saw that. And I'm pretty sure so did a lot of other people," she said.

"Come on. Let's grab Jess and sit down. I can't wait to see them on the big screen," Marianna said. She picked a smaller loveseat where she could see the screen and Alix.

"Look at all the food. I bet you none of it gets eaten. They'll probably just trash it," Andrea said.

"I'll find out. I can't imagine they would. I guess they donate it to shelters," Marianna said. She knew that sometimes the people her aunt catered for asked them to take the leftovers. Her aunt always brought them to the North Hollywood Unhoused Services.

When the lights dimmed, everyone scattered to find a place to sit. Alix appeared on screen and the applause and hollers drowned out anything that they said. Once the place quieted down, people were able to hear the exchange between Alix and Heather.

"She's pretty, but she has resting bitch face," Andrea whispered.

"Shh. You're right, but shh. We don't want to get kicked out." It was hard for Marianna to peel her eyes off Alix and try to enjoy the show. Heather was pretty, but she was fake flirting with all the contestants. Alix showed up at the halfway mark and asked Heather how things were going. They looked so dapper in their dark blue suit and white shirt. Alix was doing everything they could to make Heather more engaging, but she was too busy looking for the next person to slide out of the limo rather than to interact with Alix. Alix stepped aside to let the next bachelorette introduce herself.

"Hi, my name is Violet. I like romantic walks on the beach, volunteering at animal shelters, and quiet nights in. It's so nice to meet you. I'm looking forward to spending more time with you and seeing sparks fly between us."

Everything else faded away. Marianna didn't hear what Heather said back to Violet. She barely felt Andrea tug on her arm or Jess grab at her waist. She just knew she had to get out of there immediately. Her limbs felt heavy and she stumbled over a small table before making her way to the back of the room. She had no idea where she was going but knew there were doors behind the curtains that would eventually lead outside. Panic weighed her down. Anger kept her moving. How was this even possible? She pushed open a door and blinked at the sunlight. Where was she? She kept walking trying to put as much distance between her and the studio.

"Marianna! Marianna! Where are you?"

Andrea and Jess burst out the side door and ran toward her. "There you are. Come here," Andrea said. She pulled Marianna into a hug. "I'm so sorry."

The side door swung open a second time. Marianna looked up to find Alix standing close with total confusion on their face.

"Are you okay? What's wrong?" they asked.

Marianna took a step back. "You need to go back inside. Don't worry about me. I'll be fine."

Alix turned to Andrea and Jess. "Can anyone please tell me what's going on?"

Andrea angled her body so she was between Alix and Marianna. "Your contestant Violet? She just happens to be Marianna's ex-girlfriend Vee."

CHAPTER FIFTEEN

"Everything okay?" Tobey whispered as she walked Alix to the posh couch where they, Xander, and Kitty were viewing the episode.

"Sorry about that. One of my friends wasn't feeling well." Alix apologized and sat down. They tried to look cool and collected, but inside they were shaking. As much as they wanted to be there for Marianna, they couldn't skip this party. They would have to call Marianna the first chance they had.

"You look great up there!" Xander smacked Alix's knee. Alix didn't like the contact but thanked him.

"I knew you'd slay it," Kitty said. She reached over and squeezed Alix's arm. "This is just the start for you. I expect big things. The camera loves you."

Alix, feeling sick to their stomach, could only nod and smile. They kept their attention on the rest of the show and when it was over, thanked everyone until they could get away and check on Marianna. They were shaking by the time they got to their office for privacy. It was ten, but Alix couldn't believe she was asleep. Alix hit the number and waited. When it went to voice mail, they hung up and called back.

Marianna answered the phone without saying hello. "I'm sorry I left. I shouldn't have done that."

At least she answered. Alix sat down in relief. She wasn't mad at them. "No, it's okay. I completely understand. I'm in shock, as you obviously are."

"Just so you know, I'm over her. I just was surprised to see her on screen. And truthfully, angry at her."

Alix could tell Marianna was holding back. And the shitty part of everything was that Alix couldn't tell Marianna anything about the show. They couldn't tell her that Violet wouldn't make it to hometown dates. Or how Heather wasn't into her. Alix almost smiled. The two most conniving and mean women on the show were perfect for each other but didn't know it. Sadly, Heather was leaning toward a plastic surgeon who was very sweet and kind and in it for the right reasons. Alix predicted that Heather would poison the relationship the moment they got engaged. All of that had to remain in the strictest of confidence or Alix could lose their job and all the credibility they'd amassed in the little bit of time they'd been on the Hollywood scene. The sponsorships, the contracts, the queer visibility could disappear if they said anything. As much as they wanted to tell Marianna anything, they couldn't. They couldn't risk her getting overly emotional and accidentally telling the wrong person.

"You ran off so quickly."

"It's stupid. I'm just ultra-sensitive about her. And then wham. She's up there on the screen like a goddess getting everything she wants. Attention, fame, and probably fortune." Marianna sighed. Alix wished they could give her a hug. "It's not fair that she destroys me and then gets rewarded for it."

"I'm sorry she hurt you." Alix felt helpless. They checked the time. "Do you want me to come over and just, I don't know, be there for you? We could get pizza."

"Thank you, but no. It's been a night for you and I'm sorry that I ruined it. Please go back to celebrating. I'll be fine."

Alix could hear the forced smile and the uptick in her voice. There was nothing they could do and that sucked. "Can I call you tomorrow?"

"Sure. Please go enjoy the rest of the night. It's special for you," Marianna said.

"Good night. I hope you sleep well." They knew full well that wasn't going to be the case for either one of them.

"Good night, Alix."

Alix didn't know how to feel. On one hand, Marianna was having a terrible night and they wanted to be there for her. On the other, the episode was a roaring success. Preliminary numbers put it in the top five prime time spots. The pressure to keep it there weighed heavily on Alix's shoulders.

"Alix? Are you in there?" Tobey's voice was full of excitement. Alix rubbed their face and shook their arms away from their body. They could think about Marianna after the celebration.

"I'm here." Alix opened the door. "Is it time?"

"Time to get your party on," Tobey said. She handed Alix the jacket that they left in the studio.

"Let's go. Xander and Kitty want you to ride with them to Schmitty's house in the hills. Go celebrate with everyone, but don't forget you have *Reality Bits* at nine with Ellie Stevens. She's a big fan of the show. We'll have the car at your place at seven. You deserve it," Tobey said. Alix remembered Ellie interviewing Savannah and Lauren right after the final episode last season dropped. Tobey folded Alix's suit collar down and inspected their hair and makeup. "You look perfect. I really love that Mandee gave you flexibility with the look tonight. You look sexy." Tobey looked around. "Speaking of sexy, where's your date? I haven't seen her or her friends."

Alix had no idea what to say. They couldn't tell Tobey the truth. "She had to leave suddenly. Family thing."

"I hope everything's okay. They left their bags. If you give me Marianna's address, I can send a courier tomorrow."

An idea flickered in Alix's brain. "Oh, no. That's okay. I'm going to see her tomorrow so I'll just put them in my car so I won't forget." Tobey grabbed them before Alix could.

"I'll do it. I'm on my way home to see the kiddo. You need to get out of here. The quicker you leave, the quicker I can leave."

Alix rolled their eyes. "Thanks for the guilt trip. Okay, you win. I'm out." They followed Tobey out front to find Kitty spilling out of the SUV window waving to get their attention.

"Alix. Over here. Come on, we've been waiting for you," she said.

Alix smiled and climbed into the SUV putting ample space between them and Kitty. Kitty's excitement was infectious and Alix felt guilty for wanting to have a good time and be in the moment. It was difficult when all of this was hurting somebody they cared for.

"You did such a great job," Kitty said. She reached over and gave Alix a quick knee squeeze. There was entirely too much unwanted touching in Hollywood, Alix thought. Xander watched the exchange completely unfazed.

"Did Tobey tell you numbers are high? People love you. Viewers love the show. My Kitty knows what she's talking about," Xander said.

"Thank you for your faith in me. It's been an amazing experience," Alix said. They took the champagne flute from Kitty's outstretched hand. It would've been rude to turn it down. Alix sipped and clenched their teeth as they swallowed. Champagne to them was like beer to Buck. Hard to swallow.

"Who was that lovely woman you were speaking with before the show started? I haven't seen her at anything before. Is she with the show?" Kitty asked.

Alix dreaded bringing up their relationship status. "Marianna and her friends were my guests. Friends from the outside world." Alix forced a bored look on their face in case Kitty pressed. Thankfully, she didn't.

"Are you excited about British Columbia? Who do you think Heather's going to pick?" Kitty asked.

No way was Alix going to talk about the show even though they were in the limo with the producer. And his wife. "I'm excited to go to Canada. It'll be nice to get out of the heat. And who Heather picks is anyone's guess." They shrugged and took another horrible sip. How could something so expensive taste so bad?

"Remind me when we get to Schmitty's to introduce you to a few of my friends. They absolutely adore you," Kitty said.

Alix kept their eyes on Kitty's face even though their peripheral was picking up a lot of skin from a long slit in her dress. As attractive as she was, Alix's mind kept busy with a beautiful brunette who dressed conservatively and whose smile was breathtaking. "I can't wait to meet them. It's because of them that *When Sparks Fly* came about, right?" Alix leaned forward as though fully invested in the history of the show, but really was trying to keep Kitty from prying. It worked. She talked about Gia and Kelly until they arrived at Schmitty's house and were immediately pulled in different directions.

The party was a whirlwind of congratulatory back slaps, high-fives, and clinking of beers and Alix couldn't wait to get out of there.

"How does it feel to be the hottest person in Hollywood? You were fantastic tonight." Sam shook Alix's hand hard and fast. "My phone is blowing up for more interviews. *Hollywood Highlights* wants you next."

Alix didn't care much for the personalities on *Highlights*, but it was good publicity for both *Sparks* and them because it focused solely on the latest news out of Hollywood. "But we're leaving for Canada." Alix could feel the pressure squeezing their shoulders. "I don't know when I'll have the time."

"Oh, you can do some of them virtually. I'll get with Tobey and find out your schedule. We have to strike while the iron's hot." Another hand shaking until Alix pulled away because it was too much. It was obvious Sam was excited, but also he needed to settle down.

"We'll see. At some point I'm allowed to rest. Mandee doesn't like putting makeup on puffy eyes with dark circles. I'm not a raccoon," Alix said.

Sam shook his hands in front of him. "Oh, I just meant when you had time. Tobey can review which ones will work best for you. Just keep me in the loop," he said. He gave a crooked smile and drifted off into the crowd. Alix had about five seconds before Kitty's crew found them and pulled Alix into their conversation. It was two when Alix finally fell face down into their own bed. The alarm at six thirty made them groan. This schedule was beyond demanding. It was brutal.

❖

"Thank you for meeting me. Besides, I wanted to drop off your bags." Alix stepped inside Marianna's place and presented her with a bigger flower bouquet they forgot to give her last night. "And these." Marianna's smile grew when she saw the colorful blooms.

"That was sweet. Thank you," Marianna said. "Please, have a seat. How was the rest of your night?"

Alix stifled a yawn. Marianna had a way of relaxing them. "I got about four hours of sleep."

Marianna looked alarmed. "That's not enough especially after a full day and night. I thought today was your blackout day and then you're off to Canada."

Alix sank on the couch and stretched their arm across the back of it. "It is. For filming the show. I had an interview at nine and another one at noon. And now I'm here." It was four and they were exhausted, but seeing Marianna was a must. "I wanted to make sure you were okay after last night."

"I'm sure that looked awful." She nervously ran her hands over her hair trying to tame her curls. Alix grabbed her hand after the third time pacing in front of them and pulled her gently to sit on the couch next to them. "I was in shock. I knew she got a job, but I didn't think our paths would ever cross again."

"I know you still have a lot of anger." Alix treaded lightly. They knew exactly what she was going through.

"But I'm sure that looked terrible for you. Your only guests sprinted out five minutes into the show," she said.

"It was fine. I just told the producer you weren't feeling well. I only wished I could have left with you."

"That's the problem though, isn't it? I'm pulling your focus away from your job. What happens if they realize you're dating someone whose ex is on the show?" Marianna slowly pulled her hand away. "Why don't we put us on hold? We don't know the impact that my relationship with Vee will have on you or the show. It could have a devastating effect. I want you to be successful because you are perfect for this job. Let's just wait."

Alix missed her warmth immediately and tried to rid themselves of the dread that weighed heavily inside at the thought of losing her before they even got started. No. They were not going to let this happen. "Then you're letting her win. Your past relationship is that—in the past. I don't want her to ruin us. I like where our relationship is going. Thank you for trying to protect me, but I'm going to politely decline." Alix raised their voice. "I'm definitely not her or like her at all."

"So, you've seen her true colors then? Please tell me she makes an ass of herself on national television," Marianna said. She got up and started pacing again. This time Alix didn't stop her.

"I can't really talk about the show, but just so you know, Violet is not a nice person and it comes across on the show. I'm not surprised you don't like Hollywood types if that's who you dated last. I'm sorry, but she's awful. She puts up a super sweet front, but the cameras always get the secret conversations she has with other contestants."

"Good." Marianna's voice was full of fire. This was the position Alix never wanted to be in. They couldn't tell Marianna a lot because of privacy issues, but enough to ease her mind that good things weren't going to happen to Violet on *Sparks*.

"People have been blowing up my phone because they saw Vee on the show. Why was it so private? Don't they usually do a ton of commercials?" she asked.

Alix wondered the same thing. The show focused more on them and the new bachelorette. "Maybe because it's a rushed season? Networks don't release a lot of shows in the summer because of low viewership. That's my guess anyway."

"All of this is so embarrassing."

Alix had heard enough. They stood and pulled Marianna up and into their arms for a hug. "Here's something to think about. Your ex might be on the show, but it's my show and you just happen to be dating the host of the most popular queer dating show in the history of television." Alix brushed a curl away from Marianna's face as they leaned back to look into her eyes. "So, that has some weight, right?"

Marianna leaned her forehead on Alix's collarbone and groaned. "I'm such an idiot. You're right. Good riddance to her."

Alix cupped Marianna's chin and lifted her face so they could look into her eyes. "So, I'll not have any of this talk about needing space and holding off on our relationship. Marianna, I'm excited about you and I haven't felt like this in a long time. Not even with Savannah. I'm not going to let you walk away from us before we even get started."

CHAPTER SIXTEEN

A lix wants me to visit them up in British Columbia." Marianna slid Andrea's espresso on the table and sat in the chair opposite her.

"That's exciting and also very fast," Andrea said.

Marianna tilted her head. "It's not like that and you know it. We've barely even kissed." That wasn't entirely true. They'd kissed passionately plenty of times, but nothing more.

Andrea pointed at her. "When people ask other people to go away for the weekend, there's going to be sex. It's a known fact." She lifted her brow and blew on her coffee before taking a sip.

"It's during the week," Marianna said. Andrea rolled her eyes and gave Marianna a look. "It's just that they're going to be gone for weeks and then it's going to be hard to find time when they get back."

"Has everyone finally left you alone about Vee? I can't believe that bitch is on the show. I hope she gets dumped. And cries. You know, the ugly cry. Not the pretty tears that fall gently from her eyes, but the red, runny nose and sniffles and smeared mascara." Andrea screwed her face up in pain and faked cried, making Marianna laugh.

"You know she's not in it for love. She's going to be the girl that jumps from reality show to reality show until she ends up on *The Real Housewives* of Los Angeles or Hollywood or whatever. Gah. I'm so mad I gave her time and energy." Marianna crossed her arms and leaned back in her chair. "Why didn't you tell me?" She held up her hand when Andrea almost spit out her coffee. "Okay, okay. You told me but why didn't you make me listen?"

"Your head was in the clouds. None of us could get through to you. Vee was charming and sweet in the beginning. By the time her true colors showed you were in deep," Andrea said. She tapped Marianna's hand. "But let's not focus on her anymore. Let's talk about Alix. I feel like they are genuine and real. Any flaws? Any single brothers just like them?"

"You know, Alix does have a brother and he's supposed to visit at some point this summer for a baseball game. I don't know a lot about him except he likes horses and owns part of a tattoo studio."

"Is he hot like Alix? Like lumberjack hot? Flannel shirt rolled up to the elbows with bushy beard hot?" Andrea leaned forward. "Have you seen a picture of him?"

Marianna scowled. "Hang on. Let me text them to see if they can send a photo." She picked up her phone and shot off a text to Alix. The last thing she wanted to do was play cupid or put Alix in that position even though that was literally their job. When her phone dinged, Andrea jumped up to see the photo.

"Oh, he's really cute. Lots of tats, nice face. They look alike," she said.

"Beware. He's very private, shut off, and hates the big city." She zoomed in on the picture. "They have the same eyes. Very blue and very kind."

"Maybe invite me along to the ballgame. You never know." Andrea shrugged like it wasn't a big deal, but Marianna knew her cousin was into him.

"We'll have to time it just right so it doesn't look like a double date. But let's focus on me now, okay?" Marianna tied her hair back with a clip. Even though Wooden Box Coffee was air-conditioned, the heat from the sun was filtering in from the store front. "Do you think I should go? Now you've got me all worried about this expecting sex thing." Even though she wouldn't admit it, she already booked a bikini wax session, hair appointment, and found a cute red summer dress that showed off her tanned skin and a sliver of cleavage. It wasn't as if Marianna was embarrassed about her body, she just wasn't comfortable showing it off to everyone.

"Of course you should go. What's the plan?"

"They have Thursday off. So, fly out Wednesday and come back Friday. A quick trip," Marianna said. She played with her coffee cup, trying hard not to seem overly excited. She smiled thinking about seeing Alix again. Their relationship was still tender but there was a new level of trust since the Vee incident. Marianna didn't believe that Alix invited her up to British Columbia because of sex. She missed seeing Alix's happy face and their energy and believed Alix felt the same.

"Sounds perfect. No weekend traffic. A nice romantic getaway in the mountains," Andrea said.

"Okay, okay. Enough about that. How's it going? I feel like you've been MIA lately."

"I'm cooking everything I can think of and learning as much as I can in the kitchen, which means fewer hours at the catering business. Are you ready to pick up extra shifts?" Andrea asked.

Marianna shrugged. She wanted to be available for Alix but knew the next several weeks were going to be difficult to find time. "Sure. The school year doesn't start for a few weeks. Even then, I'm good to go. I'm so proud of you."

Andrea beamed with excitement. "My agent thinks I'm promising. Cooking shows are on fire right now. I have several auditions this summer for fall shows. I'm hoping she calls me soon with good news."

"I hope it's something fun like *Top Chef* or *Next Level Kitchen* or the new show *Million Dollar Recipe*. Can you imagine if you got on that show? The exposure would be amazing." Marianna thought about the possibilities her cousin would have if she made it on a cooking show.

"It's so exciting. You know I'm great under pressure. And if I fail, I can always take over the family business," she said.

"You're going to be a star." Marianna smiled. Six months ago she hated everything about Hollywood, but now her cousin had a foot in the door and she was watching Alix explode on the scene. "If you need anything at all, please let me know. I support you one hundred percent."

"Thank you. That means a lot," Andrea said.

Marianna's phone lit up. "Oh, it's Alix." She took a calming breath before answering. "Hello?"

"Hi. How are you?"

Their voice sent a soft ripple of pleasure through Marianna's stomach. Like the first warm breeze at the start of summer. "I'm good. Just sitting here with Andrea."

"Oh, I don't want to interrupt you."

"It's okay. We're just having coffee."

"Is she the reason you wanted a photo of my brother?" Alix asked.

Marianna laughed nervously. "Sort of. She said how adorable you are and jokingly wanted to know if you had any brothers. I remember you talked about Buck. We didn't mean anything by it."

"He's handsome, but he isn't the best company. He's super quiet and keeps to himself," they said.

"I wasn't thinking anything like that," she said, even though she totally was. "I just thought that if he comes in for a baseball game, both Andrea and I could tag along. If you want," Marianna said. She twisted a strand of hair around her finger nervously. "You probably just want to go by yourselves. I didn't mean to interject us into your plans."

"It's okay. I didn't know you liked baseball," Alix said.

Marianna could hear the pleasure in their voice. She knew enough about baseball to get by, but it wasn't her favorite thing to do in her spare time. Games were at least three hours long, not to mention travel time to and from the stadium if you could afford tickets. "I've been watching games with my dad since I was a little girl." Her father was a die-hard Dodgers fan. She had fond memories of them sitting on the couch watching the games.

"That's great. Maybe we can get a group together," Alix said.

"That sounds nice," Marianna said.

"So, I'm calling to find out if you've given any thought to coming out here. It's beautiful. The weather is perfect and everything is so green. If you're up for it, I'll arrange for you to fly up Wednesday and return Friday. But only if you want. No pressure."

"That sounds amazing." Marianna stopped second-guessing everything and made a quick decision. "Let's do it. It'll be nice to see you again." She watched Andrea fist pump the air quietly, but with conviction.

"Great. I'll have Tobey email you the information. I can't wait to see you. Oh, and tell Andrea I said hello," Alix said.

"See you soon." Marianna put her phone on the table and high-fived her cousin. "I guess I'm going to Canada."

Marianna didn't think she could get used to the Hollywood lifestyle. She was perfectly willing to fly economy and grab a Lyft, but Alix had arranged everything from the ride to the airport, to posh first class airline tickets, to a suite in the waterfront hotel. It was overwhelming. Maybe it took time to acclimate to money, but Marianna wasn't there and wasn't sure she would ever be.

We're finally done for the day. I'm on my way. I'm so excited to see you again!

Marianna didn't want Alix to know how much they affected her. *Yay! What time do you want to meet?* So much for playing it cool, Marianna thought.

How about we meet down at the bar at seven?

That gave Marianna an hour to get ready. *Perfect. I'll see you then.* She looked at the clothes already hung in the closet and decided to wear the red dress tonight. Tomorrow was a casual day where Alix wanted to go for a hike. Marianna had a feeling after a day in the sun, she wasn't going to feel like getting dolled up.

Andrea texted. *Did you make it? How's the hotel?* She had been blowing up her phone since Marianna sent her photos of first-class life.

Too bad she wasn't invited, Marianna thought. This treatment was right up her alley. *The suite is massive. Let me send you a photo of the view. It's so beautiful here. I'd FaceTime but I have to get ready. I have less than an hour before I have to meet Alix in the bar.* She snapped a photo of her view and waited for Andrea's response. She was not disappointed.

Oh my God! That's incredible. It's so beautiful there. You're hiking one of those mountains tomorrow?

I don't know. There are so many trails. That's pretty much all they do here. When Marianna checked in, the concierge talked nonstop about all the trailheads within a thirty-minute drive. She wasn't super excited about being in the sun for half a day, but she wanted to spend time with Alix so she nodded and smiled and hoped that whatever Alix had in store for them was fun and adventurous, not a twenty-mile hike with few breaks. *I'm off to get ready. I'll send you a photo when I'm done.*

Don't forget to do your eyes like I showed you.

Marianna sent an eye-roll emoji and tossed her phone on the bed. By the time she showered, and fixed her hair and makeup, it was almost seven. She grabbed her clutch and phone and quickened her step.

"Hello, wallflower. It's so good to see you." Alix took Marianna in their arms and held her for a few seconds. Not only was it good to see Alix again, but it felt wonderful being held. Marianna tried hard not to melt against them, but she couldn't help it.

"Hi, Alix. From *When Sparks Fly*." An obvious fan interrupted their hello.

Alix separated from Marianna and turned to the smiling young person who was completely oblivious they were disturbing a private moment. "Hi there," Alix said.

A warm feeling fluttered its way through Marianna's body when Alix's charming, lopsided grin popped into place. The smile wasn't even for her and it still affected her. The person put their hand on their heart.

"I'm so sorry I'm interrupting you, but I had to stop and tell you that seeing you on television changed my life." They turned to Marianna and gave her a small, apologetic smile. "Hi, I'm Jordan. Because of Alix, I was able to come out to my family and friends as trans. Having them on TV made it so much easier to explain being nonbinary." Jordan turned back to Alix. "I feel so validated and comfortable for the first time in my life. I know you don't know me, but I'd really love a hug if you're okay giving them out."

Alix held their arms out. "Definitely okay." They grabbed Jordan and gave them a hug so long that if Marianna wasn't standing right there and hadn't heard Jordan's story, she would've been jealous. She couldn't hear what Alix whispered in their ear but knew they would tell them later. Marianna teared up when Jordan's body shook with quiet sobs. It was at that moment that she finally understood how important Alix was to the queer community. It was more than just a television show. They were more than *When Sparks Fly*. She was so hung up on the Hollywood scene, that she forgot to focus on Alix and leave their TV persona out of it. Even though Marianna was within a few feet of Alix and they had just reconnected after weeks apart and fast phone calls and late night texts, Alix was focused solely on Jordan. That's why Marianna kept the relationship going. Not very many people were like Alix—caring, attentive, and genuine.

"I just had to come over and tell you how thankful I am for you." Jordan sniffled and nervously looked around.

Their vulnerability was so raw that Marianna had an urge to hug them as well. Instead, she touched their arm. "It's not a problem. Alix is a wonderful person and I'm so happy they were able to encourage you to be your authentic self. Doing what you did was brave," she said.

"Thank you, but I don't feel so brave." They took a step as though suddenly realizing they had interrupted them. "I have to go. I'm sorry again for interrupting. Have a great night." Jordan waved and scampered off into the lounge.

"I'm sorry about that. I was hoping for a certain degree of privacy for us," Alix said.

Marianna shook her head. "That was just about the sweetest thing I've ever seen. Don't apologize for helping baby queers."

Alix took Marianna's hand and pulled her close. "Thank you. That's why I'm doing what I'm doing. I have the power to influence a lot of people both in our community and the mainstream world." They kissed her hands. "But you're finally here with me and I have good news."

"What's that?" Marianna played along. She looked at Alix's full lips while she waited for an answer. She wasn't even hiding the fact that she was staring and hoping for a kiss.

"We have a private dining room so no more interruptions," they said.

A waiting server nodded at Alix and motioned for them to follow him. He opened a door that led through the kitchen and into the back of the five-star restaurant. He pulled back curtains to a private room with a table set for two and a bottle of wine in the space between the plates.

"Compliments of the hotel. We know you can stay anywhere in Vancouver and we appreciate your patronage here," he said. He held Marianna's chair out and pushed her closer to the table when she sat.

"Thank you," Alix said.

"I'll give you a moment to review this evening's specials and I'll be back in a few minutes."

"This is nice," Marianna said.

"I've wanted to eat here for a long time. A few of my friends from Portland highly recommended this place. Both hotel and restaurant. I never could afford it until now," they said.

"Wait. The show isn't here at this hotel?" Marianna was surprised. This was by far the nicest place in Vancouver from what she gathered from the internet.

"Oh, no. They are on the other side of town. I see enough of them throughout the day," they said.

"That makes sense." Marianna folded her arms and rested her elbows on the table. Not out of rudeness, but to put herself closer in Alix's space. "Hi."

Alix didn't disappoint. They leaned forward and brushed their lips against hers. "Hi. Thank you for coming up here. I really appreciate it."

Marianna was trying hard to keep her energy level from bubbling over. Playing it cool when her blood was racing was hard, but she did it. "It's beautiful here. And I know time together will be difficult in the next few months. The show is wrapping up and school starts soon. What happens after the show?"

"My contract is for one season and two weeks after the final episode drops. I'm sure I'll have to do some interviews. After that, I might guest host for some of the talk show hosts who want breaks over the holidays. I don't know really. I might even sit in on your classes. Am I smarter than a third grader?" Alix laughed at their own joke.

"You'd be too much of a distraction in class," Marianna said.

"For you or your students?"

Marianna cocked her head and smiled. "How do you make your eyes twinkle? How is that even possible?"

Alix threw their head back and laughed. "It's the lighting. I had them angle it just right and made sure I was going to sit right here to maximize the brightness." They winked at Marianna.

She shook her head but laughed at Alix's antics. "And both. You'd be a distraction for me and my students," she said.

The waiter announced himself before pulling back the curtain. "Do you have any questions?"

Marianna sat up straight and paid attention. She'd barely glanced at the menu and turned to Alix. "Since your friends recommended this restaurant, why don't you order for us?"

Alix raised an eyebrow. "Challenge accepted. We'll take the tasting menu." They handed the waiter the menus and waited for him to leave. "Thank you for trusting me."

Marianna tipped her glass at Alix and took a small sip of wine. The vibe shifted from playful to a little sexy. Alix slipped out of their jacket and rolled up their sleeves.

"I'm sorry. It's a little warm in here," they said. Any opportunity to see Alix's tattoos and their smooth skin. Marianna blatantly stared. She liked the way Alix's muscles corded when they picked up their glass and how they licked their lips after tasting the rich wine. "What's on your mind?"

"I want you to kiss me," Marianna said. No sense being coy when that's exactly what she wanted.

CHAPTER SEVENTEEN

It was hard not to stare at Marianna and even harder to keep their hands off her. The red summer dress clung to her slender body and Alix had been pleasantly surprised to see a hint of cleavage. Even the length at mid-thigh gave them pause. Marianna was usually conservative about what she showed the world. This was a lot of skin and Alix was giddy.

Marianna's request for a kiss sent a jolt throughout their body. They immediately moved to her side. Alix effortlessly slid their hand behind Marianna's neck before pressing their lips softly against hers. They stifled a moan when Marianna leaned into them. When they gently pulled her bottom lip into their mouth, she deepened the kiss. Alix wrapped their arms around Marianna the best they could sitting and at an awkward angle. They wanted to be closer, but this wasn't the time or the place.

Alix slowed the kiss and regretfully leaned back. "Wow. Had I known you were going to kiss me like that, I would've greeted you at the airport," they said.

Marianna licked her lips and scraped her teeth across her bottom lip. "This is going to be a fun trip."

Alix liked that Marianna was getting more comfortable around them. She wasn't normally flirty so this version of her was a nice surprise. "Check, please!" Alix joked.

Marianna smiled. "We have time. Speaking of, what's the plan for tomorrow?"

Alix inwardly groaned. Just when they had momentum, Marianna pulled back. She was sexy and Alix was attracted to her. Every time they saw her, it felt like the first time seeing her and that lightheaded feeling was proof that everything about this was right.

"Spending time together. I was thinking hiking and just enjoying each other's company in a beautiful place. I don't think a lot of people will bother us on the trail," Alix said.

"I'm sure it will be fine. And after watching you with that fan in the bar, I want you to know that I think what you're doing for the trans community is amazing. Even if I'm still not convinced it's all real on the show," Marianna said and quickly backpedaled. "I mean obviously it is because of what you went through, but some people have admitted to wanting to be on reality television to get into Hollywood. You're different."

"Hopefully, different in a good way," they said.

"Different in the best way," Marianna said. Before Alix could ask Marianna to elaborate, the next course was served. It smelled delicious. "Do you know the chef or just what your friends have told you about them?"

Alix snorted. "Okay, prior to getting this gig, I lived off grilled cheese sandwiches and anything I could cook in my air fryer. Now that I have the means to eat out and taste all the foods I've always wanted to, I'm going to do it. My brother can cook, especially fish, but it's not like I could just insert myself at his table. Whenever we went camping, he would cook whatever fish we caught and it was delicious. He always had a bag of mixed spices so everything he prepared tasted like we ordered straight from a restaurant."

"I want to meet him. He sounds like he's been a major influence in your life, especially when you were a young adult," Marianna said.

Alix nodded. "Once you get past his gruffness, he's kind of cool. Tell me about your brother. You don't talk about him much."

"We fought a lot growing up. He hated having his little sister tag along to everything. And my mom made him watch me whenever they went out. Usual sibling stuff. He was nice to me after he decided my friends were hot. He started hanging out with us once he knew

Chloe thought he was cute. And the twins always laughed at his dumb jokes." Marianna laughed at a memory. "Really, he ignored me in high school. He was a football player and I was and still am a total nerd. We didn't have a lot in common growing up."

"How about now?" Alix asked.

"We get along okay. I don't call him every day, but I see him at a lot of family dinners. At least he's not trying to date my friends now. I don't think he ever really got over Chloe."

"I feel the same way about my brother. It's like he poured his heart and soul into the business. I can't tell you the last time he went on a date. Well, that I know of," Alix said.

"Well, Andrea seemed pretty interested in meeting him. Maybe we can introduce them when he comes to visit," Marianna said.

"The studio has a suite at Dodger stadium that holds about twenty or thirty people. Let me reach out and see if I can secure it. We'll throw a party. See if they hit it off in a no-pressure environment," Alix said.

"Always a matchmaker."

"Well, aren't we all? I mean, you know somebody in your life who is wonderful but can't catch a break finding a soul mate and you think you know the perfect person for them and the cycle starts," Alix said.

"I love it."

"Would the rest of your family be interested in going? We'll need plenty of people there."

"My aunts, uncles, and cousins could easily fill half the suite. I can't imagine anyone in my family would say no to the Hollywood treatment," Marianna said.

Even the three feet between them at dinner was too much space, and finally after it was over and they were done sharing a delicious crème brûlée, Alix closed the gap.

"I'm tired of sitting all the way over there," they said.

Marianna delicately cupped their face and ran her fingers down their cheek. "I'm glad. I was getting lonely so far away from you."

Alix tried to smile, but their emotions were thick and heavy. They were sure it was supposed to be humorous, but neither of them was laughing. Alix held Marianna's fingers up to their lips and kissed them. Why did she always know how and where to touch them that instantly turned them to mush?

"You have such a soft and light touch." Alix wanted to feel Marianna's fingertips press lightly against their skin. Were they at the point in their relationship where it was time to have the talk? Obviously not in the restaurant but maybe somewhere more private like Marianna's suite? Was that too forward? Were they not being forward enough?

"Let's grab a drink and take it back to the suite," Marianna said.

Alix almost knocked over the table trying to get out of the booth. They looked at Marianna sheepishly. "I have to get up and move around." They made a big production of shaking out their legs as though tiny pins pricked their skin. "Sorry about that."

"Very smooth, Alix," Marianna said. Her lips were pressed tightly together as though they were keeping laughter from bubbling out. The slight dimple high up on her cheek gave her away.

Alix kissed her swiftly and grabbed her hand. "Let's head to the bar first. Should we bring a bottle to the suite or would you rather have a cocktail?"

Marianna shrugged. "Let's see what they have."

Alix guided them through the maze of tables and smiled at the patrons whose eyes grew big as they recognized them. The goal wasn't to mingle and talk to fans, but to finally have private time with somebody they cared about. And Marianna didn't need her face plastered online. Now that the show was underway, Alix was getting a lot more attention. Tobey was doing a great job of fielding calls, emails, and posting things on the socials, but it was still overwhelming.

What Alix really wanted was for the world to know that they weren't available. That there was somebody special in their life, but they weren't sure Marianna was ready for that kind of attention. Once fans found out, they would probably reach out and overwhelm Marianna with both good and bad attention. But Alix was selfish and didn't want to stop the relationship from happening either. In all fairness, at least in Alix's mind, Marianna knew the consequences from the last leaked photo. Yet here they were, in a popular bar, holding hands and leaning into one another to talk. Their body language screamed couple.

"What sounds good?" Alix asked.

Even though Marianna wasn't trying to be sexy, watching her chew on her bottom lip was making Alix's body swell in places that was borderline painful.

"You might be on to something with a whole bottle. What happens if we get thirsty?" The way Marianna was looking at Alix was anything but innocent. Nobody was that naïve. She was outright flirting.

"I can have the front desk send up some water."

Marianna grabbed the wine and two glasses and leaned against the bar. "Sounds great. Shall we?"

Alix didn't hesitate. "Let's go." They walked hand in hand to the elevators where Alix hit the top floor.

"Are we on the same floor?" Marianna asked.

"We are but safely apart," Alix said. When the doors closed, Alix put both hands on either side of the handrail so Marianna was boxed in. "Have I told you how wonderful it is to see you? I feel like I'm a million miles away from home, and seeing you makes me feel grounded. Thank you."

Marianna reached up and straightened Alix's collar. "I'm happy to be here, too."

Alix leaned their full body against Marianna and kissed her soundly. It wasn't a sweet hello kiss, but the kind of kiss that left them both breathless. Alix had never felt Marianna's body flush against theirs, and it was heavenly. It was hard not to grind their hips against hers. The ding of the elevator doors brought them back to reality.

Alix slowly moved away, breathless, and completely aroused. They cleared their throat and held their hand against the door. "This is us," they said.

Marianna pressed her fingers to her lips and walked out of the elevator. The only noise in the hallway was their soft footsteps.

"This is me." Marianna stopped in front of a door marked eight-fourteen.

Alix pointed down to the next door. "And this is me. Not to give you the wrong impression, but I got us adjoining suites only because of privacy. I didn't want people to follow us up and not be able to hang out when we wanted."

"People do that?" She shook her head slowly when Alix nodded. "That's awful." She unlocked the door and motioned for Alix to enter.

"I'm going to unlock my door. I'll meet you inside. Give me five minutes," Alix said. They quickly raced to the bathroom to freshen up. Keeping it casual, Alix left the suit jacket off, untucked their shirt, and kicked off their shoes. They were a bit wrinkled but still felt fresh. "Knock, knock," they said after unlatching their side of the door. Alix almost groaned at how dumb that sounded, especially since they also used their knuckle to actually knock. They took a step back when Marianna opened the door and held their breath when they saw her. She had let her hair all the way down and had kicked off her shoes. She was taller than most of the women Alix dated. It was refreshing to not bend down to kiss somebody.

"Come in," she said.

Alix left the door open to their suite and took the glass of wine from Marianna's hand. "Thank you."

"No, thank you. This is a beautiful suite and the view is magnificent," she said.

Alix's eyes never left hers. "Breathtaking," they said. They were rewarded with a deep blush on Marianna's neck and cheeks. Was she nervous? "I want you to know that I'm not expecting anything here. I genuinely like you and enjoy our conversations. I don't want you to think I brought you here…" they trailed off hoping Marianna understood what they were implying.

Marianna sat on the couch and patted the cushion beside her. "I trust you, Alix. You could have anybody you want and you picked me. I know you're not looking for a one-night stand. I know what's in your heart. I also know that you would never expect anything from me."

Alix held her hand. "Thank you for trusting me. Of course, I want to move this relationship at your pace." They leaned into Marianna's touch. She stroked their cheek with her thumb. "I can't wait to touch you. I want to feel your soft skin and find out what you like and find out what you taste like and what you sound like when you...well, you know."

Marianna's shaky exhale told Alix she was just as turned on as they were. In a move that completely surprised Alix, Marianna straddled their lap. "Is this okay?" she asked.

Alix's mouth went dry and they stifled a moan at how close her body was and how warm Marianna's core felt against their thighs. "Definitely okay."

Marianna leaned back and ran her fingertips up and down the buttons on Alix's shirt. "Can I unbutton this?" she asked.

Who was this woman on their lap? Thirty seconds ago, Alix was afraid just the conversation about furthering their relationship was bold, but Marianna took it as a green light and Alix wasn't complaining. They reached up to help her unbutton it. They felt Marianna's fingers rub the fabric of their binder and stop.

"It's my binder. I wear it when I wear suits so that my shirts fit me better," they said. Alix leaned forward and slipped the shirt off. It wasn't too late to stop, but it didn't seem like either of them wanted to.

"Is it okay to touch? I read that some nonbinary people don't like to be touched here. I don't want to do anything that you don't like," Marianna said.

Alix took Marianna's hand and placed it on their flat stomach. "I don't mind it at all. You can touch my chest, my nipples, but not my sides." Marianna froze and looked at Alix with eyes so wide that they couldn't help but laugh. "It's okay. I'm just really ticklish there."

Marianna smiled and grazed her nails over the spandex material. Alix liked how she was interested in it and how it made them feel as opposed to just wanting it off right away. "Still okay?" she asked.

Alix nodded as their skin twitched under her touch. "Oh, yeah. That's nice." They closed their eyes while Marianna continued to touch. She ran her fingertips over Alix's forearms and traced a few tattoos. "I like it when you do that."

"That's the cool thing about tattoos. People want to touch them," she said.

Alix cracked open an eye. "Let me know if you want one and not only will I design it, but I'll also actually tattoo it."

Marianna laughed softly. "You're rusty. I'll pass. Or maybe Buck can give me mine."

"I would hate that. Not because I'm jealous, but because you have such beautiful skin and it would be a shame to let anyone else ink it." Alix ran their fingertips over Marianna's thighs right along the hemline. They smiled when chill bumps followed the path of their fingertips. "Or touch it besides me." Marianna ran her fingers up Alix's neck and raked her short nails along the nape of their neck. "That feels amazing," Alix said. Their eyes drifted shut even though they were more than alert than ever at the nearness of her.

She was warm, soft, and very close. Alix could feel the heat radiating between Marianna's thighs and moaned with longing. This was going better than they wanted or even expected. They meant it when they said taking time was important, but it was hard with Marianna pressing her body into their lap. Her intent was clear. Alix had the green light for at least some heavy making out. They continued stroking Marianna's thighs until they either had to move on or go underneath her dress.

Marianna cupped their face. "It's okay." Not only was her consent sexy, but a power surged through Alix that was more than lust because it radiated from their heart. They would unpack this new feeling later. Right now, having Marianna in their arms was the most important thing.

"Are you sure about this?" Alix asked.

"I like the way you feel and the way you touch me," she said.

Alix pulled Marianna closer to their core. Their hands slipped under her dress and stroked the silky, delicate skin on the inside of her thighs. When they reached the line of her panties, Alix stopped. Marianna rocked her hips closer to Alix's hand and moaned when Alix's knuckle brushed softy against her pussy. Even through the satin barrier, they felt Marianna's heat, her wetness, and a slight quiver in her thighs. Alix deepened the kiss and pressed harder against her panties. They didn't care that the material separated their fingers from her pussy. They still rubbed their thumb up and down her slit. She moaned and moved her pelvis with each stroke. Alix slipped one hand around the back of Marianna's neck and cupped her pussy with the other hand. With little effort, they pushed the material aside until the only thing they felt were her swollen lips.

"You're so soft and smooth," they said. Alix watched Marianna's face as they rubbed two fingers up and down her slit. Her mouth was slightly open and her breath raspy. When Alix grazed her opening, Marianna bit her lip and closed her eyes. Alix loved the way her tongue peeked out from between her full lips and how her hips tilted down against their hand.

Very slowly, very carefully, they entered Marianna. Her slick walls grabbed at their finger. Alix clenched their teeth at how tight she was. They pulled out quickly and repeated until Marianna begged them to stay inside.

"I feel like I'm ready to explode. I want you to fuck me, Alix." She breathed against Alix's mouth.

Something almost primal took over. Alix stood with Marianna's legs wrapped around their waist and carried her to the bedroom. "Hold on to me." They ripped the comforter and sheets back. Alix gently placed Marianna sideways on the bed before unwrapping her legs and pulling her panties off. As much as they wanted to taste her, right now being inside of her meant everything. Alix slid their forefinger inside all the way and watched as Marianna arched her back slightly. When they pulled out again, Marianna frowned.

"Stop stopping," she said. It was more of a moan and confused Alix.

They stopped completely and leaned over her. "What? Am I doing something wrong?" they asked.

Marianna nodded. "You keep stopping. Stay inside of me. Give me more. I won't break, I promise," she said.

Alix didn't hesitate. They slipped two fingers inside of her, waited for her to adjust, and gave her what she asked for. Marianna spread her legs to accommodate Alix's fast movements. Her nails dug into Alix's arms and her gasps were swallowed by Alix's mouth. When Alix's thumb touched her clit, Marianna's hips jutted against Alix's hand. This was happening way too fast. As much as Alix wanted to see Marianna's body shake with an all-consuming orgasm, they also wanted to slowly peel off her clothes and enjoy every inch of her. They stretched out beside her, pulling her into their arms and nuzzling the side of her neck.

"I want this to be perfect. I'm so sorry I'm rushing this. You deserve better." The soft glow of the light from the living space spilled into the bedroom giving Alix just enough light to see Marianna's face and body. Her chest heaved with every fast breath and tiny beads of perspiration dotted her hairline.

"I regret nothing," she said. Her voice was low and her touch shaky. Alix kissed her softly and ran their hand down her neck and rested their fingers in the soft swell of her breasts. Marianna put her hand on top of Alix's. The weight felt like more than just a touch. Alix leaned down and placed a small kiss on her collarbone.

"Have I told you how happy I am that you are here?" Alix asked before capturing her lips in a searing kiss.

"You have. I'm thinking that maybe it's time to show me and not stop," she said.

CHAPTER EIGHTEEN

As much as Marianna appreciated Alix's respect and how they stopped because they were worried about the situation not being perfect, she was frustrated. She wanted Alix. She wanted Alix to touch her and for them to be intimate. Not just with their bodies, but with feelings. She wanted a cocoon that was just them for as long as possible, but Alix clearly thought they'd crossed a boundary. They were consenting adults in a new, monogamous relationship. What better way to seal it than having sex? Maybe she scared Alix by taking control. Maybe straddling them wasn't the best idea.

"Is something the matter? Did I do something wrong?" she asked.

Alix quickly pulled her into their arms. "Not at all. If anything, I'm in awe of you." They brushed her long hair from her face.

Marianna put her hand on Alix's. "Then why did you stop?" She hated that she sounded borderline desperate, but she was confused.

"Because I want to do this right," Alix said. They stood and pulled her into their arms. The kiss made her weak in the knees and she clutched Alix's hips to keep herself steady. Now wasn't the time to argue. She gave the control back to Alix and let them take the lead.

Alix slowly turned her so her back was to them. She smiled when she felt Alix tug on the zipper pull, but the smile dropped when they pulled her against their chest while they ran their fingers down her neck, breasts, and her waist. Her dress was a burden and she wanted it off. She wanted nothing between her and Alix. As if reading her mind, Alix slipped their fingers under the straps of Marianna's dress and let it pool around her ankles. With her panties already off, she was completely naked. Even though she wanted Alix's clothes off, too, there was something sexy about Alix partially dressed and her with nothing on. And as much as she wanted to turn around to face them, this was exciting, too.

"You are such a beautiful woman, Marianna." Alix's voice was almost a whisper. Their mouth was right next to her ear so she heard every breathy syllable.

She leaned against Alix so they could run their hands over her breasts. She was aching with need. Alix was too gentle, but remembering that they wanted it to be perfect, Marianna lifted her arms and locked her fingers behind Alix's neck. She was exposed and at Alix's mercy. She was never this wanton. There was something about Alix that made her want to let loose and give and take everything. She gasped when Alix squeezed her nipples and shivered as the ripple of pleasure with a hint of pain rushed through her blood. Their hands traveled down her hips to meet again at the juncture of her thighs.

Marianna shamelessly put her heel on the siderail of the bed to give Alix better access. They pressed their hand against her mound and rubbed her slick, swollen pussy until she whimpered and lost the strength to stand. She sat on the edge of the bed and looked at Alix. Their blue eyes were almost black. Marianna leaned back on her elbows and stared at Alix. She bit her bottom lip as she watched Alix's gaze travel over her body. When Alix unbuttoned their pants and let them fall to the floor, Marianna wanted to pull them on top of her, but this slow disrobing was just as hot. They removed their binder but kept their boxers on. Marianna didn't question it. She decided to save questions for later when there wasn't a raging fire of desire between them.

"Come here," she said. Alix obliged and slid on top of her and nestled their hips between Marianna's legs. She slid her arms around Alix's back and held them close. Sex was finally happening and she was ready. She already knew what it felt like to have Alix inside her, but she wanted more. She wanted Alix's mouth all over her body. "Nothing is off limits," she said.

Alix nodded. "Thank you." They sucked Marianna's bottom lip into their mouth and ran their tongue along her upper lip.

Marianna locked her ankles behind Alix's waist to get more friction against her core. While slowing down felt like the right emotional thing to do since it was their first time, her body hummed with the need to release the pressure Alix had built up over the last several minutes. Alix leaned up on their elbows and Marianna groaned at the pressure that pushed against her clit. She knew with a few hip wiggles on her part, she would come, but she also knew that was selfish. Alix was trying so hard to do the right thing and Marianna owed it to them to be with them in the moment.

"You feel so good," she said. Her voice sounded low and husky as though whiskey burned in her throat. Her body ached with need. Had she ever been this turned on before? Alix kissed her cheek and moved down to bite and suck on her neck. Marianna gasped and dug her nails in Alix's shoulders. She wasn't prepared for that much power to come from such a sensitive spot. Her body bucked up against Alix's and she knew she only had a sliver of control before she would let go and do everything she could to reach the pinnacle of passion.

Alix let go just in time and moved their mouth to suck her nipples hard and soothe the flash of pain with their tongue. It was another pull closer to cresting. Marianna bit her bottom lip and willed herself not to come until Alix's mouth was on her pussy with their fingers deep inside. She had been waiting for this moment and she wasn't going to release this beautiful orgasm until Alix was ready for it. She whimpered when she felt Alix's hot tongue swirl downward to finally reach the apex of her thighs.

"Yes. Please." She couldn't help but run her hands through Alix's hair and help guide them. When she finally felt the wet heat of their tongue, she spread her knees and placed her heels on the soft mattress. Alix slipped two fingers inside and pressed their tongue to her clit. She clawed the sheets to keep her from drifting away into a sea of ecstasy. "Yes, Alix. Just like that."

Not that Alix needed guidance, but Marianna couldn't help the words of encouragement from bubbling over. It had been so long and Alix was building her up to have an amazing orgasm as though they'd been doing it for years. She strained to hold back the rush but everything Alix was doing felt amazing. Their fingers filled her perfectly. She moaned with every push, every lick, every suck. When her legs started shaking, she knew it was time to let go. She yelled out as a delicious orgasm rolled over her body several times, leaving her shaking and sweaty. She clutched Alix when they crawled up and cradled her in their arms. She felt tears prick the back of her eyes as her emotions circled around in her heart trying to stick a landing that was wobbly. She was never good at sex without love. Her heart always got involved.

"Are you okay?" Alix rubbed Marianna's back and smoothed her hair back from her face. She felt Alix tug at the sheets and cover them up. With her head on their chest, she wasn't sure if the rapid beating was hers or theirs.

After several deep breaths she answered. "Yes, I'm good. Really good. Just trying to catch my breath." She felt Alix's laughter rumble under her ear and their arms squeeze her in a hug. "Are you okay with me touching you?" Marianna leaned up to look at Alix.

They looked serious but nodded. She slowly reached out and ran her fingers across Alix's abdomen. Even in the semi-darkness, she could see the outline of muscles. She traced her hand over Alix's hips and down their thighs. She knew Alix was strong, but their clothes never hinted at muscles this defined. It was nice. They were soft and hard and even though Marianna wanted to touch them all over, she wanted to be respectful. And she wanted reassurance. "Can I touch you here?" Her hand hovered above Alix's boxers. Alix answered her by guiding her hand down to the soft cotton.

"You can touch me anywhere, but I don't like penetration."

Marianna nodded and burned that in her mind. There were so many other ways to give them pleasure. She touched Alix's flawless complexion. They were sexy and confident. Every part of them that made the whole was perfect. Marianna never thought she had a type, although her previous lovers identified as lesbians and were mostly feminine. Dating someone masc was new. It was a totally different experience and she was all in. After Andrea planted the seed that sex might be in the equation, Marianna had scoured the internet for information about sex with nonbinary people. She knew it made her a nerd, but she didn't want to accidentally make Alix uncomfortable.

"Can you take these off?" Marianna pulled on the soft fabric of their boxers. Alix didn't hesitate and stripped them off immediately. "I think you're stunning. Every part of you, Alix." The small, pleasurable noises that Alix made with every kiss she placed on their body encouraged Marianna to continue her trek. She stroked their thighs and pushed them apart with her hands. Alix's hips lifted expectantly and greeted Marianna's mouth.

"That feels amazing. Your mouth sucking me off feels so good."

Alix was painfully hard and already close to orgasming. Marianna tried to go slow to savor the experience and the excitement of someone new, but Alix had other plans. They dug their fingers in her hair and yelled out when they came. It was too fast. Next time, Marianna wasn't going to let Alix take control. Next time. She smiled and placed soft kisses on Alix's thighs as she waited for the quivers to subside.

"Why are you smiling?" A light note of humor trickled through the breathiness of Alix's voice.

"I mean, I just got here," she said. She never joked during sex. She barely spoke during it, but something about Alix made them feel comfortable even in such a vulnerable state. As much as she wanted to continue, Alix was too sensitive so she moved back up to rest in the crook of their arm. They greeted her with a deep kiss that jumped-started her heart and sensitive spots. She was tired, but their energy was electric.

"That was incredible," Alix said. They lifted Marianna's chin and kissed her softly this time. "Thank you for trusting me."

Marianna's heart melted. "Thank you for being so sweet and gentle with me." She felt her cheeks flush as she recalled her promiscuous behavior in the other room. It was unfamiliar passion that she still had to process. Was she just getting more comfortable with her body or did Alix bring out this behavior? She placed her hand on Alix's stomach and even though she wanted to stay in this moment and listen to them talk, her eyelids reluctantly fluttered shut.

❖

"At some point, you're going to have to wake up."

Marianna moaned and snuggled under the covers completely unaware of where she was. It was the weekend, right? Why was Andrea at her apartment? Once the haze cleared and she realized she was in Vancouver with Alix, she jerked her head up and looked around. Alix was sitting in a chair near the bed. The smell of tea wafted in the space between them.

"What time is it?"

Alix, fully dressed for their hike, sat on the side of the bed and kissed Marianna softly on the lips. "It's hiking time," they said.

Marianna pulled the covers over her head. Why did she sleep in? She wanted to sneak away and brush her teeth and shower before they woke up. Alix playfully tugged on the sheet. "Why don't I answer a few emails while you get ready and we can eat a little breakfast?"

Disappointment weighed her down. She wanted to wake up in Alix's arms and stay in bed all day, alternating between having sweet sex and falling asleep with their arms and legs entangled. She wanted to close the curtains and pretend time didn't exist. Had last night not happened, Marianna would've been down in the lobby anxious to go on an all-day hike. But last night did happen and her emotions were scattered and bouncing around in her chest. She wanted the fairy tale magic of staying in bed for two days after having sex for the first time. Alix looked happy but also seemed distant. Dawn had brought a shift in their energy.

Marianna made herself smile. "Okay. I'll be done in a flash." She waited until Alix went into their suite before jumping out of bed and racing to the bathroom. There wasn't time for a long, hot shower to give her sore muscles relief. Her shower was fast and her makeup light. She slipped into pants with deep pockets and a long-sleeved T-shirt. She'd borrowed Andrea's hiking boots, which were luckily her size. After throwing her hair back in a braid, she was ready for whatever Alix had in store.

Alix knocked on the door that was ajar. "You look adorable," they said. They brought in a tray laden with breakfast. Smells of sweet waffles and peppered bacon assaulted her nose. Alix placed the tray on the small table. "Earl Gray and also coffee if you want it."

"You remembered," Marianna said. Why was she so shy this morning?

"Of course I did." Alix topped off their coffee. "Thank you again for a wonderful evening." They snatched a piece of crispy bacon from one of the plates and poured two small glasses of orange juice.

The moment Marianna stopped fixating on why Alix wasn't doting, she realized Alix was, but in a way she wasn't familiar with. They handed her a cup of tea the minute she opened her eyes. They gave her privacy to get ready and had a hot breakfast in the room with her favorite food waiting when she was done. It was very thoughtful. "I'm sorry I slept so hard."

Alix reached across the table and squeezed her hand. "You had a busy travel day and needed to sleep. I just didn't want to miss any more daylight."

The smirk on their face made Marianna pause, then laugh. "Ha ha ha. It's only ten. How long is this hike? I'm a city girl. I don't know what will happen to me in too much nature."

"I met you doing yoga in the park. You'll probably kick my ass."

"Challenge accepted," she said. This was nice. Joking and having fun with somebody special. She ate her breakfast and peeked inside the small backpack Alix handed her. "What's in here?"

"Water, protein bars, crackers, bug spray, and sunscreen," Alix said.

"Why is yours so much bigger?"

"I have more water and a hoodie just in case it gets cold. Today's high will be low seventies and although that's the perfect temperature, I want to be prepared. Are you ready?"

Alone time in the woods with the most popular single queer person in the world? "Hell, yes," Marianna said.

CHAPTER NINETEEN

N ot only did Marianna keep up, but she almost led the entire hike. Alix was expecting to baby Marianna and hold her bag, but she matched them step for step and even helped them when they stumbled over a few loose rocks on the side of the trail.

"Is there anything you can't do?" Alix drained half their water bottle and chewed on a protein bar, trying hard not to look so winded. "I'm trying to be all cool and collected and not gulp in giant breaths of air and you're all rested and perky." They stripped off their T-shirt so they were down to a black sports bra and hiking pants. It was only seventy degrees, but the sun was blazing hot and Alix didn't want to sweat so much in front of Marianna. Judging by her appreciative up-and-down of Alix, Marianna didn't mind at all. Alix made sure their muscles popped when she was looking.

"You look sexy as hell," she said.

"Mm. Thank you." Alix placed a swift kiss on her lips.

"I approve. And don't feel bad about me kicking your butt. Remember, I got to sleep in this morning," Marianna said. She kissed Alix after taking a sip of their water. "Thank you."

"For letting you sleep in?" Alix asked.

She cupped Alix's chin. "For inviting me and making me come on this hike. I like what I see. Truthfully, I wanted to stay in bed, but this view is spectacular."

Her meaning was clear and also a surprise. "You wanted to stay in bed?" Alix pulled Marianna into their arms. "Why didn't you say anything? Here I'm trying to impress you and you're telling me this now?" They kissed her softly at first, but their passion flared as though the time between last night and this very moment didn't exist and they were back in the privacy of Marianna's room. Alix broke apart only to pull her off the path for privacy in case there were others on the trail. They slid their hands under Marianna's shirt to stroke the soft skin. "You're very soft. And very beautiful." They knelt and placed a small kiss on Marianna's stomach. A shadow of panic crossed her face when Alix looked up. She wasn't comfortable making out in public. Alix stood and kissed her full lips instead. "I just wanted you to know that." They looked at their Apple Watch. "We only have three miles to go and then we can get back to the hotel, eat a light snack, and do whatever you want this evening. I have no plans."

Marianna arched her brow and smirked. "No plans? None? After my heartfelt confession?"

Alix pressed their hips against Marianna's and held her close. "I'm more of a spur-of-the-moment person, but by the time we get back from our hike, I'll have the night figured out."

"I'm limited on clothing," she said.

Alix shot her their best flirtatious look and looked her up and down. "I don't think we have to worry about clothing later."

Marianna laughed and grabbed Alix's hand. "Let's get out of here. Three miles is going to take us about an hour."

"At least it's mostly downhill from here, according to the map." Alix handed Marianna their phone to look at the trail. "It's so nice that there aren't many people. I thought for sure it would be packed. Maybe because it's a weekday." Alix shrugged and slipped their phone in their pocket.

"I thought maybe you bought out the park." Marianna smiled at Alix and squealed when they started chasing her. When they finally caught her, Marianna waved them off. "I'm just kidding. You're very sweet and I know you're not showing off."

"I'm definitely trying to impress you, but not showing off. I wanted you to be comfortable. Besides, Tobey was the one who set up everything. She deserves some credit, too."

"I like your assistant. She seems very nice," Marianna said.

"She likes you, too, and she likes to pry. She wants to know more about you," Alix said. They didn't want to ask Marianna how she saw their relationship. They were intimate less than twenty-four hours ago. That intensified their relationship, but it didn't define it. Marianna nodded.

"She and Andrea chatted at the party. They have a lot in common," Marianna said.

"You're right. They both like reality shows. They're both on the fringes of Hollywood. If Andrea ever wants a ticket to any of the shows, let me know. The studio films a lot of sitcoms and things. Even the tours are cool. You know, if you're into Hollywood." Alix knew they were toeing the line, but after last night it seemed like Marianna's edges were softer toward them. "Are you? Into Hollywood?" Alix took a sip of water as though nothing was riding on her answer when everything was.

"I don't know that I'm into Hollywood, but I'm into you, Alix Sommers."

Alix was going to keep the playful banter, but the cameras weren't rolling and they were tired of trying so hard. They stopped and put their hands on Marianna's hips. "I'm into you, too, Marianna Raines. I'm happy you gave me a chance." They kissed her again. A calmness blanketed them and even though Alix's heart was pounding, they found peace with her answer. Suddenly, there wasn't a rush to get back to the hotel. Time felt like it was on their side. They slowed their pace and pointed out interesting things in nature like how the Pacific dogwood flower extended all the way up the coast and how the fir trees reminded them of the hikes they took with Buck in the Cascades outside of Portland. "I really miss being outside. The city is overwhelming at times."

"The city is overwhelming all the time," Marianna said.

"How come you never moved?" Alix was genuinely curious. They were always fascinated by people who had deep roots and rarely traveled. For some, it was lack of finances, and for others, it was a level of comfort. There was something to be said about knowing everyone and everything in a community.

"The thought never crossed my mind. I mean, my whole family lives in SoCal. I would have to start all over somewhere new."

"It's ridiculous how expensive Southern California is. I mean, Portland is, too, but not nearly as bad," Alix said. They pulled Marianna off to the side when a large group of people met them rounding a corner. "I have family in the Midwest and it's unbelievably cheap to live there."

"Yeah, but they don't get this." Marianna swept her arm over the view of the vast, beautiful landscape.

"They have to drive a long way to get near an ocean or even a mountain range," Alix said. "Would you always want to live in California?"

"I don't know. I mean, it depends on the situation. I know it's a giant world, but I've never really had the means to travel. I'm sure that if I grew up in different places, I'd have a different view. Plus, I think I'm the kind of person who would love every single place. Like, I could see myself living here. It's so beautiful. There's city life and nature a stone's throw away."

"But it's also cold and if this is summer, I'll never last. I need the sun and heat," Alix said.

"Is it hot in Portland?"

"We get the four seasons so we learn to appreciate the heat and the cold," Alix said.

"Do you miss it?"

Alix nodded. "I do. I need to get back for a quick trip once the show is over." They wanted to invite Marianna but that was months away and a lot could change. Baby steps, they reminded themselves.

"Would you like to grab a quick drink before we get back to the hotel?"

"I'd love that. What did you have in mind?" Marianna asked.

"We could try that cute little place with the blue-and-white awning. They boast having the best Aperol spritz in Vancouver." Alix shrugged and opened the car door for Marianna. "I mean, we shouldn't pass that up, right? The best, Mar." It was the first time they called her that.

"Well, if the sign says it's the best, we should find out for sure," she said.

Alix watched Marianna pull down the visor to quickly check her reflection. She slammed it up before Alix reached the driver's door. She was a combination of sweet and sexy and it was adorable that she was trying to hide that she didn't just check her reflection. Most girls Alix dated before would do that openly and worry about if their lipstick was smeared. Now that they thought about it, nobody they dated before was like Marianna. Not even when they lived in Portland and inked for a living.

"Why are you smiling?" Marianna asked when they slid into the car.

"I'm happy. You make me happy," they said. They didn't even try to hide how big and wide their smile was. Everything was going great. Marianna was okay with their public persona. She saw them for who they really were.

❖

They had the whole night and most of the morning before Alix had to be on set. They were counting down the hours not because they were anxious to be rid of Marianna, but because they wanted to know every minute they had left. They were falling for her organically and not in front of cameras in a controlled environment, and it felt wonderful. They turned when they heard a knock on the already opened door.

"Hi."

Marianna stood in the doorway between their suites wearing a little black dress and low strappy heels. Her long, curly hair flowed down her back and a small silver necklace clung to the soft spot right below her throat.

"Wow. You're breathtaking." Alix walked over and carefully brushed their lips against hers, mindful of her makeup.

Marianna wiped Alix's bottom lip with the pad of her thumb. "Perhaps I need to invest in smudge-proof lipstick," she said.

"Just so you know, we're going to be kissing a lot."

"Noted. Also, just so you know, I always melt a little when you wear this color blue." Marianna put her hand on Alix's shirt and rubbed small circles on the soft, smooth material. Alix bit back a moan. As much as they wanted to forgo tonight's plans, they also didn't want Marianna to think they were only interested in one thing, regardless of what was said on the hike. Instead, they thanked her, held her hand, and took the elevator down to the lobby where they were greeted by the concierge who informed them that their car had arrived.

"Wow. A stretch Cadillac SUV," Marianna said. She ran her fingers across the butter soft leather bench. "This is nice. Does the show always provide a driver? Not that I'm complaining."

"I just like it when someone else drives. Especially in high traffic cities. In Portland, I either rode my electric bike to work or my motorcycle. It was easier to get around that way," Alix said. They put their hand on Marianna's leg.

Marianna stroked the top of their hand. "Plus, it gives us time to…talk." She looked expectantly at Alix's lips. "How much time do we have until we get to the restaurant?"

Alix rolled up the privacy glass that separated them from the driver after checking the route. "We have at least twenty minutes. What's on your mind?" Marianna pushed their hand under her dress. She leaned back and relaxed her knees giving Alix easy access. They kissed her hard and fast and when they tried to pull away, Marianna locked her fingers behind Alix's neck to keep them in place. Her mouth was hot and her probing tongue delved deep into Alix's mouth. Marianna's kisses made Alix's knees weak. She sucked Alix's bottom lip and ran her tongue over it until they couldn't stand it.

Alix broke away. "Let me taste you, Marianna." They knelt between her legs and placed a trail of kisses up her thighs.

Alix didn't care that her fingers were in their hair. Marianna's acceptance of this moment meant everything. They pulled her hips closer to their mouth. The position was awkward for both but they didn't mind and she didn't seem to either. Alix flicked their tongue across Marianna's clit several times while they slid two fingers in and out of her pussy, building her up as quickly as possible. Marianna pumped her hips against Alix's mouth, wanting release. Alix pressed their arm across her hips to keep her from bucking too hard. Being held down made Marianna moan even harder. She stretched her arms along the back of the seat. As much as Alix wanted a better position, having sex in the back of a limo was both invigorating and surprisingly sexy. The tension had been building all day, and as much as Alix wanted to be reserved and wait, they simply couldn't. Marianna was so wet and tight and as much as Alix wanted to come, too, making Marianna orgasm was everything right now.

"I'm so close, Alix. I'm so close." Her voice was a raspy whisper punctuated with short gasps of breaths.

Alix sped up their hand and kept the rhythm of their tongue. Marianna's body tensed and her hips stopped bucking. She clutched Alix's shoulders and kept her orgasm as quiet as she could. Alix watched the last few shudders as Marianna rode the orgasm for as long and as quietly as she could. When she opened her eyes, Alix melted at the intensity of her look. They slipped out of her, careful not to touch her dress.

"Don't move," Alix said. They pulled a napkin from one of the cabinets to wipe their hands and carefully clean up Marianna. Alix felt Marianna's hands on their lapels and pulled them up so they could kiss.

Marianna licked her lips. "You taste like sex."

"I taste like you," Alix said. They weren't used to women being so chatty about their sexual experiences. It was a nice change. They raised an eyebrow when they felt Marianna's hand on their pants.

"Is this okay?" she asked.

Alix nodded solemnly. They weren't expecting anything in return, but now that Marianna's hand was close, their energy ramped up. "Definitely okay." They unbuttoned their pants and pushed them down to rest at their knees. Limos were big except when you wanted to have sex. Alix slid down their boxers and moaned when they felt Marianna's fingers press against their crotch.

"We only have a few minutes." Alix breathed against Marianna's mouth.

She leaned back enough to look in Alix's eyes. "Then I'd better hurry."

Alix tried to keep their eyes open but failed. It felt too good. Marianna moved her fingers up and down slowly while Alix rocked their hips against her hand. "That feels amazing." Alix kissed Marianna on her lips then moved to scrape their teeth over her earlobe and down the smooth skin of her neck. "Faster." Alix was getting close. They put their hands on the back of the large bench and braced themselves for the rush of heat and pleasure to every part of their body. Alix didn't make a lot of noise during sex, but they bit back a roar when the orgasm hit. Instead, they squeezed the leather and tensed their body as wave after wave pounded them. They threw their head back and gasped for air.

"I think we're almost at the restaurant," Marianna said.

"Shit." Alix pushed back and quickly pulled up their boxers. They handed Marianna her panties and worked on getting their clothes on and presentable. They both finished about the same time and sank on the bench right when the driver knocked on the door to announce their arrival. Alix looked at Marianna and they both laughed. "Are you ready?"

CHAPTER TWENTY

A re you sure it's okay for me to be here?" Marianna looked around before entering Alix's trailer. She ran her fingertips over Alix's nameplate screwed into the siding before entering.

"I don't see why not. The contestants and Heather are far enough away. We shouldn't run into anyone except maybe Tobey. And she will certainly announce herself," Alix said.

After the limo ride and the long night of exploratory and extremely satisfying sex, Marianna was tired. It was the kind of exhaustion that she wasn't used to, but she welcomed it. She could sleep when she got home. "I feel like I'm in high school sneaking around with somebody."

Alix pulled the door shut. "Did you sneak around a lot back then?"

"Not at all. I don't know why I said that. What about you? Did you sneak around?" Marianna didn't lose her virginity until college. High school was a series of crushes on straight girls hoping they would realize they were in love with her followed by bouts of depression when she realized that wasn't going to happen.

"Yes. My parents had their hands full with me and Buck."

"I was such an angel compared to you. See, the trick is to get your older sibling to get into as much trouble as possible so that you can get away with murder," Marianna said. They both knew she wasn't a troublemaker no matter how hard she pretended. "Speaking of, when am I going to meet Buck?"

"I texted him to look at the schedule and let me know possible dates. I'm excited for it. We're going to make this meet-and-greet happen. You know what they say. Love happens when you least expect it," Alix said.

It wasn't as if Marianna was in love with Alix, but the word coming from their lips slipped inside her ear, completely missed her brain, and drilled itself into her heart. She felt her pulse quicken in an irregular fashion and told herself to exhale and inhale until her brain kicked in and took over. It was hard to put up roadblocks on somebody so seemingly perfect as Alix. She stumbled over Alix's words. "Yes. True. So, I'm in. Whomever you need me to invite, I will."

Alix's phone buzzed in their pocket. They pulled it out and apologized before answering. "Hey, Denise. What's going on?"

Marianna could hear bits and pieces of the conversation but tried not to. It wasn't any of her business. She was there to spend a few more minutes with Alix before the driver took her to the airport. Instead, she walked around the trailer. The decor was contemporary with gray, black, and white as the predominant colors. A splash of red popped up in small decorative pillows on the couch and a yellow flower vase full of daisies added brightness to the room. There was a bed in the back of the trailer that looked like nobody ever slept in it.

Marianna felt Alix's arms snake around her waist as she was gently propelled forward and landed on the bed with a soft bounce. She laughed and twisted so she could face Alix. "I would never leave this trailer. It's the perfect size. I think it's bigger than my shoebox of an apartment."

"It's pretty plush. I haven't slept here yet. We're only using these for the two weeks we're here filming."

"And at the mansion, you have your own room, right?" she asked. She lightly touched Alix's lips with her fingertips and ran her thumb over their smooth skin. They didn't have a single scar, mole, or freckle anywhere visible. Marianna found it fascinating especially with how much of a daredevil Alix was. Alix had scars on their leg from a motorcycle accident and a three-inch jagged scar on their left side from when they fell out of a treehouse. Their right elbow had two puckered circles from arthroscopic surgery as a teenager, but their face didn't have a single blemish.

"Yes. I stay there a lot when we do several takes. I'm not a pro like Lauren was, so our days and nights stretch into longer stints."

Marianna shifted her body so she was under Alix. She spread her legs to be comfortable, but the moment their cores touched, her clit swelled with need. The air shifted from playful to sexual in the span of a breath. Alix rolled their hips and Marianna moaned. "You don't have time for this," she said, hoping she was wrong. Even though she was sore from the past two days, she wanted Alix again.

"Denise said the contestants were just now waking up and it would be at least an hour before they needed me," Alix said. Marianna was going to say something flippant like "I need you" but was silenced when Alix kissed her soundly and stretched their body to cover hers. "How do you feel about strap-ons?"

Her mouth dropped open a bit at the thought of Alix fucking her that way. She nodded and tried to slow her heart. It was almost painful how hard her clit was throbbing as though all the blood in her body instantly rushed to it and pounded against the delicate skin cheering her to say yes. "I like that idea very much." She smiled as Alix's smile grew.

"Stay right here."

Marianna thought about removing most of her clothes and slipping under the perfectly made bed, but Alix told her to stay put. She leaned up on her elbows to find Alix digging through their suitcases. They held up a bag and slipped into the bathroom. Well, that was presumptuous, she thought, as Andrea's words about expected sex echoed in her brain. But also, she didn't care. She wanted this. Deep down she'd wanted to have sex this weekend. She'd wanted to advance the relationship. So far, Alix hadn't been like the other people she'd dated, but their relationship was still fresh and exciting. Before she could get further in her head and doubt every decision she ever made about Alix, they returned. It was hard not to notice the bulge in the front of their pants. Marianna swallowed hard. Alix's cheeks were flushed and their eyes were darker than Marianna had seen before.

"Hi," she said. Really? Of all the words, of all the opportunities to be and sound sexy, she says hi.

"Hi," Alix said. Only their word was said with meaning and dripped with promise.

Marianna felt a little overwhelmed at the excitement that coursed through her veins. When was the last time somebody took charge like Alix? Never. The answer was never. She crawled backward on the bed until her head hit the pillow. Alix followed.

"Are you good? Is this okay?" Alix asked.

Marianna swallowed hard and nodded. "This is perfect." Her words had barely left her mouth before Alix claimed her lips. It was the kind of kiss that made Marianna want to feel every part of Alix's body on hers. She pushed at Alix's clothes anxious to get them off while they pulled at hers. She felt their rapid heartbeat in her fingertips. When their skin touched hers, her nipples hardened. "You feel so good."

"Hopefully, we're both about to feel better," they said.

Marianna knew it wasn't said egotistically. They both were excited. She had used vibrators and dildos with previous lovers, but never as a strap-on. Alix pulled off Marianna's panties and reached between her legs to stroke her pussy.

"You're so wet. And tight. I don't want to hurt you," they said.

Marianna watched as Alix pulled down their boxers. The dildo was thicker than she expected. While they added lube, Marianna took a moment to appreciate Alix's body in full daylight. Their white sports bra was tight across their chest emphasizing tan, muscular abs and colorful tattoos that popped in the light. Alix put a dab of lube on their fingers and rubbed Marianna's slit until she moaned and lifted her hips, desperately wanting Alix to penetrate her.

"Are you ready?" Alix asked.

Marianna licked her lips and swallowed hard. "Yes." Shivers of anticipation rolled through her as though preparing for the orgasm she knew was coming.

"Let me know if you don't like it and I'll stop," Alix said. They guided the strap-on and slid the tip down Marianna's slit and slowly pushed inside. "Exhale," they said. Marianna did. She moaned when it broke the tightness and slipped halfway inside. She exhaled again. The tiny tremors she felt told her she was going to come hard and fast. "Are you okay?" Alix asked.

Marianna smiled and pulled them down for a kiss. Alix continued pushing in until all of it was buried inside. Marianna exhaled again and waited for her body to adjust. She studied the small beads of sweat at Alix's temples and the strained muscles in their neck.

"Are you okay?" she asked.

Alix made a sound that was a cross between a laugh and a moan. They nodded and opened their eyes. It was looking in their eyes at that moment when Marianna felt the slip. The crack around her heart feathered out and all doubt drifted away like dust. Alix was in this relationship as much as she was.

"I'm trying very hard not to come," they said.

"Go slow then."

Bursts of pleasure wracked Marianna's body with every thrust of Alix's hips. When they sped up, she lost all track of everything other than Alix. One orgasm exploded, then another. Every part of her body shook. She clutched Alix until they came loudly and beautifully and dropped their head on her shoulder. Marianna wrapped her arms around them and stroked their hair. Her legs felt numb and she was surprised she had control of her arms, but she held Alix close while they both caught their breaths. Alix shifted their body and gently pulled out. Marianna felt like she had to say something. She needed to get these feelings out but was afraid it was too soon. And sometimes sex had a way of sugar-coating a relationship, especially after an experience like that, but what was the right thing to say?

"That was more than incredible. I'm in another world right now," Alix said.

When Alix's trailer door opened and Tobey announced herself, they both jumped out of bed and scrambled to pick up their clothes from the floor.

"Alix, are you in here? You have to be on the set in twenty minutes."

Alix quickly closed the small bedroom door. "I'll be out in ten. Thank you," they yelled.

"Okay. I dropped off today's outfit. See you soon," she said.

Marianna blew out a held breath and quickly pulled the dress over her head. "That was way too close."

Alix kissed her swiftly. "I need to jump in the shower. I'd take you with me, but it's kind of small."

Marianna was dying to wash up but knew she only had to get to the airport and then home. She could wash up after Alix was done. "Go. You're the one who has to work. I can wait." A hard kiss landed on her still tingling lips.

"I'll be quick," they said.

No way was Marianna leaving now that people were milling about. They didn't need the distraction or the questions. She grabbed a clean pair of panties from her overnight and straightened out her dress. She wanted to send Andrea a message about what just happened, but that conversation was best in person. Alix walked out wearing a towel around their waist and their binder.

"It's all yours. I just need to throw on today's outfit. Mandee will work on my hair and makeup. Did you get a chance to meet Mandee at the screening?"

Marianna pulled Alix in her arms. "I don't want to talk about your people. I'm still reeling from the incredible sex we just had." She felt Alix soften.

"I'm sorry. I was so exhilarated and then Tobey opening the door made me crash. I didn't want her to see you. Not that I think she would say anything. It's her job to protect me and my interests."

"I don't think Tobey would say anything either. She seems pretty cool." Marianna gave Alix another kiss before pulling away. "But also, she doesn't need to see either of us naked."

"Well, not you. I honestly don't know if she's seen me naked. Quite a few people have but that's kind of to be expected. Quick wardrobe changes."

Marianna playfully growled and grabbed Alix's hips. "Well, let's hope they keep it professional. I don't like all eyes on you."

Alix pushed several wild curls behind Marianna's ear. "They aren't looking at me lustfully, I promise. Mandee is straight and my stylists are either gay or married or both."

Marianna pursed her lips together and shook her head. "Okay. I believe you. Now go get ready and I'm going to wash up. Don't leave without saying good-bye."

"Never. I might step outside to answer a few calls, but I promise to take you to the car before you leave."

Alix dropped the sweetest, softest kiss on her lips. They smiled at her and pointed to the bathroom. Marianna slipped inside. Alix was right. While the bathroom was a decent size for a trailer, the shower wasn't designed for two. She tied up her hair and stood under the stream for about five minutes to rinse off the smell of their sex and investigate the new marks Alix accidentally made on her body. She dried off quickly and dressed again hoping the steam from the shower would press out the wrinkles in her dress. It wasn't too bad.

"Alix? Are you in here?" someone called from inside the trailer.

Marianna froze behind the bathroom door. Shit. Who was here? She remained as quiet as she could, but when she turned to gather her stuff, she accidentally knocked over her purse and its contents scattered everywhere.

"There you are. Come out here. I have something I want to show you."

The voice was somewhat familiar and sounded like somebody was trying really hard to sound sexy. That pissed her off. She quickly gathered her lip gloss, wallet, mascara, gum, and earrings off the floor and shoved them back into her purse, ensuring the clasp was secure.

The person knocked again and rattled the doorknob. "Don't be shy now. Come on, baby. Unlock the door."

Baby? What the fuck? Marianna squared her shoulders and pulled the door open to give whoever was on the other side a piece of her mind, but the only thing she could do was gasp. Of all the people Marianna never wanted or expected to see again, Vee was at the top of the list and standing right in front of her wearing a trench coat and red lingerie.

"Oh, my God. What the fuck are you doing here?" Vee pulled the trench coat shut and tied the belt tight. "Wait. Are you stalking me?"

Surprisingly, Marianna kept her cool, but she couldn't keep the bitchy sneer from sliding onto her face. "Oh, please. Don't flatter yourself. Maybe you should knock before trying to force your way into somebody's personal space. Who's the real stalker?"

Vee held up her finger and ran to the front of the trailer, pushing the door open and yelling as she descended the stairs. "Security! We have a trespasser."

And to think that less than a year ago, Marianna would've done anything for her. But that was the old her. The new her just slammed the door behind Vee. Anger and disbelief made her shake. Just as she was pulling out her phone to call Alix, she heard their voice.

"What the hell is going on here?"

Marianna opened the door and pointed at Vee. "This one here decided she wanted to pop in for a visit and seduce you wearing—" Marianna paused and motioned her finger up and down. "Whatever the hell that outfit is."

Alix looked livid. They turned to Vee. "What on earth made you think it was okay to show up to my personal trailer? Go back to the set."

"This is unacceptable. I don't know what's going on here, but I'm going to have a friendly chat with Xander and Denise," Vee said. She pushed past security and marched off.

"You might want to change your clothes," Marianna yelled, hoping Vee could hear the disgust in her voice and not the shakiness. "I'm so sorry. She literally walked through the door and tried to bust in on me in the bathroom as I was getting ready," Marianna said. She couldn't stop herself from shaking.

Alix jogged up the three steps and nudged her back into the trailer. "You don't have to apologize. You did nothing wrong. She's never supposed to contact me unless it's on set. Even then, she has to go through Tobey if it's not scene-related." Alix pulled Marianna into their arms. "I'm so sorry. I don't know what the hell she was thinking." Alix tilted Marianna's chin so they could look into her eyes. "You believe me, right?"

CHAPTER TWENTY-ONE

It's a total violation of my privacy. What in the hell was Violet doing on this side of the lot and in my trailer?" Alix was seething. Not only did it look bad to Marianna, but it looked bad to the show as though there was something between Alix and a contestant.

"I need everyone to calm down," Xander said.

Alix wanted to pace in the small, makeshift conference room on the set, but there wasn't any room. Denise, Xander and Kitty, and Alix were seated at the round table while Alix's agent Sam, and Peter Meyers, CEO of Meador Entertainment, had joined them via Zoom.

Denise crossed her arms across her chest and stared accusingly at Alix. "This doesn't look good. The very last thing this show needs is another controversy."

"Then keep your contestants out of my trailer," Alix said. "The person you all need to have a meeting with is Violet, not me."

"Why was she yelling for security and accusing that woman of stalking her?" Denise asked.

"There was no stalking." Alix raked their fingers through their hair and took a much-needed deep breath. "Apparently, Violet and my girlfriend, Marianna, dated a long time ago. Seeing Marianna in my trailer set Violet off. Every single person here knows what she's like. She's making drama where there isn't. Not that it's anybody's business, but I met Marianna organically. No ties to the show. As a matter of fact, she didn't even know who I was for weeks."

"That's impossible," Xander said.

"How does she not know you or this show? Especially if she's queer?" Denise asked.

She has such an over-inflated ego, Alix thought. "Trust me, it was a big surprise. But also, I've been seeing her since before they announced the bachelorettes on television. There is no way she could've known her ex-girlfriend was a contestant on the show. She hasn't talked to Violet in over six months."

"Honestly, I don't see what the big deal is. Alix already explained themselves. Violet clearly violated Alix's space and the rules of the show especially after last year's fiasco. And they're right. We all know what Violet's like," Kitty said. Alix held their palms together and moved them up and down a few times at Kitty, thanking her for coming to their defense. Kitty winked at Alix in return. "And can we pause for a moment? Who wears a trench coat in the summer? And red lingerie?" She yawned. "The obvious color is black."

"Denise, what do we do? Isn't Heather getting rid of Violet next week? Let's just move up that timetable," Peter said.

Denise nodded. Alix looked at everyone in surprise. "So, this was always planned out? Which contestants stay and which one gets the boot?"

"Oh, don't be so naive, Alix. You were never going to win Savannah's heart. Even though you were in her top five, you were never going to be at the end. Nobody was. That season was fucked from the beginning."

Alix hated the way Denise was showing her true colors. "Was that planned? Lauren and Savannah?"

"No. Nobody knew that. Just sometimes we can see which direction the bachelorette is leaning toward. If there's a villain but she has no intentions of keeping them around, then we encourage her to keep them to boost ratings," Denise said.

Alix noticed Denise didn't show any emotion at all. This was a business even though hearts were on the line. It sucked and Alix was going to try even harder to make it better than it was before. For the sake of the future of the show. They were in it one hundred percent and could pinpoint the people who were in it for love, too. Alix could feel the heat radiating from their neck and face. They were trying hard to keep their cool, but unjust situations always pissed them off.

"It never occurred to any of you that someone who is a loose cannon on set would also misbehave off-camera?" Alix asked. Denise rolled her eyes. Kitty gave Alix a look of pity. "If Violet is threatening to sue for whatever reason even though she was completely in the wrong, remind her again she signed an ironclad contract. If she tries to make waves, it's going to backfire and she will never make a dime in Hollywood."

"I think after a second reminder, she won't be a problem. Plus, to alleviate any headaches she might cause, we're adding her to the cast of *Second Chance at Love*. She'll be back in the spotlight schmoozing with all the bisexuals and queers from several dating shows aired by Meador Entertainment," Xander said.

"*Love Fest, When Sparks Fly, Passion Island,* and *Forever Yours.*" Peter held up a finger after listing each show.

Alix's eyebrows furrowed as they thought about the shows. "But they're not all queer."

"No, but all those shows have contestants who claim to be bisexual. This will just catapult her to the front of the line." Xander sighed and leaned back in his chair. "I mean, she was going to get chosen anyway, we just didn't think it would happen this upcoming season. We need to make some quick adjustments."

Alix was getting more and more frustrated. Why were they even giving in to Violet knowing she was such a troublemaker? It felt like a test. "Fine. I just want to make it clear that there was no reason for Violet to be off set and at my trailer. She needs to understand that is completely off-limits and unprofessional. This wouldn't have happened if security had been doing their job. And where was the show's coordinator? Shouldn't she be corralling the contestants?" Alix hated that they just insulted them, but they were trying to prove their point. Nobody was holding Violet responsible. Alix stood and tried hard to keep their anger in check. "Are we done here? I need to get back to Marianna who thinks she just ruined the show just by being my girlfriend." Alix nodded as though dismissing them when nobody said anything. On the way back to their trailer they caught sight of Violet stomping with purpose toward the conference room. Tonight's recording was going to be interesting to say the least.

They called Marianna as soon as they were in the privacy of their trailer. "Hi. Did you make it to the airport?"

"We're almost there," Marianna said. Alix instantly felt relief when they heard her voice. "Are you okay? Did I screw things up for you?"

"No. It's all good." It was said with conviction that Alix didn't have.

"Do I need to stay to vouch for you or for any reason?" Marianna asked.

"You can stay for me because I miss you and enjoy our time, but not to defend me. Everything is fine over here."

"What happened?"

Alix heard the panic in Marianna's voice. "I told them Violet entering my trailer was completely unprofessional. I told them there was no way you knew anything and that we met well before anyone knew of the bachelorettes." Alix tried to sound bored as to not alert Marianna that they were still incredibly angry about it and how lackadaisical the show was being about the obvious violation. "They're going to remind her she's under contract and if she says anything, they'll sue."

"I'm so sorry this happened," Marianna said.

Her voice was shaky and Alix just wanted to be with her and pull her in their arms and tell her it was okay. "Don't be. You had permission to be there. She didn't. Please don't worry. It's going to be fine." They took a deep breath. "Did I forget to tell you how incredible today was? I know everything got shoved aside, but I loved every second we had." It blew Alix's mind at how open and willing Marianna was. Alix didn't have to turn off lights or slip under the covers when they were together. She didn't mind when Alix kept their sports bra or binder on. It was the way a relationship was supposed to be.

"It was very nice. I enjoyed it even more than I thought I would," Marianna said.

Alix felt a bit guilty. "I know it looks like I planned for us to have sex this weekend, but I really didn't. I wanted to be prepared just in case." Marianna's soft laughter made Alix's stomach quiver. They were falling for her pretty hard.

"Here's the funny thing. I hadn't thought about sex until Andrea said something about weekend getaways," Marianna said.

Her words stopped the flutters. Alix felt weak. "Did I pressure you?"

"Not at all. It was very natural. I promise you. I enjoyed it as much as you did," she said.

Alix heard the buzz of another call. "I'm happy. Listen, Mar, I need to go. They are calling. I have to be on set so I will talk to you later. Please let me know when you get home." Alix switched over to Tobey. "What's up?"

"Well, I'm cowering in the corner after dropping off lunch. What in the hell happened?"

Alix rubbed their eyes with their forefinger and thumb. A headache was starting to settle in place behind their eyes. "Violet left the set and made her way over to my trailer. Marianna opened the door thinking it was me. It turns out Violet and Marianna have history."

"Wow. Small world. Is she okay? We know how Violet can be a lot."

"It's my fault. I should've taken her straight to the airport, but no. I had to show off and give her the razzle-dazzle treatment of being on set." Alix growled in frustration.

"I take it the *Sparks* team has a solution?" she asked.

"They're not very happy with me because it changes who Heather picks this week and messes up the hometown dates." Alix wasn't sure what information Tobey was privy to. "I mean they're still figuring all that out, but at least they understand Marianna isn't stalking her."

"Well, that's good. Okay, stop stressing. Find Mandee. She needs you in the chair. You only have to announce this afternoon's date. It'll be quick," she said.

Alix was thankful that their interaction with Violet would be minimal. The elimination round was tomorrow so they would have twenty-four hours to cool down and not lunge at her next time they were face-to-face. "Thanks, Tobey. I'll see you later."

They slid their phone in their pocket and shook thoughts of the meeting out of their mind. Sam sent them a message about contract negotiations but that was before this blow up. The best thing Alix could do now was market themselves and make everyone in the industry and on social media fall in love with them so that if the show dropped them, they would have something in their back pocket. Suddenly staying in California was important. Fuck, another call, but it was one they were expecting.

"Hey, Sam. What's going on?" Alix knew Sam had more to add to the conversation. They felt if anyone was on their side, it was him.

"I was checking in. I know that meeting was harsh. I wanted to talk about a few things before you get back on the set."

"They know this isn't on me, right? Wait. Do I still have a job?"

"Yes. Don't worry about that. They're just sensitive about what happened last season. No other show has had problems except for *When Sparks Fly*. They think it's cursed. I think they just need to give it time," he said.

"Are they going to want to make a massive change? Am I out after this?" Alix's contract was only for this season. The option to host more seasons hinged on the success of Alix as host. While the show was climbing on the charts, nothing was a guarantee unless it was inked.

"I'm going to suggest maybe attending more parties and events to get seen. It's hard for them to turn you down if you have the support of the upper echelon. Get in there and rub elbows with anyone you can," he said. At least they were on the same page.

"I was thinking that, too. Any other advice?"

"Keep your emotions in check. Everyone knows you love your girlfriend, but maybe keep her off the set until the show wraps up."

Alix wanted to argue that they didn't love Marianna, but none of that mattered to Sam. It only mattered to them. Did they love her? The last few days were emotional to say the least, but was it love?

"Alix? Are you still there?" he asked.

Alix shook their head. "Yes, I'm still here. Just thinking." And taking large gulps of air as the truth of his words swirled in their chest, trying to figure out if it was safe to land on their heart or not. Were they in love? Extreme like and the utmost respect, but love? That was a word they had locked away after opening up so willingly for Savannah. "You're right. I'll have Tobey get me a list of upcoming parties. I'll reach out to Kitty. She's a good ally and I trust her."

"I think that's a great idea. Kitty definitely has your back."

It was nice that Sam did, too. "She'll circulate me around to her friends and get me invited to events." Alix slowed as they approached Mandee's setup. "Sam? They understand that Violet is the one in the wrong, right? I mean, she had no business being in my trailer." As far as Alix knew, only Xander knew about the incident back at the mansion when Violet hit on them. Hopefully, Xander believed them then and now.

"I wouldn't worry too much. Just stay alert and maybe keep Marianna away from the show and the spotlight until it's done. Everything should be fine."

Alix tried to have faith, but it was hard after that shake-up even though it wasn't their fault. They just had to amp up their game and ensure the show couldn't do any better than with them at the helm.

CHAPTER TWENTY-TWO

Andrea sat on Marianna's couch with her legs tucked underneath her and a large pillow pressed against her chest. "I don't even know where to begin. I need to process this. Give me a moment." She dropped the pillow and shook out her hands. "Okay. Let's start with the sex part. I knew you'd have sex. I mean, that's what getaways are for."

Marianna took a sip of wine, suddenly regretting inviting her cousin over. "This has to be private. I can't have you telling anyone. Not even family. Alix and I need to have a defined relationship and we have to go public on their terms."

Andrea pretended to lock her lips and threw the imaginary key behind her. "Not a word will leave this room. I understand how important this is to you and Alix. So, can we agree that I was right?"

Marianna rolled her eyes. "You were right, but to be fair, I really hadn't thought about it until you put that thought into my head." Flashes of her boldness heated her cheeks as she remembered straddling Alix's lap that first night. She closed her eyes for a moment when she recalled ripping off her own dress and lifting her hips to meet Alix's strap-on. Was that something she was going to share with Andrea?

"Start at the beginning. Tell me about every kiss, every touch, every single thing. And I'll know if you leave anything out." Andrea pointed and narrowed her eyes at Marianna.

"I met them down at the bar. They were working late and we just decided to meet downstairs."

"Did you share the same room?"

Marianna swatted Andrea's arm. "No. They were very sweet and gave me my own suite." She neglected the part about the adjoining door.

"You met down at the bar and then?" Andrea asked.

"You really do want the play-by-play." Marianna threw caution to the wind and told Andrea everything. It took over an hour just to tell her their journey and answer all her questions. When Andrea seemed satisfied and Marianna had given her every little detail, she turned the conversation to Vee. "So, about the skirmish."

Andrea held her finger up to stop Marianna and downed her wine in one long gulp. Marianna looked at her incredulously.

"I can't have anything breakable in my hands." Andrea wiped her mouth on the back of her hand. "Okay, go. Tell me everything."

Marianna popped her knuckles and told Andrea about Vee trying to seduce Alix but finding her in Alix's trailer instead. "The shocked look on her face was priceless."

Andrea punched her palm. "I would've given anything to see the look on her face when she saw you instead of Alix." She held up her hand apologetically. "I'm sorry to interrupt, but I need all the details about her outfit."

Marianna snorted. "Get this. She showed up wearing a trench coat!"

Andrea smacked her arm. "Shut up, no she didn't!"

Marianna nodded. "And it was undone, and underneath she was wearing a red lacy bra and panty set. It was like I was in the middle of a really bad nineties sitcom."

"What did she say when she saw you?"

"She ran off yelling for security so I slammed the door shut so I didn't have to hear her bullshit," Marianna said far more confidently than she felt in the moment. "She turned into a raving bitch the moment she saw me. It was so weird. She was shocked but only for a second. That tells me how much I meant to her." Marianna took a moment to wonder how Alix was doing. They were very vague when she asked how things went with the producer and kind of blew past it like it wasn't a big deal.

"When was the last time you talked to Alix? Have things calmed down?"

Marianna nodded. "Somewhat. They are wrapping things up in Vancouver and headed out for hometown dates. I don't expect to see them for a few weeks."

Andrea dramatically sprawled out on the couch. "Whatever will you do without love, sweet love?" Her head ended up in Marianna's lap. She looked up at her and rapidly blinked her eyes. Marianna patted her cheeks.

"We're not in love. We're still getting to know one another. Don't forget, our lifestyles are vastly different. I'm still not sure this is going to work." As much as Marianna wanted to be all in, it was very tricky. Could she handle being in the limelight? Would Alix be more committed to Hollywood than her?

Marianna wanted the fairy tale. She wanted the happy ending where she and her partner crawled into bed every night at ten o'clock, got up in the morning, got the kids ready for school, and had date nights on Fridays. Maybe they had a dog that sometimes crawled into bed with them when it stormed. Or maybe they had a cat who liked to run across the bottom of the bed at three in the morning until one of them got up to throw them out of the bedroom and close the door. She felt Andrea's hand on her arm.

"I like Alix. I know their lifestyle isn't what you planned, but isn't that part of life? We don't know what comes next and we just roll with it. Fairy tales exist but they aren't what they used to be. We have to make them ourselves," Andrea said.

"You have us married already and we've only been dating for a short time."

"Some people just know. The sex is apparently great." Andrea fanned herself with her hand. "And Alix is very attentive, popular, wealthy, sexy, and fun."

"So why are they dating me?" Marianna didn't think she said it out loud, but Andrea quickly sat up and grabbed her hands.

"Because you're amazing. I've known you all my life. You've got your shit together, you have a good job, and you teach kids. The world will melt when they find out your job. Your heart is the biggest heart of everyone I've ever known. And I know a lot of people."

Marianna shook her head. "Look, Alix could date anyone in the world, and I mean anyone. Models, actresses, singers. Hell, they could date Hayley Kiyoko," Marianna said. She looked at Andrea and repeated. "Hayley Kiyoko."

"I'm pretty sure Hayley Kiyoko is either married or dating, but I hear what you're saying," she said. She grabbed a handful of potato chips from the bag on the coffee table and popped several in her mouth. She chewed and held up her finger as though ready to drop words of wisdom after she swallowed. "Let's do a pros and cons list." She held up her finger again. "Mom's calling. Hang on." She answered and waited a few seconds before speaking. "Let me ask her. So, Mom has two parties in the valley. One's this Saturday and one is next Friday. She wants to know if you can help. I'm going to do both. I need a new knife set."

Marianna knew Alix wouldn't be back until next Sunday. Those two events would give her enough money to be able to treat them to a nice dinner somewhere other than Clovr. Alix mentioned they liked seeing plays so maybe she could surprise them with tickets once they returned and the show was done filming. "Sure, tell her I'm in. I could use the money, too."

Andrea disconnected the call. "Now let's get back to your stunning life. What happens next?"

Marianna didn't have an answer about the relationship but remembered a conversation they had during breakfast before she left. "I know for a fact Alix's brother is coming down from Portland. I think Alix is getting the suite for Saturday the twenty-fifth so put that on your calendar."

"Count me in. Who all are you inviting?" Andrea asked.

Since she and Alix joked about playing matchmaker, Marianna downplayed it. "I'd like to invite the family since they like baseball. Our family, Chloe and Connie, Olympia, Ophelia, and Jess. Alix has a handful of people they work with they want to invite. It could be good for you and Jess and getting your big breaks." Andrea tilted her head at Marianna who quickly averted her eyes and reached for the bag of chips. Thankfully, she didn't call her out on her skittish behavior. Marianna was a horrible liar anyway.

"Okay. I'm in. I could use a little pampering. Will they have free food and drinks?" Andrea asked.

"I can't imagine they won't. Most suites, do." Marianna already dug out her vintage Dodgers T-shirt and had it ready. As much as she tried to convince herself she wasn't falling, deep down she knew the truth.

"Marianna, please run these appetizers. I don't know where Andrea is." Carrie waved her hands and moved on to the next tray of appetizers before Marianna had a chance to protest. She preferred to be in the kitchen heating and plating but knew better than to argue.

She quickly removed her apron and placed it on the corner of the counter. She smoothed her hair and flattened her white shirt. This was the part she hated. Being invisible and yet keeping a smile on her face. She gave an eye roll to no one and carefully slid the tray onto the palm of her hand. She hoped Andrea would return so she only had to make one run around the room. She shifted the tray so it was in front of her and low enough for people to reach. She kept her eyes down and weaved through clusters of the rich and famous.

"Miss? Over here please." Somebody snapped their fingers at her.

Marianna's demeanor changed from aloof to angry. As much as she wanted to ignore him, she pasted on a fake smile and walked over to him. She presented the tray while the two women with him giggled at her. Apparently, they were impressed with his ability to treat the wait staff like trash.

"We want two Manhattans and a bourbon. Neat," he said.

Marianna stared at him unsure what to do. The bar was literally three feet behind him and she was balancing a tray of food. Since she didn't want to jeopardize her aunt's business, she nodded and headed to the bar and gave the bartender the drink order. "For the gentleman and his dates directly behind me."

The bartender gave her a knowing look. Even though they were from different catering companies, the wait staff always stuck together. "On it." He gave her a knowing wink. She slid to the side of the bar to make way for people ordering drinks. Not a single person looked at her or said hello. If she were on Alix's arm, they would definitely notice her.

"Here you go." He quickly placed the drinks on her tray and gave her a sweet smile before moving on to the next patron. Now how hard was it to be nice?

She turned and in the three steps it took to get to rude dude, a very familiar face became clear in the crowd. Alix was here. For a moment, she smiled with excitement until reality crashed around her. Alix was back and didn't reach out? She heard glass smashing before she realized the drinks and appetizers on her tray had slid off, splashed on the rude man and his company, and crashed on the hard floor. The commotion drew the attention of the entire room. Marianna noticed Alix take a step away from the voluptuous woman beside them the moment they recognized her. Marianna ignored the man six inches from her face. She knew he was yelling, but she heard nothing except for the loud, rapid pulsing of her heartbeat. She stared at Alix in shock.

"What's going on here?" A well-dressed man walked over to them.

The guy brushed off the whiskey from his jacket with his hand and held it out as though it was burning his skin. He pointed to Marianna. "This idiot wasn't paying attention and spilled the drinks all over us."

"She did it on purpose." One of the ladies with him stuck her nose up in the air and looked down at Marianna.

"She should be fired. This is a two-thousand-dollar jacket."

The man who had stepped in to evaluate the situation turned to Marianna. "Please leave immediately."

She felt the color drain from her face. Was this really happening? She bent down to pick up the tray and broken glass.

"Leave it. Just go." The man waved her off.

Marianna had never been so embarrassed in her life. It was bad enough she embarrassed her family, but this happened in front of Alix. Why didn't they let her know they were back? Who was the woman they were with? She took a deep breath and turned on her heel.

"Wait!" The single word boomed through the room and echoed in Marianna's ears. She turned and watched Alix walk over to her. It wasn't until she felt their hands grasp hers that she realized they were coming to her rescue.

"It's not what you think." They turned to both men. "Xander, this was an accident and it's my fault." They pointed at the other man who was wearing his drink. "And there is no reason for you or your friends to be rude to anybody for any reason. People make mistakes. I'll pay for the dry cleaning."

"What's going on here, Alix? I'm sure the catering company will take care of this," Xander said.

Marianna wanted to smile when Alix slipped their hand in hers but too many things were happening at once. She didn't want Alix to jeopardize their career by defending her. She was also still confused as to why Alix was here with another woman and why they hadn't called her. Anger pushed aside disbelief. She quietly pulled her hand away.

The woman who walked in with Alix stood between them and the impeccably dressed man who dismissed her. "Alix, what's happening?"

"Kitty, this is my girlfriend, Marianna," Alix said.

"You're dating the help?" Xander asked. It was the way he said it that pissed Marianna off. She hated the stigma that the help wasn't good enough. She knew of several celebrities who had their own catering businesses. She bet Xander wouldn't say shit like that if it was somebody famous who was catering this party.

"There's no reason to be rude to Marianna or anyone," Alix said.

"What are you doing?" Marianna hissed. She was completely embarrassed that they had every single person's attention in the room. She recognized a power couple standing with their heads together obviously talking about them and that one actor from the blockbuster over the summer about a zombie apocalypse. What was his name? Weird that she would obsess about that right now.

The fire in Alix's eyes was unmistakable. They were pissed. "Nobody should talk to anyone like that." They faced the room. "I'm standing up for my girlfriend. Does anyone have a problem with that?"

CHAPTER TWENTY-THREE

This is highly unusual." Xander pulled Alix into a private room in order to get the situation under control. Andrea had steered Marianna back into the kitchen and the broken glass was cleaned up in record time. The only residue of the accident was a grumpy asshole with a bruised ego and a wet sleeve.

"I know you're not happy with me, but why do people have to be such assholes? I get that he was upset, but it wasn't the end of the world," Alix said.

"He's my guest. He wants the girl to leave, so she needs to leave," Xander said.

"Nobody is leaving. Alix is my guest and this is my party so let's take a breath," Kitty said. She sat beside Alix and held their hand in support. "Mistakes happen. We could all use a bit of compassion here." The fire in Kitty's eyes was unmistakable. She turned back to Alix. "Honey, tell me about her."

"That's Marianna, the same woman who Violet screamed at in my trailer." Alix tried to keep their words as politically correct as possible since everyone was trying to move on from that incident.

Kitty slapped the tops of her knees. "Small world then, huh?" she asked.

"She's wonderful. Kind and smart and always in the moment. We have great conversations about life, the future, and everything. She's beautiful and quiet and very supportive of what I'm doing.

What happened to her out there is one of the reasons she didn't want to date me. She thinks this community is full of assholes, and after that, I'm starting to agree." Alix glanced sharply at Xander.

"Perhaps I was a bit harsh," he said.

Alix put their hands on their hips. "I would never dismiss Kitty or anyone like that. She's a person. Just because she's working the kitchen, doesn't mean she's any less important than anyone else at this party." Alix twirled their finger for emphasis.

"She seems lovely. I want you to go back out there and continue fighting for her. She didn't look happy and I like her spunk." Kitty gave Alix's shoulders a quick squeeze before she dropped her arm.

"I'm in trouble because I didn't tell her I was back from location." Alix rubbed the back of their neck hoping some of the tension would disappear.

Kitty clucked her disappointment. "That's bad. If this is somebody you love, then you should want to see her first thing when you've been out of town for so long. What were you thinking?"

Kitty scolding them felt real and they couldn't exactly explain why they went straight from the plane to the party. Trying to jump into Hollywood after pushing it away was hard. "I told her I was going be home Sunday."

Kitty put her hand over her mouth. "Oh, my. Yeah, so let's figure out how we're going to save that relationship." She turned to Xander. "Are we free to go?"

Xander leaned back in a leather chair that squeaked every time he moved. He nodded and Alix gritted their teeth and stood. "I'll see you both later," he said.

Alix opened the door for Kitty and followed her out. "Guess I'd better find the kitchen and see if I can beg for forgiveness."

"Be honest and don't keep secrets. It's the key to a successful relationship. Look at Xander and me."

Alix kept their opinion about Xander to themselves. They hugged Kitty and weaved through the throngs of people who had moved on from the drama that happened ten minutes ago. They stopped a few times to shake hands, take selfies, and blow off what happened earlier. "Oh, just a mishap. Somebody spilled their drink." By the time they got to the kitchen, Alix was on edge. What if Marianna left? They pushed open the door to find eight pairs of eyes on them.

"Is Marianna okay? Is she here?" Alix scanned the room but didn't see her.

"She's in the bathroom," Andrea said. She squared her shoulders and put herself between Alix and Marianna. The message was clear.

"I really need to speak with her and explain a few things," Alix said. Andrea folded her arms across her chest but didn't budge. "Look, I know I screwed up, but it's best if she knows the truth and hears it from me and doesn't let her imagination run wild."

Andrea finally stepped aside to let Alix by. Alix knocked softly on the door. "Marianna. It's Alix. Please let me in."

"Not now," she said.

Even through the thick oak door, Alix heard the hurt in her voice. "Please." Alix wasn't going to elaborate because too many words were more detrimental to the conversation than simplicity. They tried again. "Please, Marianna." Their heart jumped when the door cracked open and they slipped into the room. "Thank you."

"What do you need to say?" Marianna avoided Alix's offer for a hug, but Alix didn't mind. This was a big step and deep down, they knew it would work out.

"We have a lot to unpack and maybe this isn't the right place. I mean, don't get me wrong, this is a really nice bathroom, but it's still a bathroom. Can we go somewhere and talk?" Alix watched the different emotions play on Marianna's face. When she finally nodded, Alix's knees almost buckled with relief. "Did you drive or should we Lyft?"

"We can borrow Andrea's car," Marianna said. She opened the door to find Andrea dangling her car keys. She snatched them from her and Alix watched a very expressive silent communication pass between them. "I'm going to go. I'm so sorry I ruined the evening, Aunt Carrie," Marianna said.

Carrie clucked and walked over to Marianna to hug her and kiss her cheek. "Don't worry about a thing. This happens more than you know and it's no big deal."

Alix knew it was probably a bigger deal than she let on but made a silent promise to rectify any fallout. They followed Marianna out to a Toyota Tercel with faded red paint and a large dent in the back panel by the passenger side. Marianna carefully placed all of Andrea's personal items from the passenger seat into the back seat. They were quiet on the drive back to Marianna's. Every time Alix tried to say something, Marianna lifted her finger.

"Not yet."

Alix's nerves were frayed by the time they got to Marianna's apartment. They locked the door behind them and immediately tried to explain. "It isn't what you think. We got done early and I was planning on surprising you, but Kitty, the woman I walked in with, pushed for me to go to her party for just a little bit. It was on my way home and it was hard to say no."

"So, who's Kitty?" Marianna's hands were on her hips and Alix tried hard not to smile. She was so beautiful even when anger brushed her features. Her cheeks were flushed and her dark eyes narrowed. Alix took a step closer.

"She's my boss's wife. She's the one who got *When Sparks Fly* off the ground. She knows I need to do more schmoozing. My agent recommended that I do more things to make myself more marketable in case they don't renew my contract."

Her anger vanished for a moment. "They would do that?"

Alix nodded. "Nothing is ever set in stone. I need for this show to be amazing this season and I need to rub elbows and meet everyone who will push for me as host for at least one more season. If not, I lose it all and I head home to Portland."

Marianna started pacing. "So, if you get high ratings and people tell your boss how much they love you as host, they'll extend your contract?"

Alix, feeling the hostile energy between them shift into something less terrifying, sat down. "I won't accept an extension. It would have to be a brand new one. This was a trial season. So far, it looks good, but I will never assume anything in this business."

"Wait. Were you being honest with me about the whole Vee thing? Did you get into trouble for it?"

Alix rubbed their face and sat back. "I didn't get into trouble, but I can tell they aren't happy about it. They're afraid of any fallout from your past relationship with a contestant and your present relationship with me." Alix held Marianna's hand.

"I can't imagine they would get rid of you. It's the best time to have a queer dating show and you're doing such a great job. It took Lauren Lucas a long time to get to where you are," she said.

"Thank you, but also I stepped in after a season where none of the contestants were successful. They are trying hard to make this work for Heather and whoever's left. They don't want another scandal with the host."

Marianna sat next to Alix. Even though her body was stiff, it was an offering. "Why don't we have a drink and you can tell me what is actually going on? I feel like you're protecting me, but I need to know everything."

Alix took her hands. "I'd like that." Marianna was allowing the conversation to continue and that was a good sign.

❖

Alix sneaked out of Marianna's bed to answer their phone. "Hello?"

"Alix. It's Tobey."

"I know. I saw your name on my phone. What's up?" They scratched their head and looked around. The shades were pulled but gray light seeped in from the sides. "It's barely light outside." They pulled their phone away to check the time. "It's only six."

"Have you checked social media yet?"

Alix's heart sank. It was never good when somebody called about something going viral. "No. Tell me. Quick."

"Somebody videoed you with Marianna at the party last night."

"Shit. What's the fallout?"

"Alix. Your stock just jumped way up. Not only because you defended her in front of big Hollywood players, but because you're dating somebody who works a normal job. They love how grounded you are. This is amazing news."

"Wait, what? I can't believe somebody shared that." Alix started pacing and lowered their voice. "I barely remember what happened."

"I'm sure everyone's going to call you so I wanted to give you a heads up. I sent you a link to one of the posts. You might want to tell Marianna so she can be prepared."

Fuck. "Thanks, Tobey. I'll check it out." Alix quickly checked the link. The video was shaky, but it showed them making a grand romantic gesture and holding Marianna's hand. The comments scrolling across the bottom were very sweet. Mostly. They tiptoed back into the bedroom and rubbed Marianna's back until she stirred.

"What's going on?" she asked. She rubbed her eyes and held her hand over her mouth when she yawned. Instead of waking up, she rolled over and snuggled against Alix. They carefully brushed her hair out of her face. Marianna groaned. She was not easy to wake up.

"I know it's early, but we need to talk." Alix kept their voice low and calm, but Marianna's eyes flew open in alarm.

"That's never a good thing. When people say we need to talk. Especially when they wake you up," she said. Her voice was sleepy, but she was alert.

"It's not bad, but your phone is probably blowing up and we need a plan."

"What happened?" she asked. She clutched the sheet to her chest in alarm.

"We went viral last night. Somebody filmed us at the party," Alix said. They pulled up the video and let Marianna watch. "I'm only concerned because now reporters are going to be looking for you and I want you to be prepared."

Marianna looked at Alix confused. "What do you mean?"

"They're going to want to know everything about you. Some of them will be nice and some of them will be mean. I want to prepare you for what might happen. Hopefully, everyone will leave you alone, but I doubt that."

Marianna picked up her phone and showed Alix her screen. A lot of missed calls by Andrea, Chloe, Jess, and one last night from Marcus Stroud.

"Who's that?" Alix pointed at his name.

"That's my boss."

CHAPTER TWENTY-FOUR

Marianna peeked through the blinds in her kitchen. "How did they find me so quickly?" A handful of reporters were camped out in the courtyard below her front door. Alix was probably used to the attention, but it was more than Marianna was comfortable with.

"Call your apartment management. Apartment complexes are private property and those vultures need to back off. Wait. I'll call Tobey. She'll handle it," they said.

Marianna liked the protective side of Alix. This relationship was both refreshing and now scary. What was going to happen? Was this her new life? Was she going to be followed everywhere? Did she answer questions? She shivered thinking about going to school, the grocery store, or even Clovr. Shit. How was her family going to handle it?

"Okay, Tobey's calling the cops. They'll push the paparazzi back to the sidewalk. We'll have to sneak out the back entrance."

She took a deep breath. "What are the rules here? Do I just say 'no comment'? Will they dig up dirt? Are they going to mess up my life?" Marianna sank into Alix when she felt their arms circle her waist.

"Don't talk to them. The minute you answer one question they think you're best friends and will want to know about our sex life," they said.

Marianna turned to face Alix. "I'll tell them it's amazing and they all should be jealous." She pressed her cheek on Alix's shoulder and held them close. She was nervous. Not for herself, but for everyone in her life. And would anyone say anything bad about her? The only person who came to mind was Vee. Fuck. The show could silence her during production, but their past was before Vee got on *Sparks*. She would definitely lie about everything. But then Marianna had receipts, and if Vee was smart, she would walk away and continue her Hollywood life without trying to destroy them. Marianna had so much dirt, not that she wanted to play that way. She was getting worked up over nothing.

"I'm sorry about all of this. I'm sure it will die down, but everyone is going to know who you are. Are you out at work? Or is this going to screw everything up for you?" Alix asked.

Marianna touched Alix's face. "Most people know about me at work. I'm more worried about my family. I don't want their lives to be interrupted."

"I have an idea. I told the world that you're my girlfriend last night. If that's true, why don't we make it official?"

Marianna felt her insides turn to mush and looked at Alix. "What do you mean?"

Alix shrugged. "Why don't we post a photo on the socials? Get ahead of it, you know?"

Marianna didn't have social accounts since becoming a teacher, but the idea of being publicly linked to Alix made her feel anxious. "Should you check with somebody from the show on what we should do? I don't want you to take a hit."

"People love love. There will always be haters, but I can call my agent and ask him what he thinks I should do. He'll talk to the right people. I doubt I'll suffer."

Marianna felt the tension in Alix's body even though they acted like it wasn't a big deal. She groaned when her phone rang. It was her mother. She looked at Alix. "I definitely need to take this." She blew out a breath. "Hi, Mom."

"Honey, are you okay?" It was sweet that her mother was checking on her when it should've been the other way around.

"I'm good. I guess you know what's going on."

"Your brother sent me the video. I'm so proud of you and Alix. You both handled yourselves wonderfully," she said.

"Thanks. We're hiding out this morning. Alix is getting the press pushed out of the courtyard. I'm going to have to miss dinner tonight." Marianna had planned to meet her parents for dinner, but with Alix back and everything in limbo, it was best to hunker down. Alix held up their finger and retreated to the bedroom. She could hear them talking to somebody and figured it was their agent. The sooner they knew what they should do, the less stressed she would be. Free-falling wasn't a feeling Marianna liked. She lowered her voice. "Mom. It's going to come out that Vee and I dated. That's going to look suspect to everyone because my partner and my ex are both on the show." Marianna struggled over what to call Alix and made a mental note to officially ask upon their return.

"You worry too much. Some people might be jerks about it, but Alix has your back, your family has your back, and you have wonderful friends in your corner. You've led a beautiful life and I can't imagine anyone saying anything bad about you. You're my perfect angel."

Marianna's heart softened. Her mother had so much faith in her. And she knew her mother would fight for her. "Thanks. Mom. I'm sorry about all of this."

"Why? I'm happy that my baby found somebody who loves them and is protective of them. I'm not sorry about anything."

She wanted to correct her mother and say it wasn't love, but could it be? She was definitely more guarded around Alix which wasn't fair, but she wanted to be one hundred percent sure that this is what she wanted. What kind of life would they have? "Thanks, Mom. Alix is off the phone. I'm going to go talk to them. I'll keep you posted." She disconnected the call and sat next to Alix. "What did he say?"

"He's going to talk to their marketing team and figure out the best course of action. I'm glad Xander already knows the whole story so this won't be a complete surprise," they said.

Marianna held their hand. "You should've just let things alone last night. I appreciate it, but look at the fallout."

"I wasn't going to let someone speak to you like that. Besides, ninety-nine percent of it is good. Sam said so many people are rooting for us. This is really good for me and the show. I'm just sorry you're getting dragged into it." They put their arm around Marianna's shoulders. She leaned into them. "We should probably come up with a ship name. Like Alimar or Marlix. Oh, I like Marlix. Hashtag Marlix," they said.

"Speaking of ships," Marianna said. She looked at Alix. "What do you want me to call you? If I'm your girlfriend, are you my partner? Significant other? Baby?"

Alix laughed. "Partner is fine. I'll pass on baby." They laughed again. "Baby."

"What? You don't like it?" It was nice to hear Alix relax for a minute. "I guess I can just say partner. Maybe I can call you baby when it's just us?"

Alix tickled her softly. "Absolutely not, but thank you for asking." They stifled a yawn.

"You're tired," Marianna said. They had make-up sex until two in the morning and Alix had woken them up at six. "Hell, I'm tired. And the adrenaline is wearing off. Maybe we should try taking a nap?"

"I don't know if I can sleep," Alix said.

"Or maybe we can work off the stress," Marianna said. She stood and pulled Alix up. "I mean if we're stuck here, we might as well have fun."

❖

Marianna tried to be quiet in the kitchen. Alix was finally asleep after two orgasms. She cut up an apple and put a spoonful of peanut butter on a plate. As much as she wanted to avoid the online chatter about them, she couldn't help herself. Before she even reached for her phone, a rapid, insistent knock at the door startled her. She jumped up to answer it, afraid the incessant rapping would wake Alix up. Through the peephole, she saw Andrea with a large brown bag tucked under her arm. She quickly opened the door. "Get in here," she said harsher than she intended.

"I brought lunch in case you couldn't get out," Andrea said. She put the food on the counter. "Where's Alix?"

Marianna put her finger up to her lips. "Shh. They are finally sleeping. It's been a day."

"You haven't answered your phone. I called you and sent you a thousand messages. I finally called your mom and she told me what was going on." Andrea smacked Marianna on her shoulder.

"I'm sorry. I thought I sent you a message. It's been bonkers over here. I turned off my phone after the press found my number." Marianna's stomach rumbled as the sharp smell of garlic and roasted tomato filled her nose. "Food. I'm so hungry."

"New recipe. I figured you couldn't get out. There are quite a few reporters on the street. They raced over to me until I gave them the finger. They backed off once they realized I wasn't you."

Marianna pulled Andrea into a hug. "Thank you for looking out for me. I have no food in the apartment except for a few apples, oranges, and ramen." She lowered her voice. "I can't feed Alix ramen."

"There's plenty here to go around. When does Alix have to leave?"

"I don't know. I mean they just did the hometown dates so I think they might have a few days. I'll find out when they wake up."

Marianna fixed drinks while Andrea quietly pulled plates from the cabinet. They always worked smoothly and efficiently together. She grabbed a piece of freshly baked bread and tore it in half. She did a little happy dance as the bite almost melted in her mouth. "I'll work for you if you ever open a bakery."

"Wait until you try this sauce. Then you'll want to work at my restaurant."

"I'm sure it's fantastic. It's too bad I didn't inherit the cooking gene. I got the eating gene but not the talent."

"See, there's where you're wrong. You can identify most ingredients in anything made. I'm almost as good as you, but not quite." Andrea heated up a plate of pasta in the microwave for a minute before handing it to Marianna. "Tell me what's in this."

"No hint? Like what kind of sauce?" Marianna asked. She speared a few penne with her fork. One bite wasn't enough. She took another and chewed while Andrea waited not so patiently in front of her for feedback. When Marianna reached for the third bite, Andrea pulled the plate away.

"Review first," she said.

Marianna rubbed her stomach. "It's amazing, cousin. The garlic and tomato are perfectly balanced. There's definitely roasted red pepper. Some kind of nut? Hazelnuts? Did I get it right?"

Andrea held up her hand for Marianna to quietly smack it. "Perfect. It's a Romesco I've been playing with."

Marianna poked it with her fork. "It's fantastic. I like the hint of sweetness. It's delicious." She wondered how long it would take Andrea to bring up last night. She figured the next ten seconds of silence would be the transition time. She was right.

"Start talking. Leave nothing out. What happens now?" Andrea grabbed her plate from the microwave and a piece of bread and sat with Marianna at the small drop leaf table.

"We wait to hear back from Alix's agent. He's figuring out how to combat what surely will feel like a staged show or conspiracy or whatever. Even though Alix says we've done nothing wrong and we haven't, it's going to make all of us look bad that I dated Vee and now suddenly I'm dating the host of the show. I mean, the press is going to have a field day with it." She felt nauseous when she thought of the fallout. Would they shut down the show? Fire Alix? How would Vee come out of this? Hero? Villain? It was all too much. She pinched off a piece of bread, dipped it into the sauce, and took a hearty bite. Her aunt always told her the best way to fight off nausea was by eating. She was probably joking, but she knew she needed the energy.

"They'll figure it out. This is nothing compared to what they had to deal with last season. At least Alix isn't running off with a contestant," Andrea said.

"They'd better not be." Marianna grew jealous thinking about some of the women on the show throwing themselves at Alix. The whole situation with Vee showing up at Alix's trailer still pissed her off. How many times was that going to happen? Marianna had a jealous streak and this was a whole different level.

"I think it was very sweet how they stood up for you last night. I was so mad at the time, but watching the video shows how much they really care for you. It's wonderful and the world thinks so, too. Right now, you're heroes. Let's hope they can figure out a good way to spin this. Ride that high out." Andrea grabbed her hand. "Does this mean you're an item?"

Marianna felt the heat spread out over her body when she thought about her and Alix being a couple. It was new and exciting, but also terrifying if it meant turning her life upside down. She was content. She loved the kids she taught. The insurance was decent. She was finally out of debt. Her apartment was little but nice. Her family was supportive and she had good friends. Was a relationship with Alix worth the upheaval?

"We're a couple. For now," Marianna said. "Unless this becomes unbearable and I lose everything." She pointed to the window indicating the paparazzi.

"Look, I know it's awful, but I feel like this is just a flash in your life. I mean, yes, Alix is important, but they're not Taylor Swift or Jennifer Lawrence. Hollywood gossip always dies down. I should know because I'm an expert about the scene. This might be the biggest thing right now, but in two days, the media is going to move on to the next hot story. You just need to wait it out. They can't be on school property, they can't be at your door. Eventually, they'll go away," she said.

"It doesn't mean I'm not going to worry. It's stressful for me, but worse for Alix. I don't want them to lose their job. They believe in what they're doing. Not only is the show important to them, but I've seen firsthand how the queer community loves them. How being visible on a prime-time show has allowed people to feel validated. It happened in Canada. It's happened here. I don't want to be the person responsible for taking that from them. It would break my heart to see them broken because of me."

PERFECT

Chapter Twenty-five

Just be yourself. It's going to be okay." Alix held Marianna's hands and looked her square in the eyes. "We're going to hear what they have to say and if we agree to it, we do it. I won't let them walk all over us."

"I know. I trust you."

Sam popped out of the conference room. "Are you ready? And don't worry. I think they've come up with a resolution."

Alix had never seen Sam look so unkempt. Did he even sleep last night? His hair was combed, but he hadn't shaved. His red polo was wrinkled and his khakis hung loose from his hips. They smelled coffee on his stale breath and noticed his shoulders sagged from the weight of the last twenty-four hours. "Thanks, Sam. This is my girlfriend, Marianna."

"It's nice to meet you. I'm just sorry it's not under better circumstances. Are you ready? Let's go in and listen to what they have to say," he said.

Ordinarily, Alix would have opened the door and allowed Marianna to pass through first, but they were in protective mode so they tucked her behind them and walked in ready to fight.

"Hello, Alix. Marianna, it's nice to see you again. I apologize for before," Xander said.

Alix was surprised to see eight people seated around the conference room table. They recognized Xander and Denise, but nobody else.

"Everyone, this is my girlfriend, Marianna." They pulled a chair out for her and sat after she did. Alix wanted to dive in and either defend their relationship or throw out suggestions as though they did something wrong, but instead, they remained quiet and leaned back in their chair. Their anxiety was at a ten, but hopefully they came across as cool and collected.

"The events of last night brought out a lot of good publicity for *Sparks*. But it also brought out something that we weren't prepared for. Marianna and Violet's history. We recognize that it's not anybody's fault and we're trying to come up with ways to jump ahead of it," a woman next to Xander said. She was wearing a gray tailored blazer with a crisp, white button-down shirt. Her blond hair was pulled back in a tight bun and a pair of black-rimmed glasses perched on her nose.

"Who are you?" Alix asked. "Not to be rude, but I want to know who I'm talking to."

"I'm Becca Elway. I'm a communications specialist hired by Meador Entertainment when potential scandals threaten the integrity of their shows. I'm here to get ahead of this situation and come up with a solution that benefits everyone."

"Thank you. Hi, Becca. I'm Alix. What did you have in mind?"

"We think we've come up with something and hope we have everyone's support." Becca nodded in unison with everyone at the table. "*Sparks* is very comfortable with entertainment reporter Ellie Stevens and we know you've interviewed with her. We'd like for you and Marianna to have an exclusive interview with her that will air hopefully tomorrow."

Alix wanted clarity. "What kinds of questions will she be asking?"

"She'll start off with normal questions about your relationship like how you met and your first date." She turned to Marianna. "She'll pull you into the conversation by asking you things like what's it like to date a celebrity? What did you think of Alix? Very simple and sweet questions that are designed to build viewer trust. She'll then talk about the video and why you stood up for Marianna and then the conversation will turn to Marianna's past with Violet."

Alix felt Marianna tense beside them. They grabbed her hand and linked fingers. "Will it be an attack?"

"Absolutely not. Ellie is on our side, but will ask the hard questions," Becca said. She took off her glasses and rubbed the bridge of her nose. "She'll ask Marianna how long she and Violet dated and when did she find out she was on the show. We'll have the questions ahead of time. Nothing will be sprung on either of you."

Alix knew this was all about Xander and the studio covering their own asses. The good thing was that the interview saved them, too. He could have thrown them under the bus, but that would've been bad for the show and bad for Meador Entertainment. Everyone wanted *Sparks* to succeed, especially after last season. "When will the interview take place?" Alix asked.

"Tonight," Becca said.

Alix felt Marianna's fingers squeeze theirs. "That's really soon for both of us."

"We have coaches on their way to help you both feel comfortable answering the questions. Alix, you have experience with interviews, but we want Marianna to be comfortable, too. If we don't address this now, it might go sideways and *Sparks* will be accused of scripting the show."

Alix almost snorted since they'd found out that *Sparks* did, in fact, have a soft outline of the show. Still, they understood exactly what was at stake. They just needed to have a private moment with Marianna before agreeing to anything. "Can you excuse us so that we can talk about it?"

"Of course. There's an empty office next door," she said.

Sam walked out with them but excused himself. "I'll be out here making calls." He wiggled his phone in his hand as though they didn't believe him.

"Thanks, Sam." Alix opened the door to the office. They sat in one of the plush leather guest chairs. "I know that's asking a lot, but how do you feel about this?"

"I'm scared shitless. I've never been on television before. I'm worried about my students, my school, my parents, my friends, but mostly I'm worried about you," Marianna said.

Alix slid the chair closer to Marianna. "What do you mean?"

"What if I say something stupid?"

"You won't, but also, they have amazing editors. I've done a lot of interviews with a lot of people and it's amazing how much gets scrubbed."

"How long will it be?"

Alix shrugged. "I don't know. And we don't have to do this."

"But this will help all of us, right?" she asked.

Alix stood and pulled her into a tight hug. "It will. And maybe reporters will leave all of us alone. Like Andrea told you, it won't take long for another scandal to push this one aside. Not that this is a scandal, but you know what I mean."

Marianna looked up at Alix. "Then we should do it. Let's review the questions and with you next to me, I think we'll do okay."

Alix was surprised she was so agreeable. Not that she doubted her, but she was proud of her. This was a lot to ask of someone who swore off Hollywood and someone in a new relationship. "Thank you. I think this will get a lot of people off our backs."

Alix opened the door and nodded at Sam who obviously had been right outside. He didn't even pretend to worry about getting caught.

"Let's get this rolling," he said.

Becca gave them a list of questions the show had already approved. "Marianna, do you have any pictures of you as a baby, a toddler, a child, and maybe even photos of you and Violet? We need to have them to show during the interview."

"I can ask my mom to send me some pictures. The only photos of me and Vee are on her Instagram."

"You don't have any others?" Becca raised her eyebrows and looked at Marianna over the frame of her reading glasses.

"Do you have photos of your ex-partners on your phone?" Marianna asked. "I don't. It was a toxic relationship and I wish I could erase her from my memory and life."

Becca pointed at her. "Okay, so our team will help you phrase that better. We want this to be as civil as possible."

"What time are we recording?" Alix asked.

"You'll head over to the studio in a few hours. We'll do hair and makeup and wardrobe. During that time, you'll review the questions with the team and practice answering them. Marianna, do you have a best friend or sibling who would be willing to go on camera and talk about you? I know this is short notice," Becca said.

Alix immediately thought of Andrea and Chloe. Both were outgoing and passionate about their relationships with her. Hell, her whole family would fight beside her. They waited patiently for Marianna to answer or ask for help.

"Andrea for sure," she said.

"What about Chloe? Or Jess? Or both?" Alix asked.

"How many people do you want?" Marianna asked.

"We can't promise they'll use everybody's interview, but call whomever you think will do a good job. We'll send cars. Tell them to bring several outfits. We'll do hair and makeup," Becca said.

Marianna stepped away from the table to make the calls. Alix kept their eyes on her the whole time. Everything was happening so fast. It was four in the afternoon. The interview was scheduled at seven. If everything went well, *Reality Bits* would post the interview tomorrow.

"All three are in." Marianna sat next to Alix after hanging up.

"Great. Give us addresses and we'll send for them," Becca said.

Alix held Marianna's hand more for her strength than providing comfort. They were starting to understand the significance of this moment and how everything was riding on this interview. They hoped Marianna wasn't as stressed as them and tried to keep a soft smile on their face for her. When Marianna turned to them, there were tears in her eyes. Alix felt as though a giant needle pierced their heart.

"This is really happening, isn't it?" Marianna asked.

"I love it when people meet organically. Nothing against the show, Alix, but it's so refreshing to hear your love story after everything you went through to get to this point," Ellie said.

Alix focused on the word love. Nobody said anything about love. Talk about being thrown for a loop. They smiled and focused on their words, not the emotions that pushed against their ribcage and squeezed their heart. "Finding your person can happen when you least expect it."

"Marianna, what was your first impression of Alix?"

Marianna looked at Alix and gave them the most heartfelt smile. "I thought they were very attractive and very smooth. I mean, Alix literally caught me before I smashed into the driveway." She paused and smiled fondly. "The thing that hooked me was how focused they were on me. I've never had that before."

"But you wouldn't give them your number. Why?" Ellie asked.

"I recently got out of a relationship and needed to take time to heal. Plus, I have two jobs and used that as an excuse not to date. I didn't have time," Marianna said.

Alix was so proud of Marianna. She was calm and sweet and they could tell that even Ellie was smitten. The stylist assigned to them had picked a blue sleeveless dress that gave her a sexy schoolteacher vibe. Marianna pushed back against Mandee about the amount of makeup until she saw initial test photos.

"Let's talk about your last relationship. I think everyone was surprised to find out that you once dated Violet who is on *When Sparks Fly* now." Ellie paused.

That was Marianna's cue. Alix felt Marianna stiffen. This was hard for her. "I was surprised that she was on the show." Marianna stressed the word I. "We broke up months before I found out. I attended the *When Sparks Fly* screen party as Alix's guest and was shocked to see her as a contestant."

"What do you say to people who think you're this mastermind who planned all of this?" Ellie asked.

"Planned what? The service industry in Hollywood isn't that big. I met Vee, I mean Violet, at my friend's restaurant. She was the hostess there."

"You had to know who Alix was though," Ellie said.

"I don't watch a lot of television. If I do, it's usually something low-key like *Animal Planet* or *The Great British Baking Show*." Marianna gave a small shrug.

"It took several weeks until she agreed to go out on a date with me. I did everything but beg." Alix almost kissed Marianna right then. The playful banter continued because the important question was answered and explained.

When they finished, Ellie leaned over and complimented Marianna. "That was amazing. This interview along with your friends' and cousin's character dialogues will shut down a lot of the gossip. Your cousin just finished and she nailed it." Ellie tapped her earpiece signaling somebody just clued her in.

Alix gave Ellie a quick hug and whisked Marianna away to a quiet corner. "Thank you for doing this for me."

"For us. I don't want anyone to suffer because of our relationship. I just hope the fallout is minimal," Marianna said. She put her arms around Alix's waist and moved into their arms. It was more than just a hug. They held her tightly until they felt her shoulders relax.

"You were great!" Andrea, completely unaware of ruining the private moment, smacked both of them on their shoulders at the same time. "Also, I got really amazing makeup tips from your person, Alix."

Alix pulled Andrea into their embrace. "Where are Jess and Chloe?" they asked.

Andrea pointed behind her. "I think they are finishing up. They said I did a good job. Also, I'm in love with this studio. The pampering is amazing."

"Let me check to see if it's okay that we get out of here. And we'll go back to my place. I have some level of privacy," Alix said. They excused themselves to find Sam or anybody who was in that boardroom to give them the green light to leave. They were both exhausted. Alix found Xander talking to somebody in a suit and hovered, hesitant to interrupt.

"Alix. I'm glad you're here. I want you to meet someone. This is Allen Mondale. He owns the studio," Xander said.

Big dog came in for this mess. Alix shook his hand. "Nice to meet you, Mr. Mondale. It's an honor to be on the show."

He nodded and looked down at Alix as though studying them with disdain. Alix stood tall and met his eyes. "Xander tells me a lot has happened in the last twenty-four hours."

"Definitely some ups and downs. I know this wasn't the publicity the show wanted given last season, but I appreciate everyone coming in to make this happen today," Alix said. They could feel the sweat trickle down their back.

"Let's hope it pays off," he said.

"I'm sure it will," Alix said. They made a mental note to send fruit baskets or whatever Tobey thought to the people who made this happen. If Ellie Stevens said it was helpful, then they believed it. She was the voice of reality television and if she liked you, she made sure everyone liked you. They turned to Xander, hating that they were asking permission like a child. "We finished the interview. Do you need us to stick around?"

Xander moved his pressed lips from side to side as he thought about it. Alix wondered if he wanted Alix to sweep the floors or take out the trash. Honestly, they would do it if asked. Anything to still have a job. Even if they weren't considering them for next season, they still had time to make this one hit number one.

"I think we're done here," he said.

"It was nice to meet you, Mr. Mondale." Alix gave a curt nod and turned on their heel to flee the scene. If they didn't get out of here soon, they were going to fall from exhaustion or get caught up in another conversation. They found Sam scrolling on his phone near the set. "Sam. We're leaving."

"Wait. You should see this," he said. He handed them his phone and smiled a huge cheesy grin.

"What?" Alix grabbed his phone and tried to process what they were seeing. There were over ten million views on the video from the party. This morning it was almost a million.

"Read the comments," he said. He scrolled through as though they couldn't do it themselves. "Look at this! Everyone is in love with you two. The show is mentioned in almost every post. This is going to put the show in the number one spot regardless of what happens with Violet." He leaned closer so that only they could hear. "You're a star, baby."

CHAPTER TWENTY-SIX

"Thank you for letting me stay here until this boils over."
Marianna had been to Alix's place before, but that was
when things were lighthearted and flirty. Today felt heavy. She
dropped her bag and curled up on the couch next to Woody.

"Are you sure you want to go to work tomorrow? It might be
nice just to take a day off," Alix said.

"Marcus assured me there wouldn't be a problem at work.
Apparently, I'm not the first person to be affected by the media," she
said. She chose her words wisely, not wanting to upset Alix. She felt
like this was all her fault anyway. "Plus, it'll be good to get my mind
off things. Eight-year-olds don't care about Hollywood gossip."

"Let's hope the teachers are the same," they said. Alix crossed
their arms and blew out a deep breath. They looked worn-out.

Marianna scooted closer to Woody and patted the cushion
beside her. "Let's not even talk about today. Or tomorrow. Let's start
a movie and fall asleep out here in twenty minutes. I'll set my alarm
for six and we can figure out a way to get to the school then."

Marianna knew Alix's two-seater would expose them too much
to the paparazzi but if that was their only option, then so be it. She'd
deal with it tomorrow. When Alix sat, Marianna changed directions
and put her head in their lap. She smiled when she felt their fingers
massage her scalp. This was nice. Alix streamed a random movie on
Netflix and Marianna fell asleep before the opening credits finished.

"Mar. Marianna. Wake up. Let's go into the bedroom. It'll be more comfortable."

She felt Alix gently shake her shoulder and she reluctantly woke up. "What time is it?"

"It's midnight."

"I feel like I've been asleep for hours." She sat up, careful not to crush Woody, and dragged her body to Alix's bedroom. Her arms and legs felt like heavy chunks of wood, but she managed to step out of her clothes and slide between the fresh sheets.

She felt Alix slip in beside her but she didn't move until her alarm woke her up. She fumbled around until she found her phone on the nightstand. Maybe a hot shower would help. She placed a small kiss on Alix's forehead.

"Time to get up, love." She froze once the word love passed through her lips. A part of her hoped Alix hadn't heard it, but then a lighter part of her heart wanted to shout the word again. Was she in love? Or was the situation just incredibly emotional and her mind was over-emphasizing what she was feeling?

Judging by how Alix's muscles tensed for a few seconds, they heard it, too. Rather than awkwardly try to explain, Marianna carefully left the bed and padded to the bathroom. The water was a few degrees warmer than she normally liked, but it felt good against her sore muscles. She gave a little gasp when Alix slid in behind her.

"I can't believe you left me."

Marianna turned to face them. "I tried waking you, but you seemed determined to sneak a few extra minutes in." She motioned for her and Alix to trade places so they were under the hot stream. While their eyes were closed, Marianna took a moment to appreciate the water rushing over their body. She loved every part of Alix. Love was a funny, complicated word and even though she swore she wouldn't open up to another person like she did with Vee, she couldn't help it.

"Nope. I'm going to spend every second I can with you," Alix said. "Especially since today is going to be a whopper. The interview isn't until tonight, as far as I know, so we have another thirteen hours to get through before the world hears our story. Are you sure you want to go to school?"

Marianna knew Alix heard her when she called them her love so why were they acting like it didn't happen? Maybe it was a conversation for another day. "I want to go. It'll make the day go by faster. If I stay here, I'll just chew my nails and wear a path in your nice area rug."

Alix pulled her close. "There are ways I could keep your mind off things."

"Definitely incredible things, but I don't think I'll be great company. After school, maybe we can DoorDash and watch *Reality Bites.*" She nodded at her plan and placed a kiss on Alix's shoulder. "Hold that thought and maybe you can do those things to me tonight."

"Sounds like a promise. Let's get you to school. We have plenty of time. Do you want to stop through a drive-thru and grab some coffee and food? I'm sorry I don't have anything here," Alix said.

Marianna put her hand on her stomach. "I'm too nervous to eat. Plus, I can grab something in the cafeteria." She also had breakfast bars in her desk.

The traffic around the school thickened. Between the normal school traffic and the small cluster of reporters standing on the public sidewalk, it was bad, but not as bad as she expected. Marianna popped on her sunglasses and was thankful Alix insisted on putting up the ragtop. Alix put their hand on her knee.

"You doing okay?"

She was, up until two reporters approached the car. Alix honked until they moved enough for them to drive past. The buses were due to show up in ten minutes. This was total disruption to the normal flow of drop-off traffic.

"This is bananas," Marianna said. She pointed to a tall, older man in a suit standing by the administration office. "There's Marcus. I'm just going to pop out here."

"Are you sure?"

Marianna leaned over and kissed Alix. "I'm sure. And I'll wait until you or your driver is out front before I leave the school."

"Have a nice day, dear."

"I'm glad you still have your humor. I'll text you later. Be careful." Marianna scrambled out of the car and hustled toward Marcus. He immediately turned to shield her from the cameras across the street.

"Happy Monday," Marcus said.

"I'm sorry about all of this. I never thought it would affect my life this much."

He waved her off. "It's okay. We've done this before. About four years ago, the choir teacher dated Jaxon Stone and it was just as hectic. This will die down, too."

Marianna was still in college when that happened so she had no reference. Plus, this was all about timing. If it was just people wanting to find out about her, it wouldn't be a big deal. It was the video. Marianna had seen it several times and her emotions grew every time. The protectiveness and fierceness that Alix showed was unmistakable. Butterflies took flight in her stomach every time she watched it. She walked the short distance to her classroom and sat on a chair in the back of the room so lookie-loos would think she wasn't there. She was only close with a few teachers.

Andrea texted. *You make it to work okay?*

Yes, but there are several reporters outside. Luckily they are staying on the sidewalk. Marianna's blood was hot just remembering the cameras pressed up against Alix's windshield ten minutes ago.

Do you need anything? Like a bodyguard? Andrea could always make her smile.

No thanks. Alix is having a car pick me up. We're going to be at their place tonight to see the show.

I'm watching it. I'm not missing it for the world.

Thanks for doing this for me. It was such a simple phrase that meant so much.

I love you. Plus, you're going to make me famous.

Marianna laughed out loud, liked the comment, and put her phone away. The students would be filing in soon. Like clockwork, the first student ran into the classroom, slammed his bag on the floor like a receiver who just caught a football and yelled, "My teacher is famous!" So much for little kids not paying attention to Hollywood news. This had long day written all over it.

❖

"Have you seen it already?" Marianna pointed to Alix's giant television.

They looked at her guiltily. "I haven't seen the whole thing, just little snippets," Alix said.

Marianna whined. "Why didn't you show me?"

"Because you were working and I didn't want to add to your stress level." Alix handed her a plate of chicken nachos and a margarita. "Look at how much food they gave us." They had ordered from a Mexican restaurant not far from Alix's place.

Marianna ignored the fact that they changed the subject. She already knew that dating Alix meant she wasn't privy to everything in their profession. She would have to be okay with that or this relationship would fail. "Look, it's almost on. I'm so nervous." She pointed as the show before *Reality Bits* ended and the block of commercials between them started.

"I'm sure it's fine. Sam would have told me if there's an issue."

To see herself on television was surreal. She found her flaws first and after realizing there wasn't anything awful, began focusing on the interview. Alix was gracious and kind and so comfortable on camera. Their hair was artfully messy and slightly different than they normally wore it. It was adorable. Why didn't Marianna notice that last night?

"I can't believe how quickly they threw this together," she said.

"I thought so, too, but most news channels do more in less time. This is what they're trained to do," Alix said.

"I can't imagine how much it cost the show to hire Becca Elway's company."

Alix snorted. "I can almost guarantee they have them on some kind of retainer. Now, shh, I want to hear us be wonderful together."

Marianna took a sip of her margarita to keep her hands busy and to let the tequila settle her nerves. She wanted to walk around to expel the energy that her anxiety stirred up, but she didn't want to disturb Alix's viewing of the show. What if she tanked? What if she ruined Alix's career? When the part came on when Ellie mentioned their love story, Alix grabbed the remote and hit pause.

"This is what I wanted to talk about."

Marianna's eyes grew wide. "What do you mean?" There was only one thing they meant, but that was incomprehensible.

"Our love story." Alix turned to face Marianna. "Look, I know you didn't watch the last season of *Sparks*, but I went in with an open heart and open mind. I wanted to find love. I thought that was with Savannah, but it wasn't." They stood and walked over to the window to look out at the ocean.

Marianna wasn't sure if she should say something. Instead, she put her drink down and quietly walked over to Alix. She put her hand on Alix's shoulder and held them from behind. "I'm sorry you got hurt."

Alix turned. "When I first met you, I knew that I wanted to date you and you kept turning me down. I'm glad you did because it made me think about what I really wanted in a relationship and if I was ready to open up again." They ran their thumb over Marianna's chin and right below her bottom lip. "The answer is yes. I want this to work, Marianna. I know it's early and people might think I'm jumping in too soon, but I think about you nonstop. I can't wait for your texts. I enjoy talking on the phone. I can always tell how you're feeling because it comes through in your voice. I know when you're tired, when you're happy, and when you're sad. My heart flutters when you are near." They took her hand and placed it over their heart.

Marianna looked deep into Alix's eyes. "I feel the same way. I fought you for all the wrong reasons. Thank you for not giving up on me. On us."

"Marianna. I love you. I know it seems fast, but I can't help it. I feel so good with you. You make me feel so special and cherished." Their voice lowered. "You make me feel loved."

Emotions she buried a long time ago fought their way up to her heart. She let go. She gave herself permission to embrace her true feelings and just be happy again. She trusted Alix. Their misunderstanding the other night was just that. This wasn't going to be an easy relationship or a predictable one, but they both deserved to give it a chance. Allowing herself to think about love gave her the courage to say what had been in her heart all along. She felt tears gather in the corners of her eyes. "I love you, too, Alix."

CHAPTER TWENTY-SEVEN

This is quite the turnout, huh?" Alix put their Dodgers ball cap on backwards so they could kiss Marianna firmly on the mouth. It was adorable that she still blushed when they kissed her in public.

"I can't believe your boss just turned it over like that. This must cost a fortune every game. There's so much food and alcohol," she said.

Alix pulled her flush against them. "Can I tell you how beautiful you look? I feel my heart melting a little right now." The vintage T-shirt was tight and accentuated her perfect breasts, but Alix wasn't going to tell her that. Marianna didn't like showing off her body and was completely oblivious when she did. Alix understood all too well about not being comfortable in their own skin. It helped immensely having a partner who was supportive and loved them unconditionally. It was only a month ago when they both said "I love you" but it solidified their relationship and made them feel like anything was possible together. They rarely spent a night apart.

"You're such a charmer, Alix Sommers." Marianna kissed Alix back. They were surprised to feel a little tongue given that they were with family and friends.

"Hey, there are kids in here," Brandon yelled from across the room. Alix gave him a nod and kissed his sister again. He raised his beer at them and shook his head.

"You know, I think Brandon and Tobey are hitting it off quite well."

Marianna nodded. "Jess is hitting it off with one of your marketing people, Lena, right? She's cute."

"Hey, now. She's okay. Not that cute." Alix playfully pinched Marianna's side.

"Honestly, I'm most excited about Buck and Andrea. Look at them in the corner not even paying attention to the game. I thought you said he wasn't one for small talk and he was all about baseball."

Alix stretched their neck to see over Marianna. "I mean your cousin is attractive and she's the kind of woman who could whip him into shape. It'll be fun to see how they play out."

"I like him. He's quiet," she said.

Alix shrugged. They knew Buck was on his best behavior, but also his body language screamed that he was into her. "It's nice to see him away from his buddies and all the woodland creatures he's befriended. I'm just happy he trimmed his beard and put on clean clothes."

"The lumberjack look is very hot right now. Maybe a few years ago it had a murder vibe, but it's gaining hotness," she said.

Alix poked her sides until she giggled. "Hey, now. My brother's never murdered anyone that I know of."

"I'm kidding. He's very sweet. I can tell you're close. When are you going up to see him?" Marianna asked.

Sparks' "Secret Reveal" episode was live this week. By now, everyone was aware that Heather was down to two contestants and that Violet got the boot. Because she had nothing to add to the conversation about her relationship with Marianna and had the right guidance from her agent, the whole messy relationship thing disappeared. Hollywood had had two scandals since theirs and even though Alix and Marianna's relationship got traction, the bad publicity did not. They were America's queer sweetheart couple, and the queers were fierce about their relationship. The show had been in the number one spot on prime time and most streaming services since the video leaked. Sam was itching to discuss a new contract, but Alix wanted to wait until it was all over. They wanted to go in with hard numbers. Xander and the entire *Sparks* crew acted like nothing happened and things were good but Alix knew they had the upper hand. They just prayed *Sparks* agreed when it was time. "Next month. Want to go with me? We can make it a quick weekend trip."

Marianna nodded. "Sure. I want to see your tattoo parlor and out-hike you on your favorite trails. It would be nice to see where you lived."

Alix groaned. "You're not missing much, but okay." They still had the lease on their loft. Buck started using the space for storage for the studio until the lease ran out. He promised it wasn't taking up too much room. "Let's see how this week plays out and what my obligations are next week." Alix was amazed at how accommodating Marianna had been in their relationship. She never assumed Alix was available or would pick up the check when they went out. As a matter of fact, their first fight was over a dinner check. It was nice being in a mature, respectable relationship. And the sex was off the charts. There was nothing wrong with Marianna other than it took forever to get to her. Traffic sucked. Her lease was up at the end of the year and if the relationship continued to be this fantastic, Alix was going to ask her to move in or suggest they find a place together.

"Why do I want to eat so much?" Marianna eyed the counter lined with baseball food. Alix had requested extra fresh fruit and vegetables with dip knowing that those were Marianna's favorite snacks.

"Because you're nervous about today." Alix kissed her ear. "And you want everything to be perfect."

"And you don't? How are you so calm? I'm analyzing every laugh and gesture Andrea makes and wondering if Brandon's just being polite or if he's really into Tobey. It's so hard to stand here and not want to jump in and ask questions and see if they're getting along." Marianna sounded more than just a normal level of stress.

Alix pulled her close again. "I'm going to tell you a secret, okay? But you can't tell anyone I told you, okay?"

Marianna looked concerned. "Because you'll get into trouble? I don't know if I can handle that kind of responsibility. What if something slips?"

Alix put their finger on her plump lips and leaned down to whisper in her ear again. "Shh. It's okay. The secret is that we have zero control over this. It's up to them now. We've given them a space to meet organically and if it happens, it does, and if it doesn't then we'll know that they never knew what we were up to."

Marianna gave them a stern look. "That's not a secret."

Alix laughed. "Playing matchmaker is hard work. Sometimes people seem like they have everything in common, but there's no chemistry. And other times, people meet and everything is perfect."

"Like us," Marianna said. She kissed them sweetly again.

"You're killing me," Brandon said.

"Leave your sister alone. She's fine. Watch the game." Anna was on her way up to get another beer. She put her hand on Alix's arm. "Thank you so much for inviting the family to the ballgame. This is so nice."

"I'm glad we have such a good turnout," Alix said. They already loved Marianna's family. They accepted Alix with open arms.

"I don't care if the Dodgers win or lose. This is such a nice time," Anna said. She grabbed two beers and kissed them both on the cheek before heading back outside to the cushioned seats.

"Let's go sit outside for a bit. I think we've been hiding too long. I need some fresh air," Alix said. Alix sat next to Anna and Marianna sat next to Jack. They knew it was a special time for her and her father. A few people were discreetly taking photos of them but neither they nor Anna seemed to care. "You're taking this celebrity thing pretty well. Thank you for understanding."

"You're the best thing that's ever happened to my daughter. I would do anything for both of you," Anna said.

"Thank you. She's the best thing that's ever happened to me. I plan to keep her in my life and keep her happy for as long as she wants me."

Anna grabbed their hand and squeezed it. "I hope it's forever."

"I hope so, too."

"Would they seriously pay me that much money? And give me a signing bonus that large?" Alix pointed to Sam's tablet where the money and terms were spelled out. Based on the success of the show and Alix's popularity, Sam wanted to capitalize on the momentum before it fizzled out for the new shows being released in the fall. The new *Sparks* season would be a winter release and would start shooting soon. The show needed Alix, and Sam was going to make sure they were both going to get rewarded over the next three years—a total of six seasons—to host *When Sparks Fly.*

"Anything else before I go in?" Sam asked. "How about a new car? One that's bigger than that deathtrap you drive now. How about a sedan? Those are safe."

"And not at all sexy," Alix said.

"You already have a girlfriend. Why do you need a sexy car?"

Secretly, Alix loved that everyone was pro-Marianna. Not that they would ever cheat on her, but if anything seemed inappropriate, all of Alix's friends and family would rat them out. And rightfully so. "There's just such freedom in a little two-seater that can zip zip through traffic."

"And zip zip into semi-trucks. I'm going to work in a reliable four-door Mercedes sedan. We'll make it black so it's sexy. It's safer and screams not only sexy but responsible adult."

Alix laughed and fell back into the chair with relief as everything they asked for was added into the final contract he would propose. It was risky, but Sam seemed to think it was feasible.

"You're more than welcome to take a walk or you can hang out here. I'm not sure how long it will take but I can call you when I'm done," he said.

"If you don't mind, I'd like to hang out here and answer some emails." Alix was too nervous to be out in public. Marianna was working so talking to her was out of the question. They had nowhere to be so they decided to stay put in Sam's office.

Sam pointed to the phone on the table. "Call my assistant if you need anything at all. I'll be in touch soon."

"Thanks, Sam." Alix pulled out their laptop to study a new clothing line that wanted them as their spokesperson. Blue Eye Cat catered to nonbinary clients. Their top-of-the-line product was custom fitted. The off-the-rack line was more affordable but still had a unique look. The brand was starting to show up in big department stores and Alix wanted to investigate further before agreeing to sign. It was a good deal if everything seemed legit. Sam's team was pulling sales numbers together based on Blue Eye Cat's forecast for the upcoming year.

Since there was a break between seasons, Sam was starting to put feelers out for Alix to attend events, rep products, and volunteer their time at animal shelters and children's hospitals. Nonprofits liked celebrities to promote their places. More exposure meant more money. Alix didn't mind helping out those who needed a helping hand. They had a platform now and planned to use it to the best of their ability.

When the door opened, Alix looked up from their laptop in surprise. "You're already back?" They checked the time. He had been gone for almost two hours even though it only felt like fifteen minutes. They closed their laptop and waited for him to say something—say anything.

"Do you want the good news or the bad news first?" he asked.

Alix took a sip of water to steady their nerves before answering. They were surprised their quivering stomach accepted the sip and the glass didn't slip from their fingers and clatter on the table because their palms were so sweaty. "Bad news first. Always the bad news first." They clutched the arms of the chair to brace themselves for Sam to tell them Meador didn't want them to host anymore or the season sucked and it was their fault. It didn't matter that Alix knew the numbers.

"I couldn't get you the Mercedes, but will a BMW work?"

"Shut the fuck up, Sam. Really? That's the bad news?" Alix jumped up and gave him a big hug. It was completely unprofessional, but this contract just put Alix on the Hollywood map. Meador Entertainment either rolled over, or Sam turned into a bulldog that wouldn't give up a thing. Probably both.

"You got everything you wanted. It's set in stone. You got the money, the vacation time you wanted, the car. They're going to rework the contract and send it over. I'll have legal review it before I courier it over to you. I'll reach out when we have it to find out where you are. Now go celebrate."

Alix slapped their hand on the table. "Hot damn. Thanks again, Sam." They shook his hand and walked out of the building. Alix felt free. There was only one place they wanted to be right now and only one person they wanted to share their news with. Alix hopped into the convertible without opening the door and pointed the car into the direction of Franklin Elementary School.

"I'm here to see Marianna Raines."

The administrative clerk who was well past retirement age pursed her lips together and stared at Alix. Her soured frown was more pronounced as she looked them up and down. "School is still in session. Do you have an appointment?"

Alix smiled. It was refreshing when somebody didn't know them. It reminded them they weren't as important as they sometimes thought. "I do."

"Alix! What are you doing here?" Marcus slipped out of his office and shook their hand.

"They claim to have an appointment with Ms. Raines, but I don't see it on her schedule."

Alix winked at Marcus. He nodded in understanding. "I'll take it from here, Mrs. Aarons. Come on through." He waved them through the security doors and walked them down to her classroom. Alix liked him even though he always tried to impress them with his Hollywood connections which weren't that great, but they humored him. He knocked on the small window in the door and waved for Marianna to come out.

"Is everything okay?" Marianna quietly closed the door and smiled when she saw Alix. "Hi, sweetie." She walked immediately into their arms. Alix didn't even mind the term of endearment.

"I'm going to leave now. Alix, try to leave before the bell or wait until everyone leaves. Your pick," Marcus said.

"I'll stick around if that's all right with Marianna."

"What's going on?" she asked after Marcus retreated down the hall.

"Contract came through and I got everything I asked for and then some."

Marianna covered her mouth to keep herself from shouting. "Are you serious? That's amazing. I'm so proud of you!"

"You're the only person I wanted to share this news with. I'm sorry I interrupted your class." The way Marianna's smile lit up her face and how her eyes danced with selfless joy for them made Alix fall deeper in love.

"Do you want to meet my kids? They're kind of unruly."

"If you think that's okay," Alix said. Marianna took their hand.

"Come on in. I'm surprised their noses aren't pressed against the glass trying to find out why I'm out here." She opened the door. "Class, I want you to meet Alix Sommers. They're a TV host."

It took all of five seconds for Alix to fall in love with them. Their bright eager faces beamed back at them. "You all know me?"

"Yes," they said in unison and dragged the word out as though it had ten syllables.

"I'm excited to get to know you all. I'm going to sit in on class if that's okay." Alix sat at Marianna's desk trying to be as inconspicuous as possible, but it was apparent the children weren't going to listen to her.

Marianna gave up on the book she was reading them. "Since you're doing a horrible job of paying attention to me, does anyone have any questions for Alix?" she asked.

Alix smiled when every single child raised their hand. They answered two questions before calling on a little kid sitting in the front row who almost made Alix cry. They repeated the question. "Why do I love Ms. Raines?" Every emotion Alix ever had about Marianna rushed into their heart and flooded their mind with memories that were made not too long ago. The way she always smiled as though Alix was the only person who mattered, the way she refused to go out on a date with them for weeks, and the way she loved them so completely. Marianna wasn't afraid of Hollywood. She was afraid of love. Alix could've been anyone and the relationship still would've happened. It was fate that pushed them together time and time again. Alix swallowed hard. "Because she's absolutely perfect."

EPILOGUE

W e can go to the beach anytime, but this pool is amazing. This is water we can frolic in," Alix said.

Marianna's head was reeling. They were standing in the backyard of a gorgeous house in Silver Lake. She kept the conversation light seeing at how it made Alix so happy. "Frolic? Since when do we frolic?"

Alix playfully tugged her close. "We frolic well together." Their meaning was clear. Marianna blushed and stepped away when the real estate broker popped into view.

"How are we feeling about this house?" The agent discreetly looked at her watch and smiled at them.

Overwhelmed. Excited. Afraid. So many emotions rushed Marianna. And intense love. She loved Alix completely. They had been together for six months and here they were looking at a house together. She had put all her trust into another person. It was such a vulnerable position to be in and the stress brought tears to her eyes. She turned and pretended to be interested in the landscape in the back of the yard.

"We're still discussing. Can you give us a few more minutes?" Alix asked. Marianna heard footsteps fading and felt Alix's arms encircle her waist. "I know this is a big step for us, for you, but I love you and I want to spend all my time with you."

"It's a big step, Alix," she said.

Their smile fell. "Do you not want to do this? What are your reservations?"

Marianna touched their face. "First of all, being with you is the most important thing."

"And that's my number one, too," they said. They placed a small kiss on her lips and tucked her hair behind her ears. "I hate missing nights when I'm working late and you're already asleep so I go home to my empty house. Well, except for Woody. I like going to bed with you and waking up with you. This house is close to the studio and it's only a fifteen-minute drive for you. It's not as close as your apartment, but hopefully, that's not that big of a problem."

"The mansion is farther, though," Marianna said.

"Only a few miles. Please don't worry. Besides, I have a driver now." Alix planted a soft kiss on Marianna's lips. "Let's start with simple questions. Do you like this house?"

Marianna's eyes grew wide, and she gaped at Alix. "It's gorgeous, Alix. How could I not love it?" It was warm and huge with five bedrooms, four bathrooms, a formal dining room, a small movie theater downstairs, and a beautiful pool with a decent backyard.

"Then let's make this our home."

Frustration bubbled up in her veins. "It's expensive. I know the mortgage is what we pay now combined for two places, but we need money for furniture and utilities. And it's not fair for you to pay for everything." She threw up her arms and stepped back from Alix. "And I don't want to take this away from you."

"I understand what you're feeling. Less than two years ago I didn't know how I was going to pay rent. Now, I have money. We can afford this. And I want us to be together," Alix said.

Fighting Alix was futile. Marianna already loved this place, but it was hard to just dive in with somebody she'd known for less than a year. "I really like the pool."

The smile on Alix's face and their whoop of delight made Marianna laugh. They picked her up and twirled her once. "Let's go for another walk-through before we tell her yes. Just because it's Christmas Eve, doesn't mean she can push us."

Marianna pulled Alix's arm. "Shh. We don't want her to hear us." The moment she accepted Alix's offer, the cloud of doubt that hung over her faded away. Alix's bright smile and happy demeanor was infectious and Marianna knew this house would be their special place. The place where they went to bed together every night and got ready in the morning together. She could picture her family sitting around a large table eating good food and Andrea and Buck hanging out by the pool on the weekends he visited.

"The master bedroom is amazing. Look at all this closet space."

Marianna held her hands about a foot apart. "Just make sure I have this much room for my things. Or better yet, I can use one of the spare rooms' closets."

"We can split the closet and I can use one of the other closets," they said. Alix had a decent wardrobe because of the show, but their wardrobe multiplied after they signed with Blue Eye Cat.

Marianna had spent more money on clothes the last six months than ever before. She wanted to look good every time she accompanied Alix to a party or an event. They grabbed her hand and brought her back to the present.

"How about we tell her yes. It's noon. That'll give her plenty of time to extend the offer before everything shuts down until Monday." Alix kissed Marianna's hands. "I love you. Let's do this." A surge of excitement ribboned with acceptance spread through her veins when she nodded. It was cute watching Alix process their excitement. They paced and ran their fingers through their hair. "Now when we need her, she can't be found."

Marianna looked outside and pointed. "She's in the car."

Alix jogged to the front door. "I'm going to tell her the good news."

Marianna nodded and walked around the living room, running her fingertip on the walls. It was unreal. She went from rejecting anyone in Hollywood to moving in with the love of her life who was a massive figure on television in less than a year. What did she do to deserve love like this? Why her? She fought Alix so hard for so long and they never gave up on her. The emotions were too much. She sat down in a plush chair, covered her face with her hands, and cried.

A moment later, Alix dropped to their knees and touched her face. "What's wrong, Mar? Are you okay?"

The concerned look on Alix's face made Marianna take a deep breath and stop crying. "I'm just happy. This is so much to process, but it's all good." She sniffled and touched Alix's cheek. "I love you so much and I'm just happy."

Alix pulled her up into their arms. "I can't tell you how happy I am, too. With you by my side, I can do anything. We can do anything together, wallflower."

"How did I get so lucky?" Marianna asked.

"Now *that* I can answer." Even though Alix's kiss was soft, there was so much power and meaning that Marianna felt weak. "You took a chance on somebody who makes people fall in love."

About the Author

Multi-award-winning author Kris Bryant was born in Tacoma, WA, but has lived all over the world and now considers Kansas City her home. She received her BA in English from the University of Missouri and spends a lot of her time reading, kayaking, collecting football cards, and binge-watching shows. Kris co-hosts *Queerly Recommended*, a podcast with Tara Scott, where they recommend queer books, TV shows, graphic novels, games, and movies to the queer community. She also raises money for animal shelters worldwide on her Patreon page.

Her first novel, *Jolt*, was a Lambda Literary Finalist. *Forget-Me-Not* was selected by the American Library Association's 2018 Over the Rainbow book list and was a Golden Crown Finalist for Contemporary Romance. *Breakthrough* won a 2019 Goldie for Contemporary Romance. *Listen* won a 2020 Goldie for Contemporary Romance. *Lucky* was a 2020 Foreword Indie Finalist. *Temptation* was an Ann Bannon finalist and won a 2021 Goldie for Contemporary Romance. *Always* was a 2022 Foreword Indie Finalist. *Not Guilty*, written under Brit Ryder, won a 2022 Goldie for Erotica. *Cherish* was a 2023 Goldie and an Ann Bannon finalist. *Catch* was a 2024 Lambda Literary Finalist. Kris can be reached at krisbryantbooks@gmail.com or www.krisbryant.net, @krisbryant14.

Books Available from Bold Strokes Books

Back to Belfast by Emma L. McGeown. Two colleagues are asked to trade jobs. Claire moves to Vancouver and Stacie moves to Belfast, and though they've never met in person, they can't seem to escape a growing attraction from afar. (978-1-63679-731-1)

Exposure by Nicole Disney and Kimberly Cooper Griffin. For photographer Jax Bailey and delivery driver Trace Logan, keeping it casual is a matter of perspective. (978-1-63679-697-0)

Hunt of Her Own by Elena Abbott. Finding forever won't be easy, but together Danaan's and Ashly's paths lead back to the supernatural sanctuary of Terabend. (978-1-63679-685-7)

Perfect by Kris Bryant. They say opposites attract, but Alix and Marianna have totally different dreams. No Hollywood love story is perfect, right? (978-1-63679-601-7)

Royal Expectations by Jenny Frame. When childhood sweethearts Princess Teddy Buckingham and Summer Fisher reunite, their feelings resurface and so does the public scrutiny that tore them apart. (978-1-63679-591-1)

Shadow Rider by Gina L. Dartt. In the Shadows, one can easily find death, but can Shay and Keagan find love as they fight to save the Five Nations? (978-1-63679-691-8)

The Breakdown by Ronica Black. Vaughn and Natalie have chemistry, but the outside world keeps knocking at the door, threatening more trouble, making the love and the life they want together impossible. (978-1-63679-675-8)

Tribute by L.M. Rose. To save her people, Fiona will be the tribute in a treaty marriage to the Tipruii princess, Simaala, and spend the rest of her days on the other side of the wall between their races. (978-1-63679-693-2)

Wild Wales by Patricia Evans. When Finn and Aisling fall in love, they must decide whether to return to the safety of the lives they had, or take a chance on wild love in windswept Wales. (978-1-63679-771-7)

Can't Buy Me Love by Georgia Beers. London and Kayla are perfect for one another, but if London reveals she's in a fake relationship with Kayla's ex, she risks not only the opportunity of her career, but Kayla's trust as well. (978-1-63679-665-9)

Chance Encounter by Renee Roman. Little did Sky Roberts know when she bought the raffle ticket for charity that she would also be taking a chance on love with the egotistical Drew Mitchell. (978-1-63679-619-2)

Comes in Waves by Ana Hartnett. For Tanya Brees, love in small-town Coral Bay comes in waves, but can she make it stay for good this time? (978-1-63679-597-3)

Dancing With Dahlia by Julia Underwood. How is Piper Fernley supposed to survive six weeks with the most controlling, uptight boss on earth? Because sometimes when you stop looking, your heart finds exactly what it needs. (978-1-63679-663-5)

Skyscraper by Gun Brooke. Attempting to save the life of an injured boy brings Rayne and Kaelyn together. As they strive for justice against corrupt Celestial authorities, they're unable to foresee how intertwined their fates will become. (978-1-63679-657-4)

The Curse by Alexandra Riley. Can Diana Dillon and her daughter, Ryder, survive the cursed farm with the help of Deputy

Mel Defoe? Or will the land choose them to be the next victims? (978-1-63679-611-6)

The Heart Wants by Krystina Rivers. Fifteen years after they first meet, Army Major Reagan Jennings realizes she has one last chance to win the heart of the woman she's always loved. If only she can make Sydney see she's worth risking everything for. (978-1-63679-595-9)

Untethered by Shelley Thrasher. Helen Rogers, in her eighties, meets much-younger Grace on a lengthy cruise to Bali, and their intense relationship yields surprising insights and unexpected growth. (978-1-63679-636-9)

You Can't Go Home Again by Jeanette Bears. After their military career ends abruptly, Raegan Holcolm is forced back to their hometown to confront their past and discover where the road to recovery will lead them, or if it already led them home. (978-1-636790644-4)

A Wolf in Stone by Jane Fletcher. Though Cassilania is an experienced player in the dirty, dangerous game of imperial Kavillian politics, even she is caught out when a murderer raises the stakes. (978-1-63679-640-6)

New Horizons by Shia Woods. When Quinn Collins meets Alex Anders, Horizon Theater's enigmatic managing director, a passionate connection ignites, but amidst the complex backdrop of theater politics, their budding romance faces a formidable challenge. (978-1-63679-683-3)

One Last Summer by Kristin Keppler. Emerson Fields didn't think anything could keep her from her dream of interning at Bardot Design Studio in Paris, until an unexpected choice at a North Carolina beach has her questioning what it is she really wants. (978-1-63679-638-3)

StreamLine by Lauren Melissa Ellzey. When Lune crosses paths with the legendary girl gamer Nocht, she may have found the key that will boost her to the upper echelon of streamers and unravel all Lune thought she knew about gaming, friendship, and love. (978-1-63679-655-0)

The Devil You Know by Ali Vali. As threats come at the Casey family from both the feds and enemies set to destroy them, Cain Casey does whatever is necessary with Emma at her side to bury every single one. (978-1-63679-471-6)

The Meaning of Liberty by Sage Donnell. When TJ and Bailey get caught in the political crossfire of the ultraconservative Crusade of the Redeemer Church, escape is the only plan. On the run and fighting for their lives is not the time to be falling for each other. (978-1-63679-624-6)

Undercurrent by Patricia Evans. Can Tala and Wilder catch a serial killer in Salem before another body washes up on the shore? (978-1-636790669-7)

And Then There Was One by Michele Castleman. Plagued by strange memories and drowning in the guilt she tried to leave behind, Lyla Smith escapes her small Ohio town to work as a nanny and becomes trapped with an unknown killer. (978-1-63679-688-8)

Digging for Destiny by Jenna Jarvis. The war between nations forces Litz to make a choice. Her country, career, and family, or the chance of making a better world with the woman she can't forget. (978-1-63679-575-1)

Hot Hires by Nan Campbell, Alaina Erdell, Jesse J. Thoma. In these three romance novellas, when business turns to pleasure, romance ignites. (978-1-63679-651-2)

McCall by Patricia Evans. Sam and Sara found love on the water, but can they build a future amid the ghosts of the past that surround them on dry land? (978-1-63679-769-4)

One and Done by Fredrick Smith. One day can lead to a night of passion…and possibly a chance at love. (978-1-63679-564-5)

Promises to Protect by Jo Hemmingwood. Park ranger Maxine Ward's commitment to protect Tree City is put to the test when social worker Skylar Austen takes a special interest in the commune and in Max. (978-1-63679-626-0)

Sacred Ground by Missouri Vaun. Jordan Price, a conflicted demon hunter, falls for Grace Jameson who has no idea she's been bitten by a vampire. (978-1-63679-485-3)

The Land of Death and Devil's Club by Bailey Bridgewater. Special Liaison to the FBI Louisa Linebach may have defied all odds by identifying the bodies of three missing men in the Kenai Peninsula, but she won't be satisfied until the man she's sure is responsible for their murders is behind bars. (978-1-63679-659-8)

When You Smile by Melissa Brayden. Taryn Ross never thought the babysitter she once crushed on would show up as a grad student at the same university she attends. (978-1-63679-671-0)